The time-clock's panel had swung open of its own volition, and an eerie purple light poured out in rhythmic pulses from within. What this signified would be hard to say, but de Marigny could soon find out. 'Wait,' he said to Moreen and Hank as he stepped forward and made to enter the clock. Except –

– Even as his hand gripped the frame of that narrow portal, *so a figure materialized there and stepped out!*

De Marigny knew him, and on legs weak as jelly went to embrace the newcomer – fell against nothing and staggered right through him! Crow was insubstantial as smoke, a mirage – a hologram!

'A ghost!' Moreen gasped. 'Is this your Titus Crow, Henri? A phantom whose grave is the time-clock? Is that why it's shaped like a coffin?' And de Marigny sensed the shudder of fear in her voice ...

By the same author

BRIAN LUMLEY

Elysia
The Coming
of Cthulhu!

Grafton

An Imprint of HarperCollins*Publishers*

Grafton
An Imprint of HarperCollins*Publishers*
77–85 Fulham Palace Road,
Hammersmith, London W6 8JB

Published by Grafton 1993
9 8 7 6 5 4 3 2 1

First published by
W. Paul Ganley: Publisher 1989

ISBN 0 586 21468 2

Set in Times

Printed in Great Britain by
HarperCollinsManufacturing Glasgow

For W. Paul Ganley, who was
there at the christening . . .

Contents

PART ONE

Far Lands, Strange Beings

1

Borea

Kota'na, Red Indian straight out of America's Old West – Kota'na, Keeper of the Bears – watched Moreen at play with a pair of cubs each bigger than herself and shook his head in admiration and amazement. The mother of the bears, huge Tookis, almost ten feet in height when she was upright, grunted and pawed the floor of the exercise cavern where she stood beside her master. Her mate was Morda, Kota'na's favourite among all the fighting bears, but Morda was not here. No, for he was out hunting with a pack of his brothers and their keepers, butchering food-beasts around the foot of the plateau for the larders of its tribes.

But the way this girl played with these cubs – without fear, laughing and biting their ears, and slapping their noses where they tumbled her – and them retaliating with howls and clumsy bounds, like puppies, but *never* going to strike her! Striking each other, certainly, with mighty, resounding, bone-breaking clouts; but not the girl, never the girl. And mighty Tookis, the mother of the cubs – the way she seemed to enjoy all of this, snorting her encouragement and thumping the floor – but if anyone else had dared to try it, maybe even Kota'na himself . . . well, good luck to him!

And at last Moreen had had enough. Laughing and panting she struggled free of the boisterous mounds of snowy fur which were Tookis' cubs, then leaned against the wall of the cavern to catch her breath. 'They're too much for me!' she panted and laughed, shaking back her shoulder-length, golden hair. 'Why, I'd bet they're even too much for their own mother! Eh, Tookis?' And she flung an arm round the great bear's neck.

Tookis thought otherwise. With a low growl she shook Moreen off, shambled forward into the fray, raised a cloud of dust where she merged with the cubs; until their massed, tussling, rumbling bulk resembled nothing so much as a small white unevenly mobile mountain. Kota'na grinned and let the play of these giant descendants of Polar bears continue for a moment or two, then stopped it with a single word. Until now the animals had been completely free, harmless in the presence of their master, but Kota'na dared not leave them alone like that. The cubs were at that curious age and would explore if they could; it would never do to have them wandering free through the many levels and labyrinths of the plateau, with mighty Tookis shambling along behind them! And so now he chained all three by their collars to the wall, on tethers long enough they might continue their game, then stepped back and let them get on with it.

'There,' he said, as the snarling, slavering and tumbling recommenced, in a very convincing imitation of the real thing, 'let them weary themselves with play. It's the best exercise I know. And while they play, will you not sit with me on the high balcony there, and look out over Borea while we talk?'

Moreen had her breath back; she stood up straight, all sixty-four inches of her, and dusted herself down. Then she gazed up in open admiration at the tall, bronzed Indian brave. He wore his shiny black hair in pigtails that fell forward to the ridges of his collarbones, and his naked arms and deep chest were marked with the unfaded scars of many a battle. For Kota'na was a great hero of the plateau's wars with Ithaqua's wolf-warriors and his Children of the Winds, and his deeds were already legended as the deeds of any mere man may be. Now he kept the bears for Hank Silberhutte, the plateau's Warlord; but more than that he was Silberhutte's friend, the highest honour to which any man of the plateau might ever aspire.

And as Moreen regarded him, so Kota'na's keen brown eyes stared back in mutual appreciation. De Marigny, man (or possibly magician) of the Motherworld, had got himself a fine woman here. She should bear him many strong sons.

The girl was lithe and supple as a withe, with wide, bright blue eyes and skin like the pale honey of wild bees. She had about her an aura, a warmth she wore like some fine fur; which had only ever been torn aside by Ithaqua, black stalker between the stars. Now, in her brown jacket and trousers of soft leather, she seemed almost boyish, and yet fragile for all that. But her unaffected grace and loveliness, and her youthful litheness, were perhaps set off by a not-quite innocence; for Moreen had seen the Wind-Walker at his worst, and no one could remain wholly innocent after that.

To have seen Ithaqua raging – to be witness to his mindless slaughters – was to have the innocence mercilessly ripped from you. And yet she had come through all of that, had succeeded against all odds to be one with The Searcher, Henri-Laurent de Marigny. Aye, mortal and fragile as all human beings are, nevertheless Moreen bore a strength in her and a power; she was a free creature of Nature, and could commune with all creatures of Nature wherever she found them. This was her power, and thus her seeming familiarity with Tookis and her cubs.

As to Kota'na's invitation: 'Very well,' she said. 'But what shall we talk about? – and please don't ask me to tell you *again* about Numinos, or of our adventures in the ice-caves on Dromos. That was a very frightening time and I would like to forget it . . .' And for a moment, anyway, the laughter went out of her wide eyes.

It was mid-morning on Borea, and the day was still and uncommonly bright. But 'bright' is hardly the right word, for Borea has no real daylight as such; it is a world which dwells in a permanent half-light, certainly in its northern regions. And that was where the plateau's vast hive of alveolate rock stood: in Borea's northland. There it towered, mighty outcrop thrust up in ages past, flat-roofed and sheer-sided, the last redoubt of Borea's free peoples against Ithaqua and his Children of the Winds.

The balcony Kota'na had mentioned lay through an archway in the wall of the great bears' exercise cavern, cut through where the cavern's wall came closest to the plateau's face. One of many such observation points, it was a wide ledge where benches had been carved from the solid rock; and beyond – only a chest-high wall separated Moreen and Kota'na from empty air and a sheer face that fell for well over a hundred feet to the icy, scree-littered foot of the plateau.

It was cold there, where the occasional draught of frigid air would come gusting in from the northern plains; and so Moreen kept on the move while they talked, hurrying to and fro on the precipitous balcony and only pausing now and then to peer out and down at some freshly discovered feature spied on the gentling snow-slopes far below. Kota'na, on the other hand, impervious to the cold, as were most of the people of the plateau, simply stood stern-faced, his arms folded on his breast.

'No,' he said after a moment, 'I will not ask about the moons of Borea: Numinos, where you were born, or Dromos, where the Lord Sil-ber-hut-te and you others destroyed the ice-priests. I have remembered it well from your other tellings, and from what the Warlord himself has told me. It is a tale I shall pass down to my children, when they are old enough to understand it; and when Oontawa their mother is old, and when I am a wrinkled, leathery Elder, then *our* children will tell it to theirs. That is the way of legends; it is how they live. No, this time I would know of the places you have seen since last you were here, and what brings you back here? And if it is not impertinent of me – for I know your man is a wizard, whose ways are hard to understand – I wish you would also say what ails

14

him? Doubtless it is a pain I cannot ease, but if I could – '

Impulsively, Moreen stood on tiptoe and hugged the tall Indian's neck. 'No wonder Hank Silberhutte loves you!' she burst out. 'And Oontawa and the great bears and your people, too. That stern look you wear can't fool me, Kota'na; it is a mask. You and your legends and tales·of derring-do. You're a romantic, that's all! You'd take the entire weight of the plateau itself on your own shoulders, if you could. The way you talk about Hank, as if he were a god! He's a man of the Motherworld. But how can I blame you when he is exactly the same? You should hear *him*, sometimes, when he talks about how you killed the traitor Northan – and then would not give up his head until Hank had seen it and forgiven you for stealing his glory?'

Kota'na held her at arm's length and raised an eyebrow at her impetuosity; but she could tell that he was pleased. He very nearly smiled. 'The Lord Sil-ber-hut-te ... says these things?'

'What? Of course he does! He can't talk about his "bear-brother" without puffing himself up first. You men!' Then she stepped back a little, hugged herself and shivered. And: 'Come on, let's walk in the plateau,' she said; and in a moment her voice was serious again.

Back under the arch and into the exercise cavern they went, where Tookis and her cubs were sprawled, panting, for the moment spent. Kota'na stopped and spoke briefly to a young Eskimo keeper, told him to tend the bears, and then he and Moreen passed on into the plateau's labyrinth. As they went, she said:

'You ask what ails Henri. Well, I'll tell you. Except, believe me, he is not a wizard. His time-clock is a wizard's device, or would seem to be, I'll grant you; and its previous owner, now perhaps he really *was* a wizard! – or so I'd judge from what Henri says of him. But not de Marigny. He's just a man, albeit a very wonderful man, and I love him. And you're right, he *is* unhappy. Which is a hard thing

15

to understand, I know. Through the time-clock he has all space and time at his command; they are his to explore endlessly. And yet – '

'Yes?'

She shrugged, and now Kota'na could see that Moreen, too, was unhappy. Because of her man's unhappiness. 'The one thing he most desires,' she finally continued, 'it is forbidden to him. The one place he would find, that remains hidden. The one voice he would hear, even across kalpas of space and time, stands silent. Indeed, the entire universe seems indifferent to his endless searching, even heedless of it. Do you know, but Henri is known as The Searcher now, on a hundred strange worlds? What ails him? It is this: someone once showed him a bright jewel place, where miracles are frequent and the impossible is commonplace – a place beyond imagining, called Elysia and said to be the home of the gods – and all Henri finds are balls of mud and rock twirling endlessly about their heart-suns. Worlds countless as grains of sand – and to him just as tasteless. Ah! – I will tell you, Kota'na – but we have seen *wonderful* worlds in the three years you say have elapsed since first we left here in the time-clock. Huge worlds of ocean, teeming with islands of turquoise and rose and agate; mountain worlds where cities stand in the clouds atop the highest peaks; forest worlds, where the air is laden with scents of a million orchids, and the nights lit with organic lanterns glowing in the beacon-trees. We found friends on these worlds you would not believe, because of their strangeness; and so many of them took us to their hearts. But no, the one friend Henri seeks has a machine for a heart!'

'*Huh!*' grunted Kota'na. 'He would seem perverse, this man you love. And yet he cannot be, because you love him. Perhaps he is under the spell of a mightier wizard yet?'

And at that Moreen had to laugh. 'Oh, he is, he is!' she

said. 'Or so Henri would have me believe, anyway. But remember, Kota'na: my fostermother, Annahilde, was a "true" witch-wife – and yet even her magic was only trickery. So you see, I don't really believe in magic, and neither must you. There are only strange people – people with weird and fantastic powers – but there is no magic. And that is a fact for Henri told me himself. No magic at all, but forces and powers and something called "science".' But as she finished speaking, and even though she continued to smile, still it seemed to Kota'na that the girl's eyes had clouded over a little.

And in her heart:

Magic? she thought. *Perhaps there is after all. For certainly Henri is ensorcelled. By a place called Elysia, and by the visions of a man called Titus Crow . . .*

At that very moment, Hank Silberhutte and Armandra, the Woman of the Winds, were having much the same conversation. They were in their cavern apartments near the very roof of the plateau, and there was a rare tension between them which had its source in Armandra's natural suspicions and preternatural senses, and in the Warlord's most *un*natural predilection for adventure.

They were telepathetically attuned, these two, but had an agreement: their mental privacy was paramount. Only in their most intimate moments together, or in time of danger or matters of pressing urgency, did they mingle their minds. For they had long since discovered that it is not well for man and wife to live in each other's pockets – nor constantly *in* each other's thoughts, literally! But now Armandra was tempted to look into her man's mind, and perhaps not surprisingly.

The time-clock was back on Borea after an absence of three years, and with it an air of adventure. And that, thought Ithaqua's daughter, was Hank Silberhutte's trouble. It was what gave him restless nights, filled his head with thoughts of a Motherworld; Earth, else long forgotten, brought him dreams of quests and adventures out beyond the farthest stars.

'Armandra,' the Warlord sighed now, pausing in his troubled striding to reach out and gently grasp her shoulders in his massive paws – the delicate-seeming shoulders of this incredible woman, human spawn of the vastly inhuman Wind-Walker – 'we've had all this before. Don't you remember the last time? And didn't you entertain just such doubts then? And what came of all your fears, eh?'

As she gazed back steadily into his eyes, so his words brought memories:

When last de Marigny was here and before they had all four – Henri and Moreen, Hank and Armandra – gone out on their impossible, peril-fraught mission to the moons of Borea, she had had plenty of time to talk to de Marigny and get to know him. She had questioned him minutely in all aspects of his past and his wanderings in the time-clock, adventures of which the Warlord had already apprised her, but which she found more immediately thrilling when retold by de Marigny. And it had been perfectly obvious to the Woman of the Winds that never before had she met a man like this one. Even in the Motherworld he had been something of an anachronism, the perfect gentleman in a world where morals and all standards of common courtesy were continually falling, but here on Borea his like had been unknown.

It had not required much effort on the handsome Earthman's part to convince her that his presence on Borea was purely accidental, that he had not deliberately sought out Hank Silberhutte in order to perform some fantastic interplanetary, hyperdimensional rescue! No, for he was on his way to Elysia, home of the Elder Gods, and only the tides of Fate had washed him ashore on Borea's chilly strand ...

Armandra came back to the present. 'Oh, yes, I

remember,' she said, unsmiling. And she tossed her long red tresses and flashed her oval green eyes. 'And I remember what followed. It finished on Dromos in the caves of the ice-priests, where you and Henri very nearly died and I almost became handmaiden to my monstrous father! As for poor Moreen, if that *beast* had had his way ...' She shuddered and left it unfinished.

'But none of that happened,' the Warlord patiently reminded. 'Instead we taught Ithaqua a lesson. That was the second time he'd tried it on, and the second time we'd bruised his ego. And now he stands off, regards the plateau and its peoples with a little more respect, spends his time and energies in more profitable pursuits. In other words, the last time de Marigny visited here it worked to the good of the plateau. Remember, too, he saved my life, snatched me from Ithaqua's wolf-warriors – who without a doubt would have given me into the hands of their terrible master.'

'He saved *your* life?' she flared up, and for the briefest moment a tinge of carmine flashed in her green eyes. 'And how often did you save his, at great risk? Oh, no, Lord Silberhutte,' (she only ever called him that when he was in the wrong), 'there's no debt between you there!'

'He hasn't come back to collect on any debts, Armandra,' the Texan released her, turned away, clenched his great hands behind his back. 'He wants nothing of us except our hospitality. He's come back as he went: a friend – come back to be with people, for however short a time – before he goes off again on this crazy quest of his. Next to Earth, which he put behind him the day he left it, we're the closest he's got to family. That's why he's come back: because this is as near as he'll get to home. At least until he finds Titus Crow in Elysia. *If* he finds him!'

Armandra stepped round in front of him. Draped in a deep-pile, white fur smock, still her figure was the answer to any man's dream, the body of an exceedingly beautiful

19

woman. Almost unchanged from the first time Silberhutte had seen her nearly six years ago, Armandra was Complete Woman. Her long, full body was a wonder of half-seen, half-imagined curves growing out of the perfect pillars of her thighs; her neck, framed in the red, flowing silk of her hair, was long and slender, adorned with a large medallion of gold; her face was oval as her eyes and classically boned. With her straight nose, delicately rounded at its tip, and her Cupid's bow of a mouth, perfect in shape if perhaps a shade too ample, the Woman of the Winds was a beautiful picture of femininity. But where her flesh was pale as snow, those great eyes of hers were green as the boundless northern oceans of Earth. Yes, and they were just as deep.

That was Armandra. When she smiled it brought the sunlight into the Warlord's darkest hours, and when she frowned ... then the fiery hair of her head was wont to have an eerie life of its own, and her eyes might narrow and take on a warning tint other than ocean green: the carmine passed down to her from her inhuman father.

She was frowning now, but not in anger. In fear, perhaps? Fear of losing this man of the Motherworld, this Warlord, this Texan whom she loved so desperately.

'And what of you, Hank?' she asked at last. 'What of *your* home?' Her frown did not lighten, and Silberhutte knew what was coming next: 'Do you, too, feel trapped here, marooned? You guard your thoughts well, my husband, but I would know the truth. The plateau must seem a very small place compared to what you've told me of those mighty city-hives of the Motherworld. And now, with de Marigny returned – him and his time-clock – '

He took her in his arms, lifted her up as surely and as easily as her familiar winds when she walked in the sky, then lowered her down until his mouth closed on hers with a kiss. And after long moments he slid her down his hard-muscled body until her sandalled feet touched the furs of the floor; and before she could speak again, he said:

20

'This – is my home. You – *are* my life. Borea's my world now, Armandra. My woman, my son, my people are here. If I could go down to the pens and take Morda and ride him out a single mile across the plain and into the Motherworld – if it was as easy as that – I wouldn't do it. I might . . . but only if I could take you with me. And for all its many wonders, the Motherworld is a common place. It has nothing like you. What would its thronging people make of a woman of unearthly beauty who walks on the wind and commands the very lightnings?' And he paused.

He might have said more: how Armandra would be lost on Earth, bewildered, a complete outsider. An alien. A curiosity. A seven-day wonder. And finally a freak. But saying it, even thinking it, hurt him worse than it would hurt her. Which was too much. And so instead he finished with:

'I love and *will* love only you. Where you are I must be. Be it Borea, heaven or hell, if you are there it's the place for me. But surely you can see that while I have found my home – the only home I need – our friend Henri-Laurent de Marigny has not yet found his. What you call my "trouble" is in fact his trouble. If you see pain in me, it's only pain for him. Moreen says he's known as The Searcher in a hundred inhabited worlds. Beings who are not men, who don't even *think* like men, understand his quest and have named him for it. They feel for him. And should I hide my feelings? No, Armandra, I'm not a child to be homesick. Nor is de Marigny, not for a home he's never seen. But it's his destiny – yes, and it's driving him to distraction. My pain is this: that I don't know how to help him.'

Now Armandra felt wretched. She knew that she did not have to look into her man's mind, that everything he had said was right in there. Yes, this strange world with its weird auroras and inhabited moons *was* his world now; but he was still a man of the Motherworld, and so felt for his fellow man, de Marigny The Searcher.

'Hank, I – ' she began, her voice full of shame. But before she could continue, and because he would not let her humble herself:

'I know, I know.' And he patted her head.

'But how can we help him?' She desired only to put things right now. 'Should I commune with my familiar winds? For they have talked to winds from across the farthest reaches of eternity. Perhaps they have heard of this Elysia.'

Silberhutte nodded. 'It's worth a try.' Then he stood up straighter and squared his shoulders, finally gave a snort and chuckled to himself. Armandra looked at him quizzically, but he only smiled and shook his head.

'What is it?' she asked, raising the corner of a golden eyebrow.

He chuckled again, then shrugged. 'Once – oh, six years ago – I set out on a vengeance quest to track down and destroy your father. I knew Ithaqua was real: not supernatural but a Being of alien spaces and dimensions. That was my *total* belief in matters concerning things not of Earth: that Ithaqua was real, and with him others of an incredibly ancient order or pantheon of Beings, the Cthulhu Cycle Deities. Also, I was a telepath. But the rest of me was Texan, and *all* of me was Earthman, in many ways mundane as any other. And instead of tracking Ithaqua he tracked me and carried me and my crew here to Borea. Since when – '

'Yes?'

'Why, see how my spheres have widened! And what's become of this vengeful, telepathic but otherwise "mundane" Texan now, eh? Warlord of polyglot peoples on an alien world; adventurer in strange moons; mate to the daughter of the one he vowed to destroy, a woman who walks on the wind and "communes" with puffs of ether

22

from the stars? And when you say: "I'll have a word with some winds I know from the other side of eternity," this man nods and answers, "sure, it's worth a try!" ' And now he burst out laughing.

Barely understanding this sudden bout of self-directed humour, but carried along by it anyway, Armandra joined the laughter; and she hugged him and clung to him for a moment. Then, arm in arm, they set out together to find de Marigny and tell him how she would try to help him ...

Henri-Laurent de Marigny was aware of some of the concern he caused in the plateau and among its inhabitants, but aware of it only on the periphery of his consciousness. His ever-advancing obsession would not allow for more than that. No, for now the quest was all that mattered. He knew it, and could do nothing about it. He suspected, too, that but for Moreen he might well have cracked long before now, that she alone was his sanity. Together they had visited many worlds with near-human, half-human, and totally inhuman inhabitants, might easily have settled on several. Oh, yes, for there were wonderful, beautiful islands galore out there in the infinite seas of space. But while they'd rested in these planets and found peace in them, it had never lasted. Always de Marigny would wake with a cry one morning, sit up and cast about, discover that yesterday's wonders and last night's marvels had turned drab on him and lost their flavour, and his eyes would grow dull while the bright dream he had dreamed receded. And then they would go to the time-clock, and at his command its panel would open and spill out that familiar, pulsing purplish glow, and it would be time to move on.

And of course he knew that it would be exactly the same here on Borea. But at least there were friends here, completely *human* friends; which was why, after these last three years of futile search, he had returned. Earth ...? That thought had never seriously occurred to him. The

Earth was beautiful but diseased, polluted by men, the one planet of all the worlds de Marigny knew whose inhabitants were systematically raping and ruining her. Indeed, even Earth's dreamlands were beginning to suffer!

And that *was* a thought, an idea, which had occurred more than once: why not give up all Elysian aspirations and dwell instead in the lands of Earth's dreams? Fine, but there are perils even in the dreamlands. And the very least of them lay in waking up! For de Marigny knew that there are certain dreams from which men never wake . . .

The dreamlands, strange dimension formed by the subconscious longings of men. A *real* place or world, as de Marigny now knew.

Gazing down from a rock-hewn bartizan at the rim of the plateau, now he smiled – however wryly – as his mind went back again to the adventures he had known in Earth's dreamlands with Titus Crow and Tiania of Elysia. For peering from on high like this was not unlike (and yet, in another sense, totally unlike) the vertiginous view from cloud-floating Serannian's wharves of pink-veined marble, where that fabulous city was built in the sky and looked out over an ethereal sea of glowing cirrus and cirrocumulus.

And remembering that wonderful aerial city, de Marigny's mind could not help but conjure, too, Kuranes: 'Lord of Ooth-Nargei, Celephais, and the Sky around Serannian.' Kuranes, yes! – and Randolph Carter, perhaps Earth's greatest dreamer, a king himself now in Ilek-Vad – and who better for the job, since he himself had probably dreamed Ilek-Vad in the first place?

Other lands and cities sprang to mind: Ulthar, where no man may kill a cat, and the Isle of Oriab across the Southern Sea, with its principal port Baharna. Aye, incredible places all, and their peoples fabulous as the dreams that made them; but not all dreams are pleasant, and the dreamlands had their share of nightmares, too.

Now de Marigny thought of Dylath-Leen in the Bad

Days and shuddered, and he tasted something bitter in his mouth as he recalled names and places such as Zura of the Charnel Gardens, the Vale of Pnoth, Kadath in the Cold Waste and Leng's forbidden plateau and hideous hinterland. Especially Leng, where squat, horned beast-men cavorted about balefires to the whine of demon flutes and the bone-dry rattle of crazed crotala . . .

No, the dreamlands were no fit habitation for such as Moreen and de Marigny – who in any case had never considered himself an expert dreamer – not yet for a while, anyway. Perhaps one day on his deathbed he'd dream himself a white-walled villa there in timeless Celephais, but until then . . .

. . . The dimension of dream, glimpsed briefly in the eye of memory, slipped away and de Marigny was back on Borea, on the roof of the plateau. Chill Borea, where for ten days now he and Moreen had been feted like prodigals until, as always, the pleasures had begun to pall; even the great pleasure of human companionship, the company of men such as Silberhutte, Kota'na, Jimmy Franklin and Charlie Tacomah.

And suddenly de Marigny knew that he was tired of his quest, and he wondered how much longer it could last before he gave in, surrendered to the hopelessness of the thing. Indeed, sometimes he wondered what had kept him going so long . . . but no, that was a lie, for he already knew the answer well enough. It lay not alone in what Titus Crow had told him of Elysia, but also in what he'd said of de Marigny himself:

'You are a lover of mysteries, my friend,' (Crow had said), 'as your father before you, and there's something you should know. You really ought to have guessed it before now, Henri, but there's something in you that hearkens back into dim abysses of time, a spark whose fire burns still in Elysia . . .'

It had been like a promise, as if in those words Crow

had willed to him a marvellous inheritance; but what of that promise now? Or could it be that Crow had simply been mistaken, that de Marigny ought never have set his sights on Elysia in the first place? What else had Titus Crow said?

'You will be welcome in Elysia, Henri, but of course you must make your own way there . . . It may well be a difficult voyage, and certainly it will be dangerous, for there's no royal road to Elysia . . . The pitfalls of space and time are many, but the rewards are great . . . When there are obstacles, we'll be watching in Elysia. And if you are where I can't reach you without aid, then I'll ride a Great Thought to you . . .'

De Marigny could not restrain a snort of derision, however inwardly-directed. Obstacles? Oh, there'd been 'obstacles,' all right! Time-travel in the clock was invariably complicated by running battles with the Tind'losi Hounds; certain worlds of space seemed friendly but were in fact inimical to human life; the space-time fabric itself had focal points mysterious and dangerous beyond reckoning; and, neither last nor least, there was no dearth of places in the continuum wherein were contained the 'houses' or 'tombs' of the Great Old Ones (more properly their prisons), where they had been locked in untold aeons past by the beneficent Gods of Eld. This had been their punishment for an act, or the massed threat of such an act, monstrous beyond imagining. The Elder Gods had pursued Cthulhu, his ilk and their spawn, through space and time and dimensions *between* the spaces we know, prisoning them wherever they were found. And so they remained to this day, in greater part: imprisoned but immortal, only waiting out the time of their release, when the stars would wheel in their great celestial orbits and finally stand *right* in pre-ordained positions in the firmament. And then, when the stars were right –

– A great hand fell on de Marigny's shoulder and he

26

gave a massive start, clutching at the rim of the open viewport where he gazed out from the bartizan. All doomful thoughts were snatched from his mind at once, and he himself snatched back to the immediate, the now.

'Henri,' Hank Silberhutte's voice was deep where he stood with an arm around Armandra, 'we thought we'd find you here. Did I startle you? It seemed you were miles away just then, right?'

'Light-years!' de Marigny agreed, turning. He managed a smile, nodded a greeting to Hank, bowed formally to Armandra – and at once felt something of their concern for him, the pain and worry he was causing them. Words of apology would have tumbled out of him then, but the Woman of the Winds had quickly taken his hand in both of hers, to tell him:

'Henri, if you wish it, I think I may be able to help you find Elysia. At least, there is a chance.'

'And what do you say to that?' the Warlord grinned at him.

For a moment, maybe two, de Marigny simply gaped at them. He knew that Armandra had senses beyond the mundane five, was aware that if anyone on Borea could help him, she was that one. And yet he had not even considered asking for her help because ... because he was de Marigny and she was his friend, and he knew that you can only beg help from real friends just so often before losing them.

'Well?' the Warlord waited for his answer. And now de Marigny gave it.

Stepping forward, he briefly, fiercely hugged the Woman of the Winds, then lifted her bodily up above him. And still words would not come. 'Armandra, I ... I ...' Then, ashamed of his own emotions, he set her down again, dumbly shook his head and backed off. And under Armandra's stern, steady gaze, finally he lowered his head.

At last she said: 'You men of the Motherworld would

27

all seem much of a kind: you have the same strengths and the same weaknesses. Fortunately the former outweigh the latter, which in any case are often . . . endearing?' Looking up, de Marigny saw that her great green eyes were sparkling.

At which her husband put arms round the shoulders of both of them and began laughing uproariously . . .

2

Elysia

There were strange stirrings in the Elysian ether, ominous undercurrents more psychic than physical, which weighed on the souls of certain dwellers in that weird and wonderful land. The source of this dawning – dread? – was intangible as yet, but to those few who sensed it, its approach was anticipated as surely as the bite of a mosquito in the darkness of a room, in those taut moments after its hum fades to silence. Titus Crow had come awake to that silence, and had known instinctively that the bite was still to come. Not immediately but soon, and not merely the sting of a mosquito . . .

Outwardly . . . all seemed ordered – as it had been immemorially in Elysia – but inside:

'There's a knot in my stomach,' said Crow, hurriedly dressing in forest-green jacket and bark-brown, wide-bottomed trousers, tightening his belt and peering out at the sky through the stone windows of the aerial castle which he and Tiania called home. And scanning that sky he frowned, for even the synthetic sunrise seemed wrong this morning, and on the far, flat horizon, the wispy clouds were tinged a leaden grey.

Tiania was only half awake. 'Ummm!' she said, not wanting to argue, her head deep in pillows.

'Something's up,' she heard her man declare. He sniffed at the air and nodded to himself. 'Why, even the clouds are grey!'

Now she was coming awake. 'Did you never see grey clouds before?' she mumbled. 'Perhaps it will rain! It's good for the gardens.'

'No,' he shook his leonine head, 'it's not that *kind* of

29

grey. It's more a feeling than a colour.' He went to her, gently lifted her head from the pillows, kissed her soft, unwrinkled brow. 'Come on, Tiania. You're a child of Elysia, and a favourite child at that. Can't you feel it? It's in the air, I tell you, and it's been there for some time. Something *is* wrong!'

At that she sat up, and Titus Crow was frozen by sudden awareness of her nearness, her beauty. It was the same each morning, the same every night: he looked at her and knew she was his, and every fibre of his body thrilled to the knowledge. Tiania had the perfect shape of a beautiful girl, but that was where any further comparison with a female of planet Earth must surely end. Most definitely!

To describe her in detail would take many thousands of words, most of them superlatives. The mind tires of searching for them, and the reader's mind would weary of absorbing them. And so, to simplify matters:

Tiania's hair was a green so dark as to be almost black, with highlights of aquamarine and flashing emerald tints. All coils and ringlets, it reached to her waist, which seemed delicate as the stem of a wineglass. Her flesh was *milk*-of-pearl, not the nacreous gleam of shell-heart but the soft glow of a pearl's outer skin. Her eyes were huge, the colour of beryl and infinitely deep, under arching emerald eyebrows in a slender, pixie face. Pixie, too, her ears and delicate nub of a nose, so that when she smiled she might well be some tomboy elf – except that she literally radiated Essence of Woman. She *was* plainly human, and yet quite alien; a girl, yes, but one whose genes had known the mysteries of Eld.

Crow shook his head in silent wonder, a ritual of his that she'd grown used to even if she didn't fully understand it. And: 'Nothing so beautiful lived before you,' he said quite simply.

'Ridiculous!' she answered, rising up and shaking back

her hair – but at the same time blushing rose. 'Why! There are flowers in the Gardens of Nymarrah – '

'Nothing human,' he cut her off.

She kissed him, began to dress. 'Then we're a match, for you're a fine, big man.'

'Ah, but just a man for all that,' he answered, as he invariably did. Which was far from true, for Crow was wont to forget now and then that since his transition he was rather more than a man. But whichever, she returned his appreciative gaze with equal raptness, for Tiania never tired of Titus Crow. What she saw was this:

A man, yes, but a man glowing with health, ageless as a rock. He looked a young forty, but that would be to grant him more than a quarter of a century! And even *that* would be a false reading, based solely on Earth-time. For rebuilt from his own pulp by a robot physician on a robot world, he had spent more than sixty years in T3RE's vats alone! And that was where he had undergone his transition proper: in the laboratory of T3RE, whose robot hands and tools and lasers had built him the way he was now. And almost literally ageless, too, for in Crow the ageing process was slowed down in a ratio of one to ten. Twenty years from now he would look more or less the same, but Tiania would have started to catch up with him. That was a problem they would face as it arose ...

While she finished dressing he pulled on boots and tucked his trousers into their tops, forming piratical bells. It gave him a swashbuckling air which he admitted to liking. But appearances were secondary in his mind now, where his thoughts were too sombre for theatrical posing. By then, too, Tiania was ready. And:

'Where are we going?' she asked innocently.

'We? *We?*' he teased her, playing down his as yet unfounded fears. 'Who said anything about "we"? But as for me, I'm off to see if I can arrange an audience with Kthanid in his glacier palace.'

31

'Oh?' she raised an eyebrow. 'And I should stay home and prepare a meal for you, right?' And she put her hands on her hips, pretending to scowl.

Inside Crow his mechanical heart picked up speed; something gnawed at him, worried at his guts; time was wasting and a monstrous cloud loomed ever closer. But still he played this lover's game with Tiania. 'Of course, woman, what else?' he barked. 'And doesn't a man deserve a good meal when he's been out working all day and returns home to ... to ...'

The smile had fallen from her face. For all their banter, now Tiania had sensed something of her man's apprehension and knew it was real. And perhaps for the first time, she too felt that leaden, stifling oppressiveness, an as yet vague but steadily increasing sensation of DOOM in the atmosphere of Elysia. Suddenly frightened, she threw herself into his arms. 'Oh, Titus! Titus! I feel it now! But what is it?'

He hugged her, comforted her, growled: 'Damned if I know. But I intend to find out. Come on!'

They hurried out from their bedroom in the base of a turret onto ornamental 'battlements' that offered a fantastic view of Elysia – or part of Elysia, anyway. To the east a synthetic golden sun burned behind a lowering bank of cloud, and an unaccustomed chill wind rippled the fields far below. There was more than the usual movement in the sky, too, where from all quarters flights of lithards could be seen wearing the bright colours of dignitaries and bearing their favoured riders north.

North? Across the Frozen Sea to the Icelands?

Crow and Tiania glanced apprehensively, speculatively at each other. This would seem to confirm their private thoughts and suspicions. He nodded his leonine head. 'And didn't I say I wanted an audience with Kthanid, in the Hall of Crystal and Pearl?'

Before she could answer there came a throb of wings

and rush of air, and up from below there soared a monstrous, magnificent shape well known to both of them. A great lithard, the veriest dragon, flew in the skies of Elysia! Oth-Neth, first representative of his race – intelligent dinosaur of doomed Thak'r-Yon, a world long since burned up in the heart of its exploding sun – alighted in a flash of bright scales, a sighing furling of membrane wings, on the battlements close by.

'Oth-Neth!' cried Tiania, and she ran to the great beast and threw her arms about his neck.

'Tiania,' the creature returned, soft-voiced, lowering its great head to facilitate her fondling.

Crow might witness this same scene a thousand times and still be awed. Here was a monster out of Earth's oldest mythologies – a *draco* out of Asian hinterlands, and all of a natural green and gold iridescence – and Tiania caressing the beast as if it were a favourite horse. No, he automatically corrected himself, greeting it – greeting *him* – like an old friend, which he was. Oth-neth, green and golden dragon from the Tung-gat tapestries, a creature such as might sport in the Gardens of Rak. And here on a mission.

Oth-Neth wore green, the emerald saddle and reins of Tiania's household. He had been sent to collect her.

'What about me?' Crow strode forward, rested a hand on the creature's flank.

'You?' Oth-Neth bent his head to look at him. 'You, too, Tituth.' (The lithard's command of human languages was imperfect: he lisped, as did all his race.) 'But you go quick, direct to Kthanid! Flying cloak ith better for you.'

Crow looked him straight in his saucer eyes. 'Do you know what's happening?'

'No,' an almost imperceptible shake of the great head. 'But . . . I think trouble. Big trouble! Look!' He turned his head to the skies. High above Elysia, beyond the flying-zones of lithards and cloaks and winged creatures alike,

33

time-clocks in all their varieties were blinking into existence in unprecedented numbers. And all of them wending east toward the slowly rising, strangely dulled sun, to the Blue Mountains and the subterranean, miles-long corridor of clocks. Elysia's children were returning from a thousand voyagings and quests, answering the summons of the masters of this weird, wonderful place.

Crow stared for a moment longer, his high brow furrowed, then hurried back into the castle. He returned with a scarlet flying cloak and quickly slipped into its harness. Tiania had already climbed into the ornate emerald saddle at the base of the lithard's neck, but she paused to lean down and kiss Crow where he now stood poised on the battlements.

'Titus,' she began, 'I – ' but words wouldn't come.

He looked at her beautiful face and form, only half-concealed by an open jacket and knee-length trousers of soft grey, and felt her fear like a physical thing; not fear for herself or Elysia, nor even Titus Crow himself – who in any case had often shown himself to be near-indestructible – but for *them*, for they had become as one person and could not be apart. And: 'I know,' he said quietly. And then, brightening: 'But we don't know what it is yet. It may be ... very little.'

They both knew he deliberately made light of it, but she nodded anyway. Then Oth-Neth launched himself from the castle's wall and soared north; and Crow's fingers found the control studs of his cloak, which at once belled out and bore him aloft; and in the next moment girl, dragon and man were flying north to join the streams of other fliers where they made for Kthanid's glacial palace ...

Crow sped on ahead. He guessed that Oth-Neth deliberately held back, letting him gain a lead and a little extra time. For what? So that he could talk to Kthanid in private? That seemed unlikely, with all these others heading for that same rendezvous. But Crow accelerated and shot ahead anyway.

And as he flew his cloak, so it was suddenly important to Crow that he look at Elysia again, let the place impress itself upon his mind. It had dawned on him that if ever he had known a real home – a place to be, where he *wanted* to be – that home was here. Now, for the first time, he consciously desired to remember it. Knowing his instincts, how true they ran, that was a very bad omen indeed. And so, until journey's end, he deliberately absorbed all he could of Elysia, letting it soak into him like water into a sponge.

Elysia was not a planet; if it had been, then it would be the most tremendous colossus among worlds. But there was no real horizon that Crow had ever seen, no visible curvature of rim, only a gradual fading into distance. Oh, there were mountains with towering peaks, and many of them snow-clad; but even from the tops of these Elysia could be seen to go on endlessly into distant mists, a land vast as it was improbable and beautiful.

Beautiful, too, its structures, its cities. But *such* cities! Fretted silver spires and clusters of columns rose everywhere, fantastic habitations of Elysia's peoples; but never vying with each other and always with fields and rivers and plains between. Even in the most abstract of cities there were parks and woodlands and rivers and lakes like bright ribbons and mirrors dropped carelessly on the landscape, yet always complementing it perfectly. And away beyond lines of low, domed hills misty with distance, yet more cities; their rising terraces of globes and minarets sparkling afar, where dizzy aerial roadways spread unsupported spans city to city like the gossamer threads of strange communal cobwebs.

Sky-islands, too (like Serannian in the land of Earth's dreams, or Tiania's castle and the gardens around it), apparently floating free but in fact anchored by the same

35

gravitic devices which powered Elysia and kept her positioned here in this otherwise empty parallel dimension; and all of these aerial residences dotted here and there, near and far, seemingly at random and at various heights; but perfectly situated and structured to suit their dwellers, who might in form be diverse as their many forms of gravity-defying architecture. And yet the sky so vast that it was not, could not be, cluttered.

Flying machines soared or hovered in these skies whereever the eye might look (or would in normal times), and through tufted drifting clouds green and golden dragons, the lithards, pulsed majestically on wings of ivory and leather. Nor were the lithards and flying craft sole users of their aerial element: a few of Elysia's races were naturally gifted with flight, and there were even some who might simply will it! Then there were the users of flying cloaks, like Crow's; and finally, today especially, there were the time-clocks . . .

But Elysia was not all city and sky and mountain; she had mighty forests, too, endless valley plains, fields of gorgeous green and yellow, and oceans more beautiful even than the jewel oceans of Earth. The Frozen Sea was one such: patterned like a snowflake one hundred miles across, its outer rim was cracked into glittering spokes of ice, while at the core a nucleus of icebergs had crashed together in ages past to form a mighty frozen monolith. Titus Crow flew across the Frozen Sea even now, and beyond it –

– There in the Icelands, whose temperature ideally suited certain of Elysia's inhabitants – there dwelled Kthanid in his palace at the heart of a glacier. Kthanid, spokesman of the Elder Gods themselves.

'Elder Gods.' They were not gods, and Kthanid himself would be the first to admit it; but so many races down all the ages of time and on a thousand different worlds had seen them as gods that the name had stuck. No, not gods but scientists, whose science had made them godlike. Beneficent Beings of Eld, they were, but not *all* of them had been benign.

Crow was across the Frozen Sea now and began to feel the chill of the Icelands. Oth-Neth's body-heat would warm Tiania, he knew, until they were down in the heart of the great glacier; and as for his own welfare: this body T3RE had built for him would come to no great harm. And in any case, it was more a chill of the spirit he felt than the frosty burn of bitter winds. For still that leaden feeling was on him.

Away in the west, beyond the ice-shard glittering rim of the Frozen Sea, he glimpsed the blue waters of a somewhat more temperate ocean, where majestic icebergs sailed and slowly melted, but then in another moment the view was shut off as he soared down over frozen foothills and set his course parallel to a procession of lithards who bore their riders doubtless to the same destination: Kthanid's council-chamber in the great Hall of Crystal and Pearl.

Kthanid: super-sentient Kraken, Eminence, Sage and Father of Elysia. And benign . . .

But there was that One born of Kthanid's race and spawned in his image who was *not* benign, that bestial, slobbering bereft Great Old One whose cause and cult Crow had fought against all his days, that one true prime evil whose seat for three and a half billions of years had been drowned R'lyeh in Earth's vast Pacific Ocean – Cthulhu! And now Crow wondered: why did *that* thought spring to mind? From where?

And he once more quickened the pace of the cloak as finally he spied ahead a frozen river of immemorial ice and the jagged crevasse that guarded the entrance to Kthanid's sub-glacial palace.

Normally Crow would show his respect, enter cautiously and continue on foot to the council-chamber, but these were not normal times. He flew the cloak dexterously into

37

the mouth of a fantastically carved cavern, then down sweeping flights of ice-hewn steps into the heart of the glacier, until at last he swooped along a horizontal tunnel carved of ice whose floor was granite worn smooth by centuries of glaciation. And now he smelled those strange and exotic scents only ever before smelled here, borne to him on a warm breeze from inner regions ahead.

It grew warmer still as the core of the glacier drew closer, until suddenly the dim blue light of the place came brighter, as if here some secret source of illumination was hidden behind the soft sheen of ice walls. Then those walls themselves, like the floor, became granite, and finally Crow arrived at a huge curtain of purest crystals and pearls strung on threads of gold. And he knew that beyond the curtain – whose priceless drapes went up to a dim ceiling, and whose width must be all of a hundred feet – lay the vast and awe-inspiring Hall of Crystal and Pearl, throne-room and council-chamber of Kthanid the Eminence.

Crow had been here before, on several occasions, but they had never been ordinary times; and now once more he felt himself on the verge of momentous things, whose nature was soon to be revealed. But . . . here was no longer a place for flying. He alighted, slipped out of the cloak's harness and folded that device over his arm, finally parted the jewel curtains and stepped through.

And now indeed he knew that Oth-Neth had been correct, that trouble, 'big trouble,' was brewing in Elysia.

Again, as always, Crow felt amazement at the sheer size of the hall, that inner sanctum wherein Kthanid thought his Great Thoughts. He stood upon the titan-paved floor of massive hexagonal flags of quartz and eyed the weird angles and proportions of the place, with its high-arched ceiling soaring overhead. Enormously ornate columns rose up on all sides, supporting high balconies made vague by the rising haze of light; and everywhere the well remembered white, pink and blood hues of multi-coloured crystal, and the shimmer of mother-of-pearl where the polished linings of prehistoric conches decorated the marching walls.

The only thing that seemed different was the absence of the customary centrepiece – a vast scarlet cushion bearing the sphere of a huge, milky crystal. Kthanid's 'shewstone' – but all else was just as Crow remembered it. Or would be, except that on those previous occasions Kthanid had seemed alone in his palace; whereas now –

– Now, where mighty Kthanid sat in his private alcove, its pearl-beaded curtains thrown back – now he gazed out upon a multitude!

At first glance it appeared to Crow that half of Elysia must be here – including several who ranked almost as high at Kthanid himself, and whose appearances were similarly or even more *outré* – for the great hall was packed. No simple council-meeting this, for not only were these High Eminences here but also representatives of a dozen different races, and lords and leaders from all of Elysia's many cities and lands and parts.

Among those assembled were several high-placed lithards, wearing their black leather neck-bands of office; and Crow at once recognized Esch, Master Linguist of the bird-like Dchi-chis, a man-sized archeopteran who bent his plumed head in a silent nod of greeting; and then there were several 'Chosen' ones: usually but not always members of manlike bipedal races whose natural beauty was favoured by the Elder Gods, including several fragile-seeming varieties Crow could only ever think of as pixies, elves or fairies. There were insect-beings, too, and squat, amphibian fin-creatures; even a solitary member of the D'horna-ahn, an energy spiral who gyrated close to Esch where they hummed electrically at each other in muted, cryptical conversation.

Of the handful of Elder Gods who were there: Crow

spied a great, gently mobile congeries of golden spheres that half-hid a writhing shape of sheerest nightmare, and he knew that this was Yad-Thaddag, a 'cousin' of Yog-Sothoth, but infinitely good where the latter was black and putrid evil. Also, in an area apart from the rest, a lambent flame twice the height of a man, tapered at top and bottom, twirled clockwise where it stood 'still' upon its own axis and threw out filaments of flickering yellow energy; and this too was a member of the elite Elder Gods, a Thermal Being born in eons past in the heart of a star, whose half-life was five billion years! And all of them here to talk, exchange thoughts or otherwise commune with Kthanid.

And Titus Crow, a mere man, summoned to a meeting such as this . . .

'*Mere man?*' came Kthanid's thoughts from where he sat upon a throne in his arched alcove. '*That you are not, Titus Crow, and well you know it. Men are not "mere" creatures; you, of all men, are not "mere." Indeed, this entire assembly has waited on* your *arrival more than that of any other.*' Crow's entrance had been noted, and in more ways than one. Now he felt the golden orbs of Kthanid's eyes full upon him, and the mainly silent throng parted to let him come forward. This he did, losing count of the strides which took him across those great hexagonal flags to the alcove where Kthanis sat at an onyx table. And there before the Elder God, a scarlet cushion; and upon the cushion, the milky shewstone . . .

3

Kthanid

Crow arrived at the foot of the huge steps up to the dais, paused there and stood straight as a ramrod, his hands at his sides, his head bowed. It was a measure of his respect; his stance told eloquently of his recognition of Kthanid, that he stood in the presence of a superior Being. Then:

'*Yes,*' said Kthanid, but directing his thoughts at Crow alone this time. '*Well, we're one and all superior in our way, else we'd not be here in Elysia in the first place. Titus, come up here to me. We need a little privacy.*' Crow lifted his head, climbed the steps. Behind him the curtains swept shut and closed the alcove in; but not before Kthanid sent out a final thought in the direction of all those gathered there: '*Please wait. Accept our apology that we exclude you from this, but its nature is such that it involves only the Earthman and myself. Only be sure it is a matter of great moment . . .*'

Now he spoke openly (albeit telepathically) to Crow, saying, '*Titus, we now stand in a completely private place. Here we two may converse, and none hear us. Wherefore you may answer as you please, without consideration to my position here.*'

'You know there's no one I hold in higher esteem,' Crow answered without hesitation. 'What could you ask me that I could refuse, or to which I might answer no?'

'*Perceptive, aye!*' Kthanid nodded. '*Indeed the seed of Eld runs strong in you. As to what it is I must ask of you –*' and he paused.

During that pause, however brief a moment, Crow took the opportunity to look fully upon this great alien scientist, truly a Great Old One, and marvelled at what he saw. There had been a time when such a sight had almost unmanned him, but now he could look at Kthanid and ignore his monstrousness. For indeed beauty lies in the eyes of the beholder, and knowing what Crow knew, Kthanid *was* beautiful.

That itself was an incredible thought, for this might well be Cthulhu himself, this mountain of semi-plastic flesh, this pulsing Kraken. But where Cthulhu's eyes were leaden and lustful, Kthanid's were golden and wise beyond wisdom; and where Cthulhu's thoughts were creeping hypnotic poison, Kthanid's were the very breath of life, Beneficence in the fullest meaning of the word. Oh, kin to the Lord of R'lyeh, that blight on universal life and sanity, this Being most certainly was; close kin at that. The folded-back wings, the great head with its proliferation of face-tentacles, the clawed feet: all told of their kinship. But where Cthulhu was mad and corrupt, Kthanid was the very soul of goodness and mercy, and his compassion enveloped all.

His compassion, yes, which even now worked against him like an acid, betraying him in what he must do, filling him with – guilt! Crow felt it flowing out from him, and was astonished. 'Kthanid, what is it? Why have you brought me here? What is it you want me to do, which at the last you can't tell me face to face?'

'*What I want you to do? Nothing. It is what I must do, for which I need your permission!*'

Impossible! Crow's mind itself must be deceiving him. Kthanid needed *his* permission before he could perform some act?

'*Titus, in your homeworld you had a friend, the man de Marigny. A good man; I myself sent him questing after you and Tiania when you were trapped in the lands of Earth's dreams. Aye, and I promised him a welcome in Elysia, even as a son, if only he return you both alive and sane to me from your travails.*'

Crow nodded. 'He did those things. More, we purged

42

the dreamlands of certain evils – though in the end that was as much your victory as ours.'

Kthanid gave a mental groan and turned his great head away. '*You cannot know the pain your words bring me . . .*'

'What?' Crow was at first bemused – then mortally afraid. The blood drained from him in a moment. 'Henri?' he whispered, 'Something has happened to Henri?'

'*No, no,*' the great Being was quick to answer. '*Be at ease over his well-being. He is well, I promise you. Indeed, soon I shall ask you to ride a Great Thought to him, in Borea on the rim of the bitter ether winds.*'

Crow relaxed a little, allowed himself a sigh of relief. 'Then you intend to keep your promise, bring him here? Whatever it is that threatens Elysia, I can assure you that de Marigny will be a useful force against it!'

'*Useful, yes,*' again Kthanid nodded. And: '*Bring him here? Use him? Ah! – and indeed I intend to use him – but in such a way! And that is why I need your permission.*'

Crow frowned, shook his head. 'Kthanid, I don't think I fully – '

'*Let me remind you,*' Kthanid broke in, '*of things you know well enow but perhaps have forgotten – or at least put to the back of your mind – during your time in Elysia.*'

And then the great Being used a skill of his to throw into Crow's mind a mass of detail, a host of memories revived, and all so thick and fast that even the mind of Titus Crow reeled at this assault on his senses; at the assault itself, and in the face of the evils it conjured.

He was reminded of the ongoing struggle between the intelligent races of the multiverse and the prime Forces of Evil, those prisoned beings of the Cthulhu cycle:

Yog-Sothoth, 'the all-in-one and one-in-all' – a slime-thing frothing forever behind his shielding congeries of iridescent power-globes, co-existent with all time and con-terminous in all space – stood high in their ranks; likewise

Ithaqua the Wind-Walker, stalker between the stars; and Hastur the Unspeakable, half-brother and bitter rival to Cthulhu, dweller in the ill-omened Lake of Hali in the Hyades. Crow knew and had had dealings with all of them, so that Kthanid's sendings merely reinforced his knowledge of them.

He knew the others of this vile pantheon, too, some of them standing on a par with the prime powers, others lower in the scheme of things or subservient to the principal beings and forces. There was Yibb-Tstll: gigantic, grotesquely manlike lord of an alien dimension beyond the borders of sanity; and Shudde-M'ell, nest-master of the subterranean Cthonians of primal Earth; and Cthugha, whose thermal flux had reversed itself and so deranged the once ordered working of his radioactive mind. There was Dagon, fish-god of the Philistines and the Phoenicians and ruler over the Deep Ones, degenerate subaqueous (and sub-human, or *once*-human) servants of Cthulhu and his ilk. Nyogtha, too, and Zhar, Lloigor, Tsathoggua and Bugg-Shash . . .

The list went on, menacing and monstrous, but central and towering over all, always there was Cthulhu, 'an utter contradiction of all matter, force, and cosmic order,' whose lunatic telepathic sendings from R'lyeh in the deep Pacific were of such morbid potency that they were responsible for much of Earth's madness, and almost all of men's nightmares in the land of Earth's dreams.

Basically the legend or history of this ancient order of near-immortal beings was this: that at a time so remote in the past as to defy comparison or definition, they had risen up in a body and rebelled against Order, invoking Chaos as the natural condition. After committing an act so heinous that even they themselves were shocked, they fled and hid in various places and on many parallel planes of existence. Outraged, the Elder Gods regrouped, followed on and tracked them down each and every one, 'chaining' them wherever they were found and placing 'spells' to hold them in their prisons or in selected regions of space-time: Hastur in the Lake of Hali in Carcosa, Cthulhu in sunken R'lyeh, Ithaqua to dwell in frozen interstellar winds and above the ice-wastes of Earth's Arctic, Yog-Sothoth and Yibb-Tstll to chaotic continua outside any known design of science or nature, Tsathoggua to black Hyperborean burrows, and likewise Shudde-M'ell and many of his Cthonians to other buried labyrinths in primal Africa.

All commerce was lost between them except for the contact of disembodied thought. In their infinite wisdom and mercy, the Elder Gods had not taken away the mind-powers of the Great Old Ones, but had merely set up barriers to keep the evil potency of such telepathic wave-bands down to a bearable level. Thus, in the loneliness of their punishment, the Great Old Ones could still 'talk' to one another, even if the power of such communications was much reduced . . .

The flow from Kthanid's mind lessened, finally ceased. And still Crow was puzzled. Why had the great Being shown him these things he already knew so well? Why refresh his memory in these morbid areas? Unless –

'Is de Marigny threatened by the CCD?' he asked. 'Is that what this is all about? Frankly, I don't see how it can be. We've *always* been under threat, de Marigny and I. No, it must be worse, far worse than that. And how is Henri involved?'

'*We are all threatened, Titus,*' Kthanid's thoughts were utterly grave now. '*Your Earth, all other worlds of the three-dimensional universe's intelligent races, the parallel places and subconscious planes – even Elysia!*'

Crow's eyes widened. 'They've risen again,' he whispered. 'Is that what you're trying to tell me? They're free again, and more powerful than ever. The Great Old Ones are back!'

'*Very nearly correct*,' Kthanid answered at once. '*But no, they are not yet "free", as you have it – not yet. But their time is close now; soon they will have the power to be free; even now the constellations move into certain patterns which never should have been. Azathoth, which you knew in your world as the power of nuclear fission, is the betrayer. The mindless nuclear chaos and confusion which spawned us all is a force of Nature and may not be denied. Out there in the vasty voids, gas clouds gather and Azathoth lights them to suns; stars are born which complete a pattern whose configuration is the one thing come down to us from a time beyond all other times; and yes, it would seem that for Cthulhu and those you choose to call the Great Old Ones – after all these eons of time – at last the stars are coming right! Look!'*

Face-tentacles reaching out toward the huge ball of crystal on the onyx table between them – that milky shew-stone whose entire opaque surface seemed slowly mobile, like a reflection of dense clouds mirrored in a still lake – Kthanid showed Crow a distant scene. For as the Earthman stared at the crystal, slowly the milky clouds parted to reveal a picture of an almost sacred place:

Elysia's Vale of Dreams, at the foot of the Purple Mountains far to the south. Tiania had taken Crow there once, to that mysterious place. Mysterious, aye; for there, cut into the royal basalt, were the Thousand Sealed Doors of the N'hlathi, hibernating centipede creatures whose slumbers had already lasted for five thousand years and were not due to be broken for as long again. And the pattern of the doors – each one of which was thirty feet in diameter, sealed with bands of a white metal that no acid might ever corrode – was as the shape of a huge whorl against the face of the mountain, like the spiral of Andromeda.

'It is the spiral nebula in Andromeda!' came Kthanid's thoughts in answer to Crow's own, however unspoken. *'Each portal indicates an especially bright star in that mighty*

whorl. Now let me show you something else – ' and again he reached out with his face-tentacles.

Now, superimposed over these thousand portals to the burrows of the immemorially dreaming N'hlathi, Crow saw Andromeda, how perfectly its principal stars matched the pattern of the doors. '*But see,*' Kthanid indicated where Crow should look, '*there are three doors where no stars exist; but at this very moment spatial debris gathers in one of these places, and in the others ancient suns bid for rebirth. Gravity forms mass ... and soon the raw and elemental power of nuclear genesis will do the rest. Ah! See!*'

For even as Kthanid had spoken, so another star had blazed up, newborn and bright, central in the circular panel of one of the great basalt doors. And now only two spaces remained to be filled ...

Kthanid turned his great head from the crystal, and at once milky clouds rolled as before across its surface. And: '*So you have seen for yourself,*' said the Elder God, '*how time narrows down for us.*'

Crow kept his patience, knew that Kthanid constructed his case this way the better for him to grasp the whole picture. And sure enough:

'*Another portent,*' said the golden Kraken in a little while. '*The giant poppies put up their shoots in the Vale of Dreams. Aye, and the N'hlathi stir in their burrows. It would seem that their ten-thousand-year cycle is broken. Soon the N'hlathi will waken and graze on the seed of the poppy, but utterly out of their season. And it is a matter of legend that this has only ever once happened before – when Cthulhu and his cohorts rose them up against universal sanity! And so you can see, this too is a bad omen ...*'

Now Crow must speak; he controlled his mental agitation, tried to ask only ordered, logical questions: 'Then the N'hlathi are harbingers of doom? I've heard it said that the history of the giant centipedes has never been written, their tongue never understood, the inscriptions on their

47

doors never deciphered, not even by the Dchi-chis. But since they would seem to have had knowledge of this now imminent coming of the Great Old Ones, to such an extent that they deliberately, correctly forecast the pattern of this fantastic omen, as a warning, surely – '

'– Surely we should have made every effort to decipher the legends of their doors long before now? Titus, our greatest scholars, linguists, calligraphers and cryptographers have worked on those inscriptions for a thousand years! It is only through the work of such masters as Esch that we recognized the pattern in the first place. Aye, and his work progresses well – work which I have only disturbed in order to bring him here, so that the Dchi-chis, too, may know of the doom hanging over us all. And so I hope to hasten him and others of his race in their work . . .'

'Why not simply wait for them to wake up?' Crow asked.

'Who can say how long their waking will take – or if it will be soon enough? Indeed, we might contact them in their dreams, but their minds are different; to disturb their hibernation might be to destroy them. We cannot risk that.'

Crow nodded, frowned, said: 'But still you haven't told me what Henri has to do with all of this. How exactly do you intend to use my friend, Kthanid? What is it you need my permission to do? And remember: it was you promised him a welcome here.'

Yet again Kthanid's mental groan. 'I remember it well enow, Titus Crow. But as you well know, there's no royal road into Elysia. Still and all, yes, I greatly desire for him to come here now – but by a route extraordinary!'

Dark suspicions growing, Crow waited, and:

'First let me say this,' Kthanid continued. 'The last time Cthulhu rose him up, we put him down. If it goes our way, this time will be the same. If not –' Crow sensed a mental shrug.

But something which had been bothering the Earthman at the back of his mind now surfaced. 'That's it!' he cried.

'That's what puzzles me. If you had the measure of the Great Old Ones way back there at the dawn of time, and if you beat them then, why not use the same process over again? After all, they've been prisoned for billions of years while your science has gone on, improving almost to infinity. So how can they possibly form any real threat now?'

'*Their threat comes in two forms,*' said Kthanid, patient as ever '*Against Elysia and us Elder Beings, whom they detest and are sworn to destroy, and against your Earth and the lesser worlds and planes of existence. We in Elysia are far from helpless against them, but what of the rest of the sane, ordered universe? Aye, and against us they have a great advantage: for while they may kill or try to kill us, our laws utterly forbid us to kill them!*'

'I begin to understand,' said Crow. 'You may defend yourselves – defend Elysia, Earth, the other places – but you may not attack, not kill. You can only trap them, prison them as before. And you don't know where they'll strike first, right?'

'*That is correct, and so we would like to be able to* direct *their first strike! More of that in a moment, for that's where your friend de Marigny comes in – with your permission. Without it – then we must seek another way. But first let me explain something else:*

'*You have asked why we do not use the same forces – the same methods – against the evil Great Old Ones that were used before. The answer is this: that we are no longer certain exactly* how *we defeated them!*'

Crow was utterly dumbfounded. 'But you were part of it – you engineered it – you *are* the self-same Elder Gods, the same great scientists who brought them down! Are you saying you've forgotten how you achieved your victory?'

'*That is precisely what I am saying! Oh, we remember the last million years with considerable clarity, but what of the three and a half* thousand *million years before that?*'

While Crow absorbed that fantastic thought, that vision of eons, so he felt the Elder God searching delicately in his mind for parallels: looking for ways to make his meaning clear. And finally:

'No single atom of my body is the same – every single one of them has regenerated many times – in three and a half billion years! Memory? Do you remember your first week of life on the planet Earth? Listen, in a time of your planet's history which I consider yesterday, many peoples spoke Latin – and who remembers how it was spoken now? Certain scholars guess. Some of them fairly closely. Your "ancient" Egyptians built great pyramid tombs, and who is there "today" to say how they built them? Your scholars guess. Indeed, you have only recently rediscovered their writing! And what man of you remembers the time when the Elder Gods shaped themselves like men and came down to mate with your daughters, which made you great? Not a one; it is the merest echo of a legend. But indeed there were giants in the land in those days. Yes, I have forgotten!'

Still Crow's mind, keen as any, could not accept it. 'There are no records?'

'Records? Do not think thoughts at me of primitive books and tapes and plastic disks, Titus Crow! The finest memory crystals turn to dust in a billion years. Metals transmute. Sand becomes stone and is worn down to sand again. Indeed, entire worlds may be born and die in that span! The records are gone, forgotten, erased, eroded, extinct. Now, like man, we live with myths and legends . . .'

'Except the N'hlathi.'

'Exactly, for they have "lived" only a few hours out of each ten thousand years. Their minds are the original minds and uncluttered, eneroded. They remember everything. And the legends are writ on their sealed chamber doors.'

Suddenly Crow felt infinitely tiny before this mighty Being and the concepts he conjured. 'You've literally forgotten more than my entire race shall ever learn,' he mumbled then. 'And yet you call me here to ask my permission ... for what?'

And at that point Kthanid told him how he would 'use' de Marigny. Crow might have argued, might even have denied him. The dangers to his friend would be ... enormous! But at least Henri would have a chance, however slim. He'd taken slim chances before, run the gantlet and lived to tell the tale; and as Kthanid had pointed out, there was no royal road into Elysia.

Finally, after long moments of thought, Crow nodded, said: 'I'll ride your Great Thought to de Marigny, Kthanid. Yes, and I'll tell him what I must tell him.'

The Eminence seemed to sigh, nodded gravely. *'I thank you, Titus Crow. Indeed, all Elysia thanks you. But before that there are things that must be done, messages to be run. Now stay here beside me and hear what I shall tell my messengers, and then we shall think a Great Thought to carry you to Borea.'*

He motioned and the curtains hissed open, and the sounds of the assembled peoples of Elysia flooded in. Then Kthanid called certain of them to attend him ...

... Some little time later four 'messengers' went out from the Hall of Crystal and Pearl and made their ways at once and swiftly to various parts of Elysia. One of these was the Thermal Being previously noted by Titus Crow among the throng, another a gossamer-winged, insect-like and ephemeral creature who carried a memory-crystal hurriedly prepared by Kthanid; both of these flew under their own power to the Corridor of Clocks beneath the soaring Blue Mountains.

Of the two remaining messengers: one was Tiania herself, who flew Oth-Neth to The Tree in the Gardens of Nymarrah; the other was a Dchi-chi pupil of Esch, specializing in the cryptic codes, enigmatic and riddlish conversation of wizards, who flew a gravity-defying airform to the spherical aerie of Ardatha Ell at the uppermost limits of Elysia's atmosphere.

In the Corridor of Clocks, the Thermal Being paused before a huge time-clock of near-indestructible glass. The four curious hands on its great dial were tipped with gold to make them more conspicuous, but their *motion* about the hieroglyphed dial was utterly eccentric for all that, which is the way of such devices. The Thermal Being considered his instructions one last time; he would carry them out to the letter, not returning to Elysia until . . . until this thing with the Great Old Ones was finished. Which meant that he might never return. So be it.

All done, he opened and entered the time-clock, flew it out of the subterranean corridor, up over the Blue Mountains, to a point in the upper atmosphere where clock and passenger both blinked out of existence in this plane and so left Elysia. And his destination was far, far away in the deepest voids of space . . .

The clock chosen by the fragile fairy-insect creature was a small grey metal cube of nine-inch sides – more conveyance than vehicle proper, and featureless except for the inevitable dial with its four bizarrely wandering pointers – into which he placed Kthanid's memory-crystal before whistling a sequence of instructions which the clock, in some mysterious way, accepted. For all its unspectacular appearance, this leaden cube was a very special clock indeed: it was not constructed to operate in the physical space-time continuum at all but in those subconscious dimensions formed by the minds of all creatures who dream. It was, quite literally, a clock of dreams, a mechanical monitor of many of the dreamlands of the psychosphere. And it, too, had a special quest: to seek out and deliver its cargo to a very special mechanical being. No sooner were the whistled instructions concluded than the grey cube grew less solid, became transparent, finally

52

disappeared in a rush of displaced air. Satisfied, the insect creature took wing and departed . . .

And in the same moment that the dream-clock passed from Elysia's conscious world, high above her cities and oceans and fields, Esch's favourite student approached the silver sphere which was Ardatha Ell's retreat. The comb-headed creature flew his airform close to the wind-riding, highly reflective surface of the sphere, adjusted his vehicle's controls to 'hover,' rapped upon a curved silver panel with the bony knuckles at the end of a vestigial wing.

'Who knocks?' the sphere dolefully inquired after a moment, asking its question in three mechanically-created languages, all of which the Dchi-chi understood.

'No one,' he at once answered, likewise in triplicate, knowing how much Ardatha Ell would appreciate so cryptic a statement.

'No one knocks, and speaks to me in three tongues? Well, then, the equilibrium is maintained, for I am not at home.'

The Dchi-chi did not even pause to consider this (Kthanid had already apprised him of the wizard's absence, at least of his part-absence) but said: 'I meant that I am no one in the great scheme of things, as I'm sure you well know, wizard. But my message is from a definite someone.' This time he had used only one language, the English of Earth, widely known in Elysia.

'And am I acquainted with this someone?'

'Should I name him, or would you prefer to fathom his identity?'

'You may couch his name in terms, if it please you.'

Knowing that it would please Ardatha Ell even more, the Dchi-chi said: 'Very well, let me say that if your cap was a conical titfer of white wizardry, his would be a crown of mighty beneficence.'

'I do not wear a head garment,' said the sphere, speaking for Ardatha Ell.

'Nor does he.'

'*Hmm!*' said the sphere, thoughtfully. 'He is mighty, he sends out messengers to do his bidding, he is good, and if he wore a crown it would be a kindly one. Hah! Clues galore – and an anagram, too! "Kind hat," indeed! Kthanid!'

'Excellent!' declared the Dchi-chi.

'What's more,' said the sphere, 'you are a Dchi-chi and likely one of Master Esch's best pupils. This is a simple deduction: who else but a Dchi-chi would be adept in so many tongues, and practised in the curious ways of wizards to boot? Oh, you are Dchi-chi, certainly, but not the very master. No, for while your riddle was merely middling, *his* are ever desperately difficult.'

'Still, I do my best,' answered his visitor with a shrug.

'Indeed, and who could ask more of you than that?' agreed the sphere on behalf of Ardatha Ell. 'And now you may enter.'

The curved panel opened outwards and formed a ramp with steps, which the Dchi-chi climbed without hesitation. And: 'Use my house as you will,' the machine voice continued, as the bird-man made his way down a shiny metal corridor toward the centre, 'even though, as you were warned aforetime, I myself am not at home and so may not welcome you.'

'Nor likely to be at home,' answered the other, arriving at Ardatha Ell's innermost apartments. 'Not yet for a while, anyway. But tell me pray: since you are not here, where then are you?'

'In the manse of Exior K'mool, a sorcerer late of Theem'hdra in the primal planet Earth, now Lord of Lith in Andromeda. We amuse ourselves with cryptical conjecturings . . .'

'Pray offer your friend my compliments,' said the Dchi-chi, staring about in amazement, 'and tell him that if ever he has need of a half-decent linguist – '

'What?' Ardatha Ell chuckled. 'Why, Exior K'mool was unriddling the stars when your remote ancestors were eggs in the nest of Archaeopteryx! But say, what bothers you now?'

'Only this,' answered the Dchi-chi with something of a gulp, 'that apparently the greater part of you is here after all!'

For there, suspended on a gravitic bed of air in the centre of this central room, surrounded in the soft green haze of glowing emerald globes that floated around him, lay the body of the wizard, horizontal where his clothes drifted lazily, weightlessly outward from him. All of eight feet tall, Ardatha Ell, but slender as a wand in his robes of floating, fiery bronze mesh. Young-seeming, and yet white-haired and with skin pale as death; his eyes were closed and sunken under purple lids, like those of a corpse. Six-fingered, his hands, with thumbs on both inside and out; and the nails of his long fingers white as wax, and lacquered black at their pointed tips. Sharp-pointed his chin, his nose too, and the bronze mesh slippers on his feet curled at their toes.

No beat showed in his breast, or if there was one it was imperceptibly slow; no breath seemed drawn or to issue from his lips; no proper signs of life were in him at all. And yet:

'I beg to differ,' came that voice from some unseen mechanical source, causing the Dchi-chi to start. 'The lesser part, surely? For this recumbent shell here is only the flesh of Ardatha Ell. The mind – which is greater by far, which is more truly *me* – that is in Exior K'mool's manse in Andromeda.'

The Dchi-chi gulped again, his gizzard contracting, and gazed all about at the room's crammed shelves and sorcerous appurtenances: the ancient books and bottles, charts and charms, even a shewstone like that of Kthanid in the Hall of Crystal and Pearl. And: 'Of course!' he concurred with a nervous *chirrup*. 'Why, this must be the very least part of you, I see that now. But, good sir, time waits for no creature and I carry Kthanid's message, and – '

' – And you must fly, little bird? And the secret of your cryptic statement – that for the time being I shall not re-enter Elysia – lies hid in Kthanid's message, eh?' The voice seemed far less mechanical now, much more vibrant and forceful. Even ominous, in a way. 'Very well, let's have that message now. Merely place your hand – or whatever you have which passes for one – on the pale brow of that sleeper there. Then think your message, or chirp it if you will, or even couch it in rhyme or riddle, and I shall receive and understand.'

Gingerly the Dchi-chi did as instructed, placed his bony bird-hand upon the brow of the suspended wizard, and . . . instantly it was as if his claw was glued there, taken root in Ardatha Ell's skull and held fast by some irresistible force! He felt his message, which he would have passed anyway, *sucked* out of him in a moment – following which he was at once released. Staggering backwards he heard the wizard's dry, mechanical chuckle. And:

'There, all done,' said Ardatha Ell. But in the next moment, in a voice more grave: 'Aye, and this is an important task Kthanid has set me. You should have said so before now, little bird, instead of posing and parroting.'

But the Dchi-chi was already fluttering his way back down the shining corridor to the outer portal. Out into the gusting higher atmosphere of Elysia he went and down the metal steps to his airform, and only then did he pause to say: 'I thank you for your hospitality, wizard. Alas, my wit is small and likewise my talent, when compared with such as yours.'

'Not at all,' said the sphere through the bluster of air, once more completely cold and mechanical. 'We all have to begin somewhere. But when next you call, first make sure I'll be at home in person to greet you, eh? Or perhaps I'll speak to your master, Esch, and tell him to let you come more often; and we can test each other's mettle with riddles, or I'll teach you some tongues you haven't even heard of yet. What say you, Dchi-chi, who fancied himself proficient in the many ways of wizards?'

Casting off, the Dchi-chi answered: 'I thank you, sir, and hardly like to appear ungrateful – but Esch keeps me very busy, and I haven't much of a head for heights – and truth to tell, I'm afraid I'd bore you very quickly!' He dipped his airform toward the fields far below.

'Ah, well! So be it,' the sphere called after him. 'Farewell, then, little bird.' And the steps flattened themselves and folded back, becoming a panel in the sphere's silver flank as before.

. . . And in the fire-floating manse of Exior K'mool where it drifted over the bubbling lava lakes of Lith, two great wizards nodded and chortled, amused for a moment by this diversion whose source lay in Elysia on the far side of eternity. And then they returned to their game of chess . . .

Tiania, the fourth messenger, sat high in the branches of the Tree in the Gardens of Nymarrah. The fork where she perched was broad as a branching path, but even if she slipped she would not fall very far. The Tree's sensitive tendrils were never far away; indeed the one that carried his powerful thoughts and emotions lay on Tiania's pulsing wrist. His leaves were huge as blankets and just as soft; his smaller branches were bigger than the oaks of Earth; all of his care and attention were centred now on this favourite child of Elysia.

Six hundred feet below, there the Tree's vast roots spread out in Nymarrah's rich soil, while as high again overhead his topmost leaves, small and lush green, trembled in Elysia's synthetic sunlight; but here in his heart sat Tiania, talking with him as they had talked a hundred times before, though rarely so seriously:

'And you *will* speak to that Tree in the land of Earth's dreams, and pass on Kthanid's message as I've told it to you, word for word?' she begged for at least the tenth time, while the Tree caressed her with the soft-furred edge of a leaf.

'I sleep and dream, too, child,' he answered in her mind. 'If that dream-Tree may be found – even on a world as far away as Earth – then I shall find him. Aye, and I'll pass on Kthanid's message. Now be sure of that: if I must dream all night, I'll find him.' He was silent for a moment, then said: 'He must be very dear to you, this Searcher?'

'He's a friend like no other,' she answered, sighing. 'But for Henri I'd not be here. He's a brother to me, a lifelong friend and companion to my man, a champion to all lesser creatures. And we treat him like this!'

'Well, then,' said the Tree's gentle 'voice' in her head, 'if he's all of these things my task is made doubly important. And lifelong friend of Titus Crow, you say? That alone were more than enough! No, I shall not fail you. But why are you alone today? Where is your Titus?'

'With Kthanid,' she answered in a whisper, 'in the Hall of Crystal and Pearl. He's there, and by now he's very likely somewhere else.'

And with that she fell silent and was satisfied to let the Tree comfort her ...

4

Familiar Winds

Ithaqua The Wind-Walker was back on Borea.

Once, three years ago, this Great Old One would have sat atop his totem temple throne four or five miles from the foot of the plateau out in the white waste; he would have sat there and scowled at the plateau – threatening occasionally with raised, massive club-like fist, or lightnings called from living, lowering skies – while his wolf-warriors and the wild Children of the Winds howled and cavorted at his great splayed feet and made sacrifice to him. And when the mood took him he would have raised up tornadoes of snow and ice, gigantic wind-devils tall as the plateau itself, to hurl shatteringly against the hollow mountain's impervious flanks.

Three years ago, aye ...

But Ithaqua's totem temple was no more; at Hank Silberhutte's bidding, Henri-Laurent de Marigny had used the time-clock to destroy it utterly, a crippling blow to Ithaqua's monstrous pride. More than that, Ithaqua himself had felt the sting of de Marigny's weird hyper-dimensional vehicle, had come to understand that the plateau's Warlord and his friend from the Motherworld had his measure. And so now he stood off and kept his distance, especially since he sensed that de Marigny had returned, and that once again the time-clock and its near invincible weapon of the Elder Gods were resident in the plateau.

Like some toxic breath of ill-omen, the Wind-Walker had come back to Borea in that same hour that Armandra called her council of tribal chiefs to attend her in the Hall of the Elders, to witness her intended communication with ether winds from all corners of space and time. And while they had gathered there at the counselling place, so he had come striding down the star-winds to Borea, evil burning in his black heart and the unquenchable lust for revenge fevering his alien blood.

And because his totem temple was no more, and also because he hated and feared the time-clock, now he perched a good six miles from the plateau on the rusting steel hulk of a British ice-breaker of the late '20s; a once-proud vessel, fashioned perhaps in the shipyards of the Weir or the Tyne and long since paid for by Lloyds of London: 'lost with all hands, somewhere inside the Arctic Circle', stranded now in the ice and snows of the white waste. There the ship lay – half-shrouded in ice, her once powerful propellers jutting up at an odd angle, monument to Ithaqua's enormous cruelty – snatched up by *him* in deranged glee and borne here through alien voids, finally to be tossed down in the snows of a strange world like some discarded toy.

And the beast himself, crouched upon the ship's flank, the carmine stars of his eyes thoughtful in his dark blot of a head where they burned on the distantly jutting rock of the plateau. For aye, he knew that Armandra talked with the winds, those traitor winds (to him) of time and space. But what his half-human daughter could do gently and without coercion, he would do brutally with blows and curses. And what secrets she could learn by simply asking, he could likewise learn with demands and threats of doom . . .

In the Hall of the Elders, Armandra was in trance.

To call that place a 'hall' were no misnomer: it was a huge cavern of a chamber, lit by many flaring flambeaux; and at its centre a fur-decked dais supporting a carved, massively ornate throne. There sat Armandra, her white hands curved over the throne's stone arms, eyes closed and regal head upright, breast slowly rising and falling under a white fur jacket.

Before her face, hanging down from the forward-curving back of the throne and suspended on a chain of gold, was the large medallion she normally wore at her neck, sigil of her supremacy over the winds. Slowly the medallion turned, its gold burnished to a blaze in the bright glare of the hall's flambeaux.

Descending tiers of stone benches encircled the Hall of the Elders, giving it the rich acoustics of an auditorium; so that now, in the near-absolute silence, even the steady sussuration of Armandra's breathing could be heard in all quarters. And certainly there were sufficient elders there to hear it! Chiefs of all the plateau's peoples they were: Tlingit, Blackfoot, Esquimaux, Chinook and Nootka, and all the old Northwest Tribes of old Earth, their ancestors brought to populate Borea in primal times by Ithaqua the Wind-Walker. There they sat in full ceremonial regalia, just as they might have sat at some meeting of the great chiefs in a northern forest of the Motherworld, watching Armandra with their eagle eyes and breathlessly awaiting her words and works.

To the left of Armandra's throne kneeled Oontawa, lovely Indian handmaiden and squaw of Kota'na; she was there in case the plateau's priestess should require assistance in this task she'd set herself: to call down before her those strange winds which forever wander between the worlds. And at the foot of the dais, at its front, there stood the warlord's small party: Silberhutte himself, his bear-brother Kota'na, Tracy (Hank's sister) and Jimmy Franklin, and The Searcher, Henri-Laurent de Marigny, and his woman Moreen. With them stood Charlie Tacomah, a modern Shawnee late of the Motherworld who had befriended Silberhutte and co. when first Ithaqua had brought them across the star-spaces to Borea – a mistake the Wind-Walker must surely rue to this very day. After the war in Korea, Charlie had travelled north in the Motherworld to write a book on the old Indian and Eskimo tribes, and there on the fringe of the Arctic he'd run foul of Ithaqua. Korea to Borea, as simple as that! He'd spent some time in the camps of the savage Children of the Winds, had finally run off to the plateau. His military experience had been useful, for he'd been a strategist; now he had a seat on the Council of Elders. But his high-ranking friends preferred that he stand here with them.

And so they all waited, and in a little while ... so it began!

For now de Marigny and the others began to hear, as if from far, far away, a keening as of winds blowing between the worlds, and the sounds issued from that now vibrating medallion where it turned on its golden chain before Armandra's drawn white face. What few hushed whispers had sounded before from the audience of elders now ceased; and as if to compensate, the humming and roaring of the throbbing medallion increased. Then –

– It seemed to de Marigny that a host, a torrent of sighing ghost-winds rushed through the chamber. They plucked at his and Moreen's clothes, played in their hair, rushed on in a curious swirl. And yet surely it was all delusion, for the flambeaux flickered not a jot but burned steadily as before! An illusion, yes, like the crashing of distant breakers heard in a shell, this moaning of winds plucked down from between the stars – or was it?

'This never fails to get to me,' came Hank Silberhutte's hoarse whisper in de Marigny's ear, causing him to start. 'She's all woman, Armandra, but there's plenty of the stuff of her father in her, too. Still, I don't have to tell *you* that!'

Indeed he didn't, for de Marigny had previous experience of Armandra's works a-plenty – but this at least was new to him. New, too, the sudden shock of her voice, where before she had been silent – that golden, bell-like voice, breaking over the ghost-ridden rush of weird winds.

The short hairs of de Marigny's neck prickled as she spoke, and he felt an electric tension in the air:

'Ithaqua has returned to Borea,' she intoned, her eyes still closed, her face white as driven snow. 'Drawn back before his time, he watches even now from the white waste. I feel his mind probing at my own, which now I fortify against him!'

Whispers of inquiry and alarm passed between the elders. Ithaqua had not been due back for a three-month yet! What, Ithaqua, back so soon? And no use to ask for what good reason, for there was never any *good* reason where the Wind-Walker was concerned. This was ill-omen indeed!

Armandra gave them no more time for speculation, however, for: '*There!*' she continued, giving a curt nod of satisfaction. 'Now I have shut him out, whose greatest desire is to know our every secret. And now I may converse with the small, friendly winds that wander all the starlanes. Not the mighty whirlwinds of time and space, spawned in the great holes and angles of existence, but their little cousins who play in the vasty voids, whose wanderings have taken them every where and when ...'

For a moment she was silent, breathing deeply, her brow furrowed in concentration; but then her face lightened, she smiled strangely, her right hand lifted and beckoned. 'Come then, little wind. Come talk to Armandra, and tell her of your travels. And speak, if you will, of the ways of Elysia and the roads that lead there.'

Her eyes remained closed but her burning hair stirred eerily, apparently of its own accord, and began to drift up weightless from her alabaster neck and shoulders. The fur of her jacket grew ruffled, as by a breeze, and her smile became broader at some small secret she alone heard whispered. And:

'This one has returned from Arcturus,' she said, 'where ten thousand ice-planets whirled about a frozen hollow sun.

63

And so fragile that great frozen star, that when he ventured inside and blew about its icicles and brittle stalactites, all crumbled and fell in and shattered into shards and motes of ice. And when the frozen sun collapsed, so its many worlds, released like shots from a sling, went bounding off into space to seek new suns; and so this small wind is very likely a father of future worlds! So he says, but I think it a clever fantasy, with which he hopes to please me. As for Elysia: *there* lies the fable, he says, for never did he talk to a wind who ever ventured there.'

Her smile faded a little as she slowly cocked her head to allow a very small breeze to rest a moment like a kitten in the crook of her neck. Invisible, that ether-gust, but it smoothed out the ruffled fur of her collar and caused her copper hair to billow there. 'And this one is sad,' she said, 'for he lost his brothers in the maw of a black hole, where they strayed too close to its rim. Now they are sucked through the hole to some other place far removed, and he fears he'll never more gust with them out in the stars we know. He supposes they might just possibly have found their way into Elysia – whereof he's heard it said that all the winds are fair – but alas, of the location of that place he can tell me nothing.'

And so it went: the ether winds came and departed at her bidding, breezes and breaths, puffs and pants, gusts and gasps of wind come to talk to Armandra. She spoke with bitter winds from the deepest regions of space, and others warmed by the exhalations of suns where they'd played. There were winds born in the mountains of green worlds on balmy summer evenings, and others whose worlds were dead now and mourned their passing as winds do. Infant breezes there were, and soughing winds almost as old as time, and all of them with their own tales to tell.

Until at the last, and just as de Marigny began to despair of ever hearing anything useful –

' – *Ah!*' sighed Armandra, clasping the arms of her

throne and sitting up yet more regally erect. 'Now here's a rare wind indeed, and a *frightened* one at that!'

Hank Silberhutte grasped de Marigny's elbow, reminder that he was not merely lost in some impossible dream or hallucination. 'This might be just what you're looking for!' the ex-Texan whispered. 'I thought she was beginning to flag, but now she's fully alive again – *see* . . . !'

De Marigny saw. A faint bloom was suddenly visible on Armandra's pale cheeks, like the flush of some strange excitement. Some unseen thing – a panicked gasp of air, perhaps – hid for a moment in a sleeve of her jacket, causing it to bell out, then burst free to rush round her head in a veritable frenzy of fear. Until: 'Be still! Be calm!' she cried. 'You're safe here, little one, from whatever it is that pursues.'

De Marigny was drawn to lean closer, caught up in what was happening.

'And this one,' said Armandra, with something of triumph in her voice at last, ' – this last small wind – he has had all the bluster knocked out of him! He's fled far and fast from a very terrible thing, almost exhausting himself entirely in the process. He is not pursued, no, but he has heard the shrieking of a gaseous intelligence out beyond the Red Medusa who *was* pursued – by the Hounds of Tindalos!'

De Marigny caught his breath as his flesh began to crawl, but he must hear this out.

'A cloud of gas, yes,' Armandra continued, 'a vapour in the voids travelling half as fast as light, and pursued by the hounds. He had a name, this intelligence, which was simply a hiss – Sssss! Or if not a name, at least that is how he thought of himself. And as he fled, so this small wind thought to hear him praying to the Great Gods of Eld in Elysia, begging of them their assistance! Then he saw the hounds where they pursued, saw them devouring the trailing wisps of the gaseous being, and when he saw how hideous they were he too fled. And so he is come here to rest and recover his strength . . .'

Armandra sighed, lay back her head a little, opened her great green eyes. Her lustrous copper hair settled down upon her head and round her shoulders, and suddenly the chamber was still and the winds were gone from it.

Then someone coughed and the silence was broken. The spell, too. De Marigny shook himself, considered all he'd heard – especially the tale of the final visitation.

It wasn't much to go on, he thought, but it had to be better than nothing. Or was it? What was he to make of it after all? A cloud of intelligent gas out beyond the Red Medusa Nebula? A vapour-being who prayed to the Gods of Eld? And yet if that incredible gas intelligence knew enough of the Elder Gods to call out to them for their aid, perhaps he (it?) might also know where they were. It was a possibility, however remote, that de Marigny couldn't ignore – made all the more urgent by the presence of the Hounds of Tindalos. Maybe out there in the star-voids a door was closing even now, a gateway to Elysia, slammed shut forever by the Hounds of Tindalos!

Oontawa was helping Armandra down the dais steps. The Woman of the Winds was not so much tired as dizzy from her efforts. Tracy, too, had gone to help support her; both girls were anxious for her, until the Warlord reached up and lifted her easily down the last two steps into his arms. She hugged him, then turned to de Marigny.

'I'm sorry, Henri, but that's as much as I can do. It seems that this Elysia is a very special, very secret place.'

He took her hand, kissed it, said: 'Armandra, you've probably done more for me in half an hour than I've been able to do for myself in three long years! At least I've something to go on now. But the effort has wearied you, and I had no right to ask you to do it anyway. So how can I ever find words to thank you for – '

He paused as there came a sudden buzz of excitement

66

from the elders close to the chamber's entrance. An Eskimo runner stood there, gasping his message. Kota'na recognized him not so much as a messenger but one of the keepers he'd left in charge of the bears that guarded the time-clock in de Marigny's chambers, and went to him at once. He returned in a moment.

'Henri,' he said, his Indian's eyes wide and very bright. 'It is the time-clock!'

'What?' de Marigny's jaw dropped as he grasped Kota'na's brawny arms. 'The clock? What of it?' His anxiety was very real, for he remembered that time from three years earlier, when Ithaqua's wolf-warriors had stolen his vehicle. 'Don't tell me something's happened to – ?'

'Happened to it?' Kota'na cut him off, shaking his head in denial. 'Oh, no, my friend – and yet, yes. The clock is where you left it under guard – but its door has opened, and a purplish light spills out!'

5

Great Thought Rider

Time-clock: a totally inadequate misnomer, thought de Marigny, as he hurried with Hank and Moreen through the plateau's labyrinth to the dwelling-caves near the perimeter where the clock was temporarily housed. It did look like a clock at first glance, like a fine old grandfather in the somewhat macabre shape of a coffin, and it did have a dial and hands; but there any resemblance to a clock in the mundane sense of the word ended.

Its weird ticking was quite irregular; its four hands moved about the hieroglyphed dial in spastic patterns patently divorced from any chronological system known or even guessed at by man; it was certainly *not* an instrument for measuring the orderly passage of time at all but rather ignored and even transgressed temporal laws. And because time is part and parcel with space – the other side of the same coin, as it were – so the time-clock transgressed against spatial laws, too.

In short, it was a vehicle for space-time travel, a gateway on all possible worlds and levels of existence, a not entirely mechanical magical carpet. Einstein would not have believed in the time-clock, and what he would have made of a gaseous intelligence riding the solar winds through space at half the speed of light ... who can say? But then again, a sea-urchin would probably experience the greatest difficulty believing in Einstein.

De Marigny, on the other hand, did believe in the clock; each time he used it his life, Moreen's too, hung by the thread of that belief. He believed in it, and he trusted it, even though many of its complexities remained way beyond his grasp. This was hardly surprising; it had been that way for Titus Crow too, in his time. But the more de Marigny used the clock, the more he learned; a slow process, true, but a sure one. It was like being a learner-driver in the latest model of some high-technology motor-car; there was always a new button or switch one had never tried before, which might well be a device for steaming rain off the windows ... but might just as easily jettison the driver through the roof!

... Finally the three arrived at de Marigny's and Moreen's quarters, passed the Eskimo guard and keeper where he stood with a pair of massive, rumbling bears, and so into the chamber where the time-clock waited. Here small circular 'windows' looked out over the white waste, and on a bleak horizon Ithaqua crouched atop the derelict ice-breaker, watching the plateau just as Armandra had seen him in her trance. Time for only a cursory glance at the Wind-Walker, however, for here was an even greater wonder; and perhaps one just as fearful, in its way.

For indeed the time-clock's panel stood open, its eerie purple light pouring out in rhythmic pulses from within. Just what this might signify was hard to say, but de Marigny could soon find out. 'Wait,' he said to Moreen and Hank as he stepped forward and made to enter the clock. Except –

– Even as his hand gripped the frame of that narrow portal, *so a figure materialized there and stepped out!*

Taken by surprise, de Marigny gasped, jumped back and almost collided with Hank and Moreen. Then he grasped and restrained the Warlord's hand where already his knuckles were white, clenched on the haft of a bright pick-like weapon snatched from his broad belt.

'No, Hank!' The Searcher cried then. 'There's no danger here. Can't you see who it is? Don't you recognize him? It's Titus Crow!'

On legs suddenly weak as jelly de Marigny went to embrace the newcomer – fell against nothing and staggered right through him. Crow was insubstantial as smoke, a mirage – a hologram!

'A ghost!' Moreen gasped. 'Is this your Titus Crow, Henri? A phantom whose grave is the time-clock? Is that why it's shaped like a coffin?' And for all that she was only half-serious, still de Marigny sensed something of fear in her voice.

Silberhutte, on the other hand, was quicker to grasp the true picture. '*Shh*, Moreen!' he whispered, putting a protective arm round her shoulder. 'This is no ghost. It's not magic but science. And Henri's perfectly correct: wherever this 3-D picture is coming from, it's certainly a picture of Titus Crow.'

De Marigny had meanwhile recovered himself and stepped back from the apparition; and as for Crow, he seemed just as bemused as the three whose eyes followed his every movement. For a moment utter confusion was written on his face; then, like a man suddenly blind, he groped his way backward until once more he stood inside the clock and was bathed in its ethereal glow. Then came his voice, that deep, rich and oh so well remembered voice from the memories of de Marigny and Silberhutte both:

'Henri? I saw you then, but just for a moment. If that was really you out there, please come inside the clock where we can talk. I'm riding a Great Thought sent by Kthanid. Outside the clock I'm largely immaterial, but in here I'm much less a spectre. Only be quick, Henri, for Kthanid can't keep this up for very long.'

De Marigny needed no further urging. With a second 'Wait!' to his friends, he stepped inside the clock and was engulfed in its pulsing light. Then for a moment two old, true friends peered anxiously at one another – and at last smiles broke out, and laughter – and finally they pounded each other's backs.

'It's you,' said de Marigny, 'in the flesh – of a sort, anyway! But how?'

'You haven't changed, Henri,' said Crow then, holding him at arms' length. 'Not a jot. Still full of questions I never have the time to answer.'

'And you,' the other returned. 'Why, if anything you seem even younger!' And then, with less levity: 'But you're wrong, Titus, for I have changed. I've been changed. It's not simply my own skin I've to care for now. But . . . I want to show you something. How long do we have?'

Crow's smile also fell. 'Minutes,' he answered. 'I'll get the very briefest warning, and then I'll be on my way back to Elysia.'

'Time enough,' said de Marigny; and over his shoulder he called, 'Moreen, will you come in here, please?'

She came at once, innocent and charming as always. Face to face with the girl, Crow's eyes opened wide in wonder and appreciation. And: 'This is Moreen,' said de Marigny. 'Born in Borea's moons of Earth stock taken there by Ithaqua. Funnily enough, she was mine even before I found her, much like your Tiania. Now we travel together.'

Crow gave the girl a hug, said to his friend: 'You'd have been pushed to find her like on Earth, Henri – or even in Elysia, for that matter.'

'Room for another in there?' came the friendly, growled query of the plateau's Warlord. And a moment later Hank Silberhutte, too, stood bathed in the clock's weird illumination. For that was another anomaly of the time-clock: that the space within it was very nearly as great as that outside!

And now for the first time it was Crow's turn to display amazement. 'What?' he said, his eyes incredulous where they looked Silberhutte up and down. 'Hank? Is it really you? My God! And how long ago since we all went at the Burrowers together, eh? And how much passed between?'

'That was . . . another world,' said the other. 'Hell, it really was! But from what I've heard, it hardly seems we'll have the time now to fill in the gaps. So Moreen and me, we'll simply stand here and listen, and try to keep patient until you and Henri get done. You're not here for the fun of it, eh, Titus?'

Crow's face quickly became grave. 'Not for the fun of it, no. My reason for being here is probably the best any sane human being could have.' He turned more fully to de Marigny. 'I might have come sooner, mind to mind, but you weren't receptive. You were preoccupied, Henri, your mind full of other things. But I know that wherever the old time-clock was, then that you'd be there too. Also, I might have simply come here – more fully "in the flesh" – in another time-clock or via this one. But with very few exceptions all the clocks are back in Elysia now, where for a little while at least they're destined to stay. This clock of yours is one of those few exceptions. Also, to use this clock as a gateway and come here physically, that would mean returning the same way: transmitting myself *physically* into Elysia. And right now nothing physical is allowed into Elysia. Which is why I rode a Great Thought, between Kthanid and the clock. It was the only way.'

'You seem physical enough to me,' said de Marigny, and the Warlord nodded his agreement.

'I felt your arms around me,' said Moreen.

'That's the clock, reinforcing my presence here. But you saw what happened to me outside – I was thin as a spook!'

'Wait a minute,' said de Marigny, frowning. 'Are you saying that something's happened in Elysia? Nothing physical is to be allowed in? And does that include me?'

'Elysia is under siege, Henri,' said Crow, 'or as good as. It's just a matter of time, that's all.'

'Under siege?' This was plainly beyond The Searcher. 'But how could a place like Elysia possibly be under siege? From whom? I mean, I – ' He stopped dead and his eyes suddenly opened wide. Then: 'This has to be some sort of perverse joke, Titus, surely?'

Crow shook his head. 'No, my friend, no joke. They're rising – and soon!'

'Who?' the Warlord could keep silent no longer. 'What is this threat? Who or what is rising?'

'*They* are rising,' Crow repeated. 'The primal threat, the Great Old Ones themselves! The stars are very nearly right, and the Cthulhu Cycle Deities are on the move again. But that doesn't mean you're excluded, Henri, on the contrary. Indeed, both you and Moreen will be welcome in Elysia. It was Kthanid himself promised you that, remember?'

'Oh, I remember all right,' the other answered, a little sourly. 'But how does one *attain* Elysia? Titus, I've searched so hard. Believe me, I've tried. Man, I've found out what you meant when you warned me that there was no royal road into Elysia. In fact, I had almost given up hope.'

Crow bit his lip, and for the first time de Marigny knew that something gnawed at him, something other than the trouble brewing in Elysia. Crow covered it quickly, said: 'You can't give up hope now, Henri, not now. No, for now you're really needed in Elysia' (and again that tortured look). Then: 'Listen, you're right about there being no royal road. I can't take you by the hand and lead you there, especially not now. But there is still a way. It's a pointer, that's all, a couple of clues, and they're the best I can do for you.'

'I'm listening,' said de Marigny eagerly. 'Whatever it is, it has to be better than groping in the dark. Just keep talking, and believe me I won't miss a word.'

'Very well,' said Crow. 'First, there are places you can try looking in Earth's dreamlands. Now we both know a little about the dreamlands but we're not expert dreamers, so don't go jumping to any wrong conclusions. It's just a place to start. Then there's – ' He paused, looked startled, grasped de Marigny's hand and held it tightly. For a moment his outline wavered, and at the same time his grip on de Marigny's hand seemed gentle as a girl's, but then he firmed up strong again.

'Titus, I – ' de Marigny was alarmed.

'The warning I told you about,' Crow cut him off. 'We only have a minute now. So listen: back in Theem'hdra at the dawn of all Earthly civilization, there was a wizard called Exior K'mool. He, too, might know something – if you can find him. And finally – '

The light in the clock was pulsing faster now, and its colour was changing through all the shades of purple to a strange foxfire blue. Crow wavered again, grew wispy as smoke, tried to grab de Marigny and hang onto him. His hands went right through; de Marigny's and Silberhutte's, too, where they tried to hold fast to their old friend. And now, at the last, Crow's voice was thin as a reed:

' – Finally there's a cloud of luminous gas out beyond the Red Medusa Nebula,' he said, as from a million miles away; but on the last word his voice grew fainter still and petered out altogether.

'I know it!' de Marigny cried. 'It has intelligence. It's fleeing from the Hounds of Tindalos . . .'

Crow was still mouthing something but the words were lost. Suddenly he seemed snatched up, whirled away. Pin-wheeling down a whirlpool of throbbing blue light, he grew small in a moment. But before he vanished completely, his voice came back one last time:

'But if you know that much, maybe you'd have discovered the rest, too. That's good! I don't feel so bad . . . about . . . it . . . now . . .'

'About what?' de Marigny frantically called after him, but only echoes came back. Titus Crow had gone, drawn back on Kthanid's Great Thought to Elysia.

Gone too the whirlpool of blue foxfire, and the interior of the time-clock pulsed purple as before . . .

6

Sssss!

Named after a creature of incalculable evil, nevertheless the Red Medusa Nebula was a thing of incredible beauty.

Way beyond the range of Earthly telescopes, in whose eyes it was the merest smudge of ochre light or series of faint radio blips, the Medusa was aptly named: not only did it have the outlines of that Gorgon's head, but also a mass of snaky filaments which could be her hair. More, it had a certain trick of hers, too: in a manner of speaking, it could turn things to stone.

The Medusa was a cancer which was eating itself; its filaments had not been flung outwards but were being *drawn* out, by a ring of great black holes where they circled the nebula and sucked off its countless billions of tons of matter into nothingness. Theory has it that matter falling into a black hole, as it approaches the speed of light, becomes motionless as time itself is frozen. And so it can be seen how this great cosmic Medusa 'petrified' her victims. But of course that was only theory, and since coming to know the time-clock de Marigny was given to mistrust much of what theory says.

Nevertheless the Medusa was a place to avoid, and so now the time-clock winged around it, hurtling at many times the speed of light (and in so doing, ruining another theory) and heading for the far side. 'Beyond the Red Medusa Nebula' had seemed to The Searcher's way of thinking to cover a very large and largely unknown region; but at the same time he (the clock) was equipped with the most sensitive scanners, and so it should not prove too difficult to locate the luminous and comparatively slow-moving Sssss . . .

When it had come to choosing a place to start there had seemed very little of choice. Theem'hdra, the Primal Land in the dawn of all Earthly civilizations? The land of Earth's dreams? But the sentient gas cloud was threatened by the Tind'losi Hounds; he (it) had called on the Elder Gods for their aid; perhaps – and for all de Marigny knew – this mission of his was simply Kthanid's way of answering that call. Another good reason was that Moreen had wanted it; indeed her love of all (or most) creatures, no matter how strange, had driven her to insist upon it. The Hounds of Tindalos were devouring the gas-being, and that was good enough for her. In the three years she had loved and travelled with The Searcher, Moreen had come to know the hounds very well; to know them, and to be repulsed by them – even Moreen.

In those same three years she'd learned something of the clock's handling, too, so that along with de Marigny she now exhilarated in its flight as they sped in that near-fabulous craft across the vast curve of space. And so at last, when the Red Medusa sprawled far in their wake: 'There!' she cried, first to detect the drama that lay ahead.

De Marigny saw it a moment later, drew it close in the clock's scanners: a glowing green cloud like some mighty comet, with a hard bright nucleus and a long gossamer tail flaring far behind. Fifty thousand miles long, Sssss, and seeming to expand enormously by the moment as de Marigny slowed the time-clock and brought it about in a great semi-circle to parallel the path of the nucleus. And back there in the tail –

The time-clock's rearward scanners left little doubt as to what was happening back there.

It was without question the hounds, but in such numbers – so vast a pack – as de Marigny had never imagined in all his wildest hound-ridden nightmares! 'By all the gods in Elysia,' he whispered to Moreen then, 'just *look* at them!'

'I have looked,' she answered with a sob, 'and I've seen.

They are like no other creatures, these hounds. They know only two things: destroy and devour.'

De Marigny nodded. 'They're the stuff of the Mythos, all right,' he agreed. 'The CCD's trackers across time's wastelands!'

To see the Hounds of Tindalos was to know them at once, but a man might see them a hundred times and still find difficulty in describing them. They were that alien! Like some monstrous four-dimensional plague, they were vampires of time that haunted its darkest angles, foraging abroad from the temporal towers of wraithlike Tindalos to hunt down unwary travellers. An uncleanliness lacking any real, living form, yet they were embodied in vague batlike shapes. They were flapping rags of evil, thirsting drinkers of life itself. And insatiable.

But since their true habitation was time itself, de Marigny found a strange anomaly here. 'A weird pack, this,' he said to Moreen. 'They run in space! I knew that in certain circumstances they can cross the time-barrier into three-dimensioned space, but this is the first time I've actually seen it. Maybe those black holes back there on the rim of the Red Medusa have something to do with it. Perhaps they've welded space and time into one here.'

But Moreen was hardly listening. Rapt to her scanners, she murmured: 'He is alive! He is . . . *aware*! And Henri, he is in pain! Not pain as we know it, but hurtful none-theless. The hounds are a slow acid that sloughs away his being, reduces his life-force, slows him down and ever more speedily devours him. They are a disease eating into him, corrupting him, killing him. It may take a thousand years, but what is that to them? Time is on their side. And all the time his agony increasing, until the hounds reach his nucleus. Then the final rending as they bring him down, the last spurting of the forces which power him, and the black debris of his passing seething forever in an endless orbit round the Red Medusa.'

De Marigny found and squeezed her hand. 'Not if I have anything to do with it,' he told her. 'We'll see about that in a little while. But first . . . Moreen, can you actually talk to it – to him?'

'Did you ever see a creature I couldn't talk to?' she asked.

'Only the hounds themselves,' he answered.

'Because they are *not* life,' she explained. 'Because they are anti-life. But Sssss is alive and beautiful. His colour, even his size is . . . beautiful! Of course I can talk to him. Only adjust your receptors, Henri, and hear him for yourself.'

Receptors: another misnomer. Like the scanners, these were not wholly mechanical; both words were simply terms for devices almost beyond mundane comprehension. To meld one's mind with the clock was to enhance one's perceptions ten-fold, while to use its sensors was to achieve the square of that effect. Through the clock's scanners human eyes might well be telescopes, or on a different scale microscopes. Hearing was so sensitized that the human ear might detect the abrasive rasp of one snowflake against the next. Tuned to the time-clock's senses, a man might 'smell' the scents of distant moons, or the decay of a dying star, or 'taste' the atmosphere and water of a planet while still a million miles away. The sixth, psychic sense was amplified, too: a gifted telepath such as Hank Silberhutte would become a thought transmitter to the stars; and as for a woman like Moreen, whose empathy with all living creatures must surely be the result of a unique mutation . . .

Oh, Moreen could 'talk' to Sssss, most certainly, but all de Marigny got was a mush of mental static. He could *not* talk to the gas-being, not possibly. To the amphibian holothurians he'd met on a mainly water-world, yes, and to the pollen-gathering apoideans of a savannah planet in Aldebaran; but these had been alive as he understood and was physically aware of life. 'Fire' to him was fire to them, and likewise 'danger', 'good', 'bad', 'joy', 'flight', 'walking', 'pleasure', 'food', and 'drink'. And of course 'life' and 'death'. Most creatures have some common ground, recognize parallel links in the chain of life. But Sssss? The gaps were too great, for The Searcher, anyway.

And so de Marigny could only shake his head in defeat. 'Then you'd better translate,' he said. 'Ask him if we can help.'

She did so, at once, and de Marigny heard her thoughts go out with crystal clarity to the fleeing gas-being – and heard them answered. The mush of psychic static altered its pitch, tone, timbre, became more controlled, more purposeful. Moreen and the gas cloud Sssss conversed.

'You know,' de Marigny told her in something of awe, 'I believe that if you'd wanted to you might even have talked to Armandra's familiar winds.'

'I would not have dared to try,' she told him in an aside. 'The plateau is Armandra's domain and her winds are loyal to her. No, I didn't try to talk to them; but when she had drawn them to her, I couldn't help but overhear a little of their conversation. Just a little, for indeed they're secretive things, winds . . .'

Again de Marigny marvelled, and almost laughed. But just then –

'He wants to know if the Elder Gods sent us. The time-clock isn't entirely strange to him for he's seen one before, quite recently. It was piloted by a – I don't know,' she paused briefly, ' – by a creature, anyway.'

De Marigny was elated. 'A time-clock was here, recently? Ask him what he can tell me about Elysia. Ask him if he knows the way there.'

Moreen put his questions to the gas cloud, and after a moment's listening said: 'He doesn't really understand the concepts of "ways" or "paths". He has only his orbit and can't remember when he might ever have deviated from it.

But he does appreciate the idea of places. He knows for instance that *this* place is usually fraught with hounds.'

'But didn't he talk to this visitor of his at all? What did the pilot of this other time-clock say to him?'

Moreen tried her best, and after a moment: 'They ... they passed a little time, that's all. Their concepts, too, were different, do you see? The creature in the clock talked in terms of pressure, temperatures and radiation, some of which Sssss understood. And he in his turn spoke in expressions of gravity, velocity, density and capacities.'

Frustrated almost beyond endurance, de Marigny gritted his teeth and cursed under his breath. One might as well try to make sense of a shooting star! 'He's talked to someone, some*thing*, from Elysia – and I can't find out what passed between them!'

Moreen ignored this very untypical outburst, continued to pour urgent thoughts in the direction of the green-glowing gas cloud. 'I'm telling him who, what we are,' she explained. 'Trying to get it over to him how important he may be to us. How far we've come and how long you've been searching. It's not easy, but ... *wait!*'

'Yes?' de Marigny felt his spine tingling.

'He understands "search"!' said Moreen excitedly. 'He, too, searches. In his orbit he seeks out dead planetoids to draw in, food or fuel to power him on his way. Yes, and he asks ... he asks ... are *you* the one called The Searcher?!'

De Marigny's mind reeled. 'He's heard of me?'

'The other time-clock's pilot mentioned you, "one who searches". He said that if Sssss should meet you in his orbit, he should tell you to look inside yourself – that the answer you seek lies in your own past, and in your future, and in your dreams!'

'What? Are you telling me now that a cloud of gas understands the concept of dreaming?'

'Of course! When he cruises in the outer attraction of

great stars and pivots about them – when he has not the need to power himself but rides the forces of gravity – then he shuts down. And like all sentient beings, Sssss also dreams.'

'Look inside myself,' de Marigny repeated feverishly. 'The answer lies in my past, my future, my dreams. And Titus said much the same thing: that I should look in the land of Earth's dreams . . .'

Moreen nodded. 'Yes,' she said, 'I'm sure that's right – but not until we've done what we can for him.'

'You're sure there's nothing more he can tell us?'

Moreen was almost in tears. 'There may be, I don't know. But I do know that the hounds are hurting him, Henri. And I know he's afraid.'

Something of her horror got through to de Marigny. For all the sentience of Sssss, he still seemed little more than a green comet to the Earthman, or would if Moreen were not there to remind him otherwise. And suddenly de Marigny felt like some merciless inquisitor. 'You tell him,' he said, applying mental brakes, slowing the time-clock's forward velocity, 'that we're going to teach these Hounds of Tindalos the lesson of their lives – or their un-lives. Tell him *bon voyage*, and I hope his orbit never decays.'

As the emerald nucleus shot forward in space, so Moreen passed on de Marigny's message. And while he primed the clock's incredible weapon, so she relayed the answer of the being called Sssss. 'He says, may your search be of short duration. Also, you're to give the Elder Gods his thanks when you reach Elysia.'

The nucleus of Sssss was already thirty thousand miles ahead now, and his flaring tail rapidly drawing up alongside. With it came the hounds, their hellish, mindless bat-chitterings menacing in the sensors. Then the clock's scanners were full of them, a mighty pack of unprecedented size.

'They feed on the substance of Sssss and they spawn,'

81

Moreen sobbed. 'They devour him, his goodness, and increase themselves.'

'Well, they're about to suffer one hell of a decimation!' de Marigny was grim. 'I'll never get a better chance than this to even up a few scores. It's impossible to miss them.'

Even before he opened fire the hounds recognized him. De Marigny, and Titus Crow before him, were matters of fearful legend now: they and the time-clock had openly defied whatever laws governed the Hounds of Tindalos. Lacking true life, the hounds could hardly 'die' as such, but they could certainly be destroyed. And this coffin-shaped clock had become a destroyer with a will!

Rotating the clock on its own axis like a top, de Marigny opened up. Pencil beams of the purest white light struck forth, shredding the evil, ethereal stuff of the hounds wherever it was met. The wispy green tail of Sssss became filled with hound debris, ragged black fragments flying in all directions, upon which others of the pack fell like a great shoal of frenzied sharks! But in a very short while de Marigny saw that he'd set himself a hopeless task; there were simply too many of them.

'This is like swatting flies in a field on a summer day!' he said. 'If we were a fleet of a hundred clocks, then we might make a dent in them. But we're not.'

'But we're going to try anyway?' Moreen was anxious. 'We won't leave Sssss to be devoured?'

Still firing, he answered, 'There has to be a better way than this. These hounds have broken the rules, left their own environment and come through into space.' He narrowed his eyes, opened his scanners on the distant Red Medusa Nebula. 'And maybe – just maybe – that's where they've made a very grave error of judgment!'

'Henri?'

'Time's their element, isn't it? And back there near the Red Medusa, there are places where time itself is frozen. According to a certain theory, anyway. Well, such theories

rarely apply to the time-clock, but as for the hounds . . . ?
It's worth a try, anyway.'

He stopped firing, deliberately sent the clock tumbling
end over end, so that it must seem completely out of
control, a simulated malfunction. This proved no discomfort at all to the clock's passengers: their space-time
machine simply compensated, and it was as if space turned
while the clock stood still.

The hounds closest to the clock had been fleeing in
disarray, but now they paused, gathered in chittering
clouds, began to fly in ever decreasing circles toward a
common centre which was the time-clock. The rest of the
vast pack did likewise.

'Henri, they're coming!' cried Moreen. 'What are you
doing? Have you forgotten that they can break through the
clock's angles?'

'I know it,' he answered, 'and so do they. I'm far more
important to them than poor old Sssss there, Moreen.
They're Cthulhu's scavengers, remember? What a great
prize we'd make, eh?'

Believing the clock crippled, the hounds closed in. Now
de Marigny could sense their psychic feelers groping for
the clock, soul-sucking tendrils of mental energy; and now,
too, their chittering was a frenzy of lust and monstrous
anticipation. And only at the last moment – when it seemed
the closest of the nightmare things must surely fall upon,
fall *into* the clock – only then did de Marigny accelerate
away from them. Not far, a short spurt, and then a pause
as he let the clock tumble once more and waited for them
to catch up. So he played them, the entire pack, like some
vast and monstrous fish on a line.

And yes, they were hooked!

Sssss was free of them now, powering himself on and on
along his orbit, his distance increasing by leaps and bounds.
They could never catch him now, not in three-dimensional
space. But in fact they had lost all interest in Sssss. De

Marigny and whoever journeyed with him, they were the new targets; the travellers, and the time-clock itself.

Now the gas-being was little more than a mote speeding away into far infinities, a green speck, gone! And now, too late, the hounds felt the irresistible attraction of de Marigny's trap: one of those greatest of black holes where it circled the Red Medusa. For he was leading them straight into its heart! Deeper still de Marigny drove, and ever faster, until even the time-clock's near-impervious fabric began to strain under the forces working upon it. And only then did The Searcher break the time-barrier and leap forward into a future where the hole was long extinct.

He did it only just 'in time'; for at this range, so close to the black hole, even time itself was beginning to bend and lose its shape. But too late for the hounds, far too late. Matter could not escape the maw of that Great Omnivore; space was warped inwards; the ethereal stuff of the hounds was flimsy as cobweb, no match at all for this vast insensate monster. Down they fell, ever faster, toward a point where time for them would freeze. And them with it.

Very few of them escaped to limp back to the corkscrew towers of dead and spectral Tindalos ...

Moreen picked up all of these mental pictures from de Marigny's mind and shuddered. 'Horrible,' she said. 'A horrible fate, even for such as them.'

'Moreen,' The Searcher answered, 'sometimes I think you're just too good to be true!' But he hugged her anyway.

And then he set course for Earth ...

PART TWO

De Marigny's Dream-Quest

1

Ulthar and Atal

'If only,' thought de Marigny, as the time-clock winged him back through time and space to the 20th Century Earth of his past: if only Elysia were as easy to discover and enter into as the dreamlands of Earth. For certainly in their diverse ways both places were parallel worlds of wonder; oh yes, and be sure that there were places in the dreamlands gorgeous enough to rival anything in Elysia.

Except ... except that not *all* things were wonderful there. No, for the lands of Earth's dreams were also of necessity the lands of her blackest nightmares.

'Tell me again of the Motherworld's dreamlands,' begged Moreen, as her man, The Searcher, began to recognize familiar constellations and knew now that he was not far from home – or at least, not far from the world which had once been his home. 'Please, Henri, tell me more of these places I have never dreamed of.'

It was true, for while she was of Earth stock Moreen had been born and raised in a moon of Borea; she had never once visited the human dreamlands of her birthright but only the subconscious, haunted dreams of her native Numinos. By no means an expert dreamer himself (and this despite the fact that he and Titus Crow had been honoured and feted there, until indeed they had become one with the stuff of dreamland's legends itself), stumblingly at first and then with more assurance, de Marigny had related yet again his earlier adventures in the strange dimension of Earth's dreams. He told of how he had gone there to rescue Crow and the girl-goddess Tiania, trapped in abysses of trauma; and how with the help of certain inhabitants of the dreamlands he had succeeded; and then how the three of them together had gone on to triumph over an insidious incursion of Cthulhu and the Great Old Ones into the subconscious worlds of mankind's innermost dreams. And when all of this was not enough for Moreen, then de Marigny went on to tell of places he knew there in that imagined yet real otherworld, and of places he'd only heard of and never (or at best only rarely) seen; places he had dreamed of long ago, which had faded now as all dreamstuff does in the cold morning light of the waking world.

He spoke of monstrous Kadath where it aches in the Cold Waste, forbidden to all men ever since the immemorial dreaming of certain hideous dreams there; and of the no less ominous icy desert Plateau of Leng, where horrible stone villages squatted about central balefires which flared continuously, while Leng's *denizens* danced grotesquely in flickering shadows to the rattle of strange bone instruments and the droning whine of cursed flutes. And seeing how Moreen shuddered at the tone his voice had taken and crept closer to him, he at once turned his attention to healthier regions of the dreamlands.

He spoke of the resplendent city of Celephais in the valley of Ooth-Nargai beyond the Tanarian Hills, whose myriad glittering minarets lie mirrored in the calm blue harbour; and of the galleys anchored there, with furled, multicoloured sails, beneath Mount Aran where the ginkgos sway in the breeze of the sea; and of the tinkling, bubbling Naraxa with its tiny wooden bridges, wandering its way oceanward; and of the city's onyx pavements and maze of curious streets and alleys behind mighty bronze gates. He made mention of sky-floating Serannian (which had always reminded him of Crow's description of Elysia's sky-islands) high over the Cerenerian Sea, whose foaming billows ride up buoyant as clouds into the sky where Serannian floats on their ethereal essence.

He talked of Zak with its many-templed terraces, abode

of forgotten dreams where many of his own youthful dreams and fancies lingered still, only gradually fading away; and Sona-Nyl, blessed land of fancy where men dream what they will, none of which might ever take on real material form; and the sea-spawned Basalt Pillars of the West where they rise from the furthest reaches of the Southern Sea, beyond which (so legend has it) lies a monstrous cataract where all the seas of the dreamlands pour abyssally away forever into awful inchoate voids. He mentioned Mount Ngranek's peak, and the great face graven in that mountain's gaunt side; and having spoken of Ngranek he could not help but mention the hideously thin and faceless, horned and barb-tailed bat-beings – the night-gaunts – which ever guard that mysterious mountain's elder secrets.

Then, because he believed that despite Moreen's fears she should know the worst and not go into the dreamlands a total alien and unprepared, de Marigny hurriedly went on to tell of the Peaks of Throk, those needle-like pinnacles which are the subject of many of dream's most awful fables. For these peaks, higher than any man might ever guess or believe, are known to guard the terrible valleys of the Dholes, whose shapes and outlines have often been suspected but never seen; and in one such place, the ill-omened Vale of Pnoth, there the rustling of the Dholes is ever present in utter darkness, where they infest mountainous piles of dried-out bones. For Pnoth is the ossuary into which all the ghouls of the waking and dreaming worlds alike throw the remains of their nighted feastings.

Finally, and yet more hurriedly, for by now Earth was swelling large in the time-clock's scanners, he made mention of Hlanith of the oaken wharves: Hlanith, whose sailors are more like men of the waking world than any others in the dreamlands – and ruined, fearsome Sarkomand, whose broken basalt quays and crumbling sphinxes are remnant of a time long before the years of men – and the mountain Hatheg-Kla, whose peak Barzai the Wise once climbed, never to come down again. He spoke of Nir and Istharta, and the Charnel Gardens of Zura where pleasure is unattainable; also of Oriab in the Southern Sea, and infamous Thalarion; and at the very last, for he wished to be done now, he mentioned Ulthar where no man may kill a cat.

And Ulthar he had deliberately kept to the last, for it was where their quest must start. Indeed, for of all the towns and cities and lands of dream, Ulthar was the one place which had its own Temple of the Elder Gods; and who better to talk to about Elysia than the priest of that temple, who himself aspired one day to a position there?

'And do you know him?' Moreen asked when de Marigny was done and the time-clock sailed in an orbit high above Earth's nightside. 'Is he a friend of yours, this high-priest of the temple?'

'Oh, yes,' he answered with a nod, taking her in his arms and settling down for sleep. 'I know him fairly well – or as well as any man of the waking world might be expected to know him. I've met him several times before: twice when I sought his help, and the last time at a banquet at the Inn of a Thousand Sleeping Cats, in Ulthar. But as for "friend" – I wouldn't presume. Ancient beyond words, he was around when the dreamlands were young! There's one thing I can guarantee, though, that he's pure as a pearl. As for his name: it's Atal the Ancient – Atal of Hatheg-Kla, who came down again when Barzai did not – and if there's one man in all the dreamlands who can help us, Atal's that man ...'

The first time de Marigny had used the time-clock to enter into the lands of Earth's dreams might well have been his last; he remembered that fact now as he drifted into sleep in the arms of Moreen, but this time he had resolved it would be different. The trick was this: to meld one's mind with that of the clock itself (for indeed it had a mind) as one fell asleep, and falling asleep to command the clock that it proceed into the neighbouring dreamlands. That way a man might take the clock with him into dreams, not merely use it as a gateway into those subconscious regions. That had been his mistake last time: to use the clock as a gateway, leaving it in orbit while he literally became stranded in darkling dreams! After that . . . but that's a tale already told.

This time he made no such mistake. His will, slipping ever deeper into sleep, clung tenaciously to the time-clock, and even more especially to Moreen; so that all three of them, man, girl and machine, entered the dreamlands as a single unit. Physically, of course, they remained in orbit, all three; but psychically they dreamed, the time-clock too. What's more, de Marigny's dreaming was accurate to a fault: the clock materialized in Ulthar beyond the River Skai, in the courtyard of the Inn of a Thousand Sleeping Cats.

There the lovers 'awakened' in each other's arms, rose up and yawned, stretched, stepped out through the clock's frontal panel into Ulthar's evening. De Marigny was not sure what welcome he might expect, or even if he'd be remembered or welcomed at all; for surely his coming again would only serve as a vivid reminder of the Bad Days, when all the dreamlands had been in a turmoil of terror. But the scanners told him that the courtyard of the inn was set with tables, and that the evening was filled with the scents of flowers in full bloom, and that already people were arriving and seating themselves outdoors for an evening meal. What they could not tell him was that the tables had been set *since* the arrival of the clock, while he and Moreen had lain 'asleep', and that the meal in preparation, like the last one he'd eaten here, was in his honour!

But when at last the lovers left the clock and its

door closed behind them, closing in the purplish glow of its extraordinary interior and leaving them in Ulthar's lanthorn-illuminated twilight ... ah, how de Marigny's 'forgotten' friends in the dreamlands crowded to him then!

Now, time is a funny business in the dreamlands; in places like Celephais or Serannian it can seem to stand quite still, so that nothing changes much. But to dreamers from the waking world who go there only rarely, it often seems that many years have passed between visits. Or perhaps it is the attitude of the dreamer himself, for it must not be forgotten that the dreamlands are themselves built of men's dreams. De Marigny's attitude – his desire – had been to enter the dreamlands 'now', not in the future or the past, and so he and Moreen had arrived at a time little changed from when he was last here. In other words, dream-time had kept pace with his waking-world time: the friends he saw now had aged a year for each of de Marigny's years – not merely an hour, and God forbid a century!

Grant Enderby was there and his strapping sons; his daughter, too, dark-eyed Litha, blushing as she thought back on earlier dreams. But she was wed now to a quarrier and had her own house close to her father's, and those had been vain dreams anyway for Henri was a man of the waking world, a tall ship passing in the night of the dreamlands. Oh, he had planned one day to build a villa here, in timeless Celephais, perhaps – what dreamer hasn't? – but these, too, had been only dreams within dreams.

Then there were dignitaries from several local districts, some of which de Marigny recognized, and the fat inn-keeper and his family – beside themselves with pride that the visitors had chosen this particular place in all the dreamlands into which to dream themselves – and finally there was the venerable Atal himself, who had been a mere boy in that immemorial year when the city's elders had passed their ordinance prohibiting the killing of cats. Atal, borne in by four young priests of the temple, reclining upon a canopied litter and dressed in his red robe of high office. His priestlings wore grey and were shave-headed, but their respect for the Master was not born of arduous ritual and service but more of love. For while he was undeniably the high priest of the temple, he was also simply Atal: which is to say that he was one of dreamland's greatest legends.

Deposited at the head of the rows of small tables – where stood a somewhat larger table – Atal's litter was tilted and part-folded to form a carved chair, where he sat beneath his gold-embroidered canopy while de Marigny and Moreen were ushered to their places of honour beside him. Then, after the briefest but warmest of greetings and introductions, a fabulous, sumptuous meal was served; and at last, when the throng began to eat and under cover of their low, excited chattering, finally de Marigny was able to talk in earnest to the high priest of Ulthar's Temple of the Elder Gods.

'I knew you were coming,' the ancient told him at once, almost breathlessly. 'You or Titus Crow or some other emissary of the waking, outer spheres. I knew it, for there have been portents aplenty! You know how the people of Nir and Ulthar fear eclipses? No? But of course not, for you are still a novice dreamer – though of course that is not said to slight you. No, for you've served the lands of your dreams well enough in your time. Anyway, this fear of eclipses all dates back to my youth and is unimportant now; but in the past month there have been two eclipses of the moon, and both of them unforeseen. Now, the orbit of dreamland's moon is at best less than entirely predictable – and never more so than recently, since the dreamlands waged a war there – but our astronomers are rarely so awry as to miss an eclipse! And as for two, that is surely unheard of! How do I read it? I'm not sure, but I know that in the Bad Days, when Cthulhu's influence was strong here, eclipses were frequent. They occurred whenever Nyarlathotep, the Great Messenger, came to spy on the dreams of men ...

'Another omen: in Serannian of the Clouds there has been a visitation, a singular thing. I have had this from Kuranes himself and know it to be true: an event has occurred there which never occurred before, and so has been the cause of much speculation. Likewise, strange thoughts have entered the dreamlands. I myself heard the merest echoes of them in dreams within dreams, and they were not the thoughts of men – but I believe they were good thoughts for all that. They came out of Elysia, I think, and fell to the ground somewhere beyond Thalarion. But who in Elysia would wish to speak to someone beyond Thalarion, de Marigny?' The ancient shook his head. 'Omens, my young friend, all of these things, and more still to come. Would you hear?'

De Marigny gazed long and wonderingly at the old man, near hypnotized by the gentle sigh and rustle of his voice. Frail and weary with years the ancient was; his face a wrinkled walnut, head sparsely crested with white hair, beard long and white and voluminous as a fall of snow; and yet the colourless eyes in that worn old face were lit in their cores with all the wisdom of the dreamlands. And so: 'Say on, sir,' said de Marigny, stirring himself up and giving the patriarch all of his attention.

Atal reached out to take his hand in a trembling, mummied paw. 'I am the priest of Their temple, as you well know, and I aspire one day to serve Them there in Elysia as I now serve Them here. In return – though of course I would not presume to bargain – it is my prayer that They shall give me back a little of my youth, so that I may enjoy more fully something of my time in Elysia, the place of the Elder Beings I serve.'

De Marigny nodded, however ruefully, and answered:

'We both aspire to great things, Atal, though I admit that at times my faith has weakened.'

Atal answered de Marigny's nod with one of his own. 'Impatience is the privilege of the young,' he said, 'while still they have the energy for it. But now is not the time for a weakened faith, of that I am sure. I *am* the priest of the temple, and I know as much as any priest of the Elder Gods knows of Elysia; except do not ask it, for even I cannot tell you the way there. What I must tell you is this: recently, though I have prayed as always, I know that my prayers have ⸱not reached Elysia. The way is barred! Prayers go unheard, unanswered, and strange thoughts no longer fall to earth beyond Thalarion; an inhuman messenger has come into Serannian, and abides there still, and no human being knows what message he brought; aye, and there have been the eclipses, and now you, The Searcher, have returned once again to dreams. Strange times, and I cannot fathom the whys and the wherefores of it all — unless, perhaps, you can enlighten me?'

De Marigny, noting that he had now acquired a dream-name — the same one by which he was known in many dozen worlds — quickly explained his purpose here in the dreamlands: the fact that while he was needed now in Elysia, which stood imperilled by an imminent eruption of the Great Old Ones, still there was no royal road to that place; for which reason Titus Crow had given him certain clues to the route he must take, clues he now pursued as best he might. Then he asked the elder to go into more detail in respect of certain of his 'portents', those singular occurrences he had mentioned:

'What of those alien thoughts,' he asked, 'which you heard in your dreams? Can you not tell me a little more? And what of this weird visitation Lord Kuranes reported from sky-floating Serannian?'

'As I have said,' Atal replied, 'the thoughts from outside were not human thoughts, but yet they were not evil or inimical to man. Indeed, they may even have had some bearing upon your quest – though I cannot swear to that. Ah, but now I see it written in your face that you will go at once into Thalarion's hinterland! So be it, but remember: that region is not much travelled. It borders on the old territories of the eidolon Lathi – lands where for long she reigned supreme – and so there may well be danger lurking there yet. However, there are others here in the dreamlands who can tell you more reliably of such things; for of late there have been such marvels and tumults and victories . . . the battle of the Mad Moon . . . Zura's treacheries, and the triumph of the ships of the dreamlands . . . an old man is hard-pressed to stay well informed.'

De Marigny frowned to himself in the light of the lanthorns and allowed himself a few thoughtful bites of food while Atal got his breath. The Searcher knew that the temple's high priest was growing weary – he was beginning to ramble a little, so that his words no longer completely made sense – else The Searcher might also ask him about those recent 'marvels and tumults and victories', and perhaps something of the war in dreamland's moon; but he was sure there would be others he could talk to of those things, which must certainly be matters of wider report. And so it seemed to him that there remained only one more thing requiring the elder's clarification.

And as if Atal read his mind, at last that ancient had control of himself sufficient to say: 'A visitation, aye, a strange new thing come into Serannian. It is a small grey metal cube,' (and he made its shape and size with his trembling hands), 'which flew out of the sky one morning when the city was just astir, and poised itself at the mainland end of that narrow promontory whereon Curator keeps his Museum. There it hovered and spun like a top in the air, seemingly sentient, a dull leaden box containing – what? And from where?

'Ah! – but let me tell you this: the strange cube was not

96

featureless. No, for upon one of its six sides it bore hands, like those of a clock – even like those of your time-clock there – and aye they numbered four and moved in a manner without rhyme or reason!'

De Marigny gasped and sat up straighter, but before he could form a question:

'Wait!' said Atal. 'Let me say on. The longshoremen and sailors spied the cube there where it spun in mid-air, dully agleam, and word was sent to Kuranes who of course came at once from his ivied manor. A great dreamer, Lord Kuranes, but this was a matter beyond even his dreaming. Natheless he questioned the box in all the tongues of the dreamlands; but it answered him not, merely spinning there at Serannian's rim, where the narrow span of the causeway goes out to Curator's marvellous Museum . . .' The ancient paused.

Now de Marigny knew something of Curator and his Museum, but not a great deal; his time in Serannian had been very limited and in the main restricted to visiting Kuranes' manorhouse. He knew however that Curator was a mechanical man, or that his body at least was of shining metal, and that both he and his Museum had existed in Earth's dreamland at least as long as Serannian; but just what the robot really was, and where he came from, and why he had brought the collection which formed his Museum's exhibits here in the first place . . . no one knew those things. It was sufficient that he did no harm – within certain limits, and provided the Museum and its contents were not threatened or interfered with – and certainly the place did contain many wonderful things. Kuranes was known to frequent the Museum with some regularity.

'I should not think,' he finally prompted the old man, 'that Curator would be much taken with this enigmatic visitor, spinning there in mid-air so close to his Museum!'

'On the contrary,' Atal sighed, once more taking up the

tale. 'For as the sun rose up and broke free of the horizon, so Curator came out and scanned the cube where it whirled; and he must have taken note of its erratic hands where they measured conjectural matters upon its sixth side; and he stared at it with his crystal eyes along the length of the bridge which connects the Museum to Serannian's rim. Then –

'A passing *weird* thing! For Curator, who has many arms, formed four of them into hands like those of the cube, all sprouting from a central place, and these he jerked and twirled in a singular fashion, duplicating to a large degree the movements of the cube's hands!'

'They talked to each other!' gasped de Marigny at once. 'Curator and this time-clock – for it can only be some sort of strange time-clock – conversed!'

'More than that,' came Atal's rustling affirmation. 'For in a little while Curator strode out along the causeway, and the leaden cube moved forward to meet him, and there in the centre of that spindly span they paused, as it were, face to face. And while longshoremen, sailors, citizens and Kuranes himself looked on, panels opened in Curator's chest to reveal a space just so big,' (again he described a small cube with his fluttering hands), 'in which without pause the enigmatic visitor located itself, ere Curator's panels closed again to fold it within his breast. And so the wonder was at an end, for without more ado Curator turned and clanked back to his Museum. And still the mystery of this meeting and its meaning remain unknown.'

'So,' said de Marigny, 'not only must I visit Thalarion's hinterland but also Serannian, to talk to Curator.'

But here Atal shook his head. 'Not possible,' he said, 'not even remotely. It is a matter of immemorial legend that no man in all the dreamlands ever spoke to Curator!'

'Never?'

'Not ever. Ask yourself these questions: does Curator

even understand the speech of men? Does he care? Is he even *aware* of any reason or purpose outside his one task of preserving and protecting his beloved Museum? But on the other hand – '

'Yes?'

'Curator has had *to do* with men – with certain men, that is. By that I mean that while he converses not, still he can make his desires known to men – especially those who would harm his Museum or attempt to disorder or even steal its exhibits!'

De Marigny frowned, tried hard to understand. 'You mean that he chastises would-be thieves?'

'He has done so, yes. And he has had occasion to merely warn others. Indeed I know of two such, er, gentlemen, cautioned by Curator, as it were – ex-waking-worlders, as it happens. And by rare coincidence, though I for one do not believe in coincidences, these same men have also ventured beyond Thalarion – ventured there and more – *and* returned unscathed! You should talk to them, Henri, before proceeding further with your quest.'

'Do you know them, these two, and where I might look for them?' The Searcher was eager.

But while they had talked something had been taking place to attract the attention of all the others at their tables: a curiosity at first, which had now grown into something so strange and wondrous rare as to be a singular occurrence in its own right. It concerned the cats of Ulthar, and it also concerned Moreen.

For during her man's conversation with the temple's high priest (and knowing the importance of their subject), Moreen, seated on Atal's left, had not interrupted but had taken the opportunity to eat; and having eaten she had then found a kitten to talk to, which had jumped into her lap from beneath the table. Now the cats of Ulthar are a special breed and have their preferences; they know good men from bad and true from false, and are mainly indifferent toward all but the warmest, purest hearts. How then Moreen's heart? For where one small kitten had coiled in her lap and purred –

– It seemed to the people gathered in the courtyard of the Inn of a Thousand Sleeping Cats that at least half and probably more than half of all the cats in Ulthar must have come to congregate here in the last half-hour, and all of them worshipping at the feet of Moreen! Of every type and size and description they were, though outside the circles of lanthorn light their colours were quite uniform; for of course it was that hour when all cats turn grey, except in the light. Kittens galore (Ulthar's cats have large litters), and huge, prowling toms, and sleek, well groomed matrons, all rubbing shoulders and straining forward; but never once a snarling or spitting, for theirs was a unity of curiosity – a group engrossment, a mass hypnotism – whose soul and centre was Moreen.

De Marigny and Atal, deep in conversation, had barely noticed the gradual encroachment and massing of the cats; but now, as all chatter died away, in the glimmer of lanthorns and perfume of Ulthar's night blossoms, and in the sudden astonished sighing of all humans who congregated there in that courtyard, they could scarce help but notice it. And more cats arriving by the minute, until the cobbles were crowded with them where they spread out in concentric circles from Moreen's feet; and the girl still petting that smallest kitten while she spoke purringly to all the cats in general. And them beginning to purr back at her, in a concerted rumbling that spoke of all the contentment in the world!

Forgetting de Marigny almost entirely, Atal took Moreen's hand and pressed it, and said: 'You must have loved cats for a very long time, my dear, and loved them well. For the cats of Ulthar are very discerning.'

'Cats?' she smiled at him. 'Is that what they're called? Oh, yes, I remember now! Cats are mythical creatures in

Numinos, only ever heard of in legends of the Mother-world, passed down from generation to generation.'

De Marigny quickly explained Moreen's origin – and the fact that Borea's moon, Numinos, had no cats, for Ithaqua had never taken any there – and Atal was rightly dumb-founded. 'And she befriends all beasts in this manner, you say? But this is an astounding thing, and as surely as all the other portents have been bad ones, this *must* be a good one! Merely to have this wonderful girl with you bodes well for your quest, Searcher.'

'Then you'll tell me where I can find these men you spoke of, who've travelled beyond Thalarion and had something of business with Curator?'

Atal nodded his old head. 'Anything you desire to know,' he said. 'Except, if I told you *all* I've heard of these two it would take all night – and half of it at least would be fabulous anyway, I'm sure – and both of us would fall asleep ere I was done. And so I'll be brief:

'They came from the waking world and were stranded here when their lives were prematurely ended in that plane. At first they seemed at odds with the lands and men and customs of Earth's dreams, they became wanderers, adven-turers, great brawlers and even thieves; but because they were artful dreamers, finally the dreamlands accepted them and gave them shelter. And rightly so, as it turned out, for now it seems they're destined to grow into legends in their own right. They are questers now, agents of ever-watchful Kuranes, and their many deeds have included keep-climbing and exploring, black wizard-slaying, gaunt-riding and far-adventuring in some of dreamland's most monstrous places. Why, it was them burned down the paper city Thalarion, and almost the wicked eidolon Lathi with it! – though I'm told she's building that awful hive once more. They were dreamland's warlords in the battle of the Mad Moon; they put an end to Zura's plot to sink Serannian; for all their roguish natures, even the King of

Ilek-Vad is said to number them among his personal friends!'

'Randolph Carter?' de Marigny was impressed.

'Himself!' Atal nodded. 'And talking of King Carter, and remembering your reason for coming here at this time, his current absence is a great pity; for Randolph Carter has been to Elysia in his dreaming and might perhaps show you the way; except that he's once again gone off, exploring in undreamed of places, ever searching for your father, Etienne, his old friend from the waking world.'

Again de Marigny turned a little sour. 'It has always been the same story,' he said. 'Like father, like son. I'm what I am because of Etienne-Laurent de Marigny. His love of mysteries rubbed off on me, and now I'm a searcher, too. *The* Searcher!'

'Aye, your destiny,' Atal sighed.

It was late now and the people were coming forward in small groups, politely nodding their farewells and good-nights as they went off to their homes. The moon had risen and the lanthorns were burning low, and even the cats were stirring now and their ranks thinning as they went off to seek the shadows. For delightful as Moreen was, there were more important things for cats to be about when the moon hung full and high in the night skies of dreamland. Which was just as well; for at that juncture there came a soft flapping of wings, and down out of scented darkness fluttered a bird of Ulthar's Temple of the Elder Ones, a pink pigeon, to alight on Atal's shoulder.

A few departing cats looked back, their almond, slant-eyes yellow in the night, and two or three lean toms might just have considered the possibility of a little fun and flying feathers; but Moreen was wise to their ways now and tut-tutted, which was chastisement enough. So off they went as Atal tremblingly took the tiny cylinder from the bird's leg and unwrapped the scrap of paper tucked inside it.

'A message,' he husked, screwing up his eyes and

drawing a lanthorn closer. 'But from where, and about what?' Then –

'*Ah!*' the old man sighed as finally his eyes focussed. 'And indeed this arrives at an opportune moment. For if you really wish to meet the two men I've mentioned – the questers from the waking world – it would seem it's now or never. Here, read it for yourself, for unless I'm much mistaken it's couched in runes you'll know – English, I believe.'

De Marigny took the note, smoothed it out on the table, read its short, sharp legend.

'HELP!' it said in black, jagged lines, 'AND MAKE IT FAST – FOR TOMORROW AT FIRST LIGHT GUDGE SENDS US TO HELL!' And it bore the signatures of David Hero and Eldin the Wanderer ...

2

Hero and Eldin

Playing *Pass The Time Before—*, David Allenby Hero, late of the waking world, where he'd been a sensitive painter of matters ethereal, and Professor Leonard E. Dingle (Psychology and Anthropology), ex-lecturer on the subconscious mind of man, had almost inevitably ended up in the doldrums of the game yet again. Hero, or more formally Hero of Dreams, as he was now known, and Eldin the Wanderer, had most recently been enumerating 'Things Ridden Upon'.

Before that they'd recalled 'Inimical Creatures, Beings or Persons Slain or Otherwise Subdued', had listed alphabetically 'Ladies Lusted After', chronologically 'Fantastic Feats', and somewhat morbidly in light of their current circumstances 'Deaths Defied'. The first of these had included a certain black wizard, species of man-eating flora and fauna, night-gaunts, dholes, zombies, termen, moonbeasts and Lengites and so on, all leading eventually to Gudge, whom they merely wished dead but who, ironically and in all likelihood, bar a large miracle, would shortly gain some notoriety in the dreamlands as *their* executioner!

The second series in *Pass the Time Before—*, 'Ladies Lusted After', had been a bad choice of subject; Eldin had led off with 'Aminza Anz', immediately breaking down in tears before the game could go any further. For Aminza, may the Lords of Dream bless her memory, had woken up on the very day she and Eldin were to have been wed, which had brought about an abrupt termination of that romance.

'Fantastic Feats' had been a good one, for both of the

questers were given to boasting a bit and vied with each other in respect of frequently recounted acts of heroism. What thief in all the dreamlands (for example) could match Hero's feat in 'cracking' a great keep of the First Ones? And who but that magnificent arsonist Eldin the Wanderer would ever have dreamed of burning down an entire city (the hive Thalarion) with his firestones? (Of that last: Hero was wont to point out that it had been done before by someone called Nero, a waking-worlder, he thought.) And so on. Alas, their most recent 'feat' had been to come a-spying for Kuranes in the Badlands back of Zura the land, where Gudge the pirate had discovered, recognized, captured and would now kill them.

Which had led them to 'Deaths Defied'. This list had been longest of all, involving not only all of the Creatures, Beings or Persons in the first series but sundry menaces such as: freezing in the upper atmosphere; drowning in a whirlpool; walking-the-plank two and a half miles over the Southern Sea; a moonbeast spell of petrifaction; being devoured by Oorn the Gastropod Goddess in primal Sarkomand; seduced to a soggy pulp by Lathi and romanced to rottenness by Zura of Zura; and so on, etc., *ad infinitum*. Except, quite naturally, this had only brought them to the current Death Defied, which being unavoidable couldn't be so much defied as simply waited upon; hence the game of *Pass the Time Before*—in the first place. For of course that pair of indefatigable dreamers were only passing the time before their mutual demise.

Except that demise was not upon them yet, and there were other lists to be considered, most recent of which had been 'Things Ridden Upon'. And boastful or not it seems highly unlikely that any dreamers anywhere could summon up a list of conveyances half so fabulous (and yet so thoroughly authentic) as that of Hero and Eldin. They had sailed a reed-tree raft across the blue lake beyond the Great Bleak Mountains, and down a whirlpool to a swamp beyond Thalarion. They'd ridden (flown) on a Great Tree's life-leaf from Thalarion's hinterland to the gardens of Nyrass the Mage in Theelys. They'd been transported 'magically' from Theelys to a mighty mountain keep, all in the blink of an eye. They'd been aboard Kuranes' ships of dream, Zura's ship of death, the eidolon Lathi's ship of paper. They'd been flown by night-gaunts across all the gulfs of dream, and vented in ethereal essence from Serannian's huge flotation system, and bustled on the back of a many-legged Running Thing through the Caves of Night in Pnoth and across the Stickistuff Sea. And that wasn't all, far from it:

They'd slid down a beam of light from Curator's curious eyes to a sky-ship in the aerial Bay of Serannian; and rushed up into higher space on a broken mast and a bag of air; and flown to dreamland's moon on a spiral moon-beam! Last but not least they'd been borne by Eeth, a moon-moth maid, to the feet (or roots) of a magical moontree; absorbed by him and transferred to seedlings, which had then twirled them back down to the dreamlands; and finally, as grotesque gourds, they'd fallen to earth on the banks of the Skai near Ulthar, where both had been 'reborn' full grown.

'And now,' Eldin morosely concluded, 'it seems we're to careen on these damned great crosses to dreamland's very core – perhaps to the pits of nightmare themselves!'

Hero could only nod (literally) and agree: 'Aye, this is another hell of a crucifix you've got me onto.'

'Is that a joke or an accusation?' Eldin asked suspiciously.

'*Huh!*' Hero snorted.

'I accept your apology!' said Eldin; and: 'You know, lad, there's a list far more important than all these others we've played with. One which we haven't considered at all as yet.'

'Oh?'

'Indeed! It's called "Narrow Squeaks Squeezed

Through", and it might just provide a clue as to a way out of this current mess.'

Hero carefully moved his head (about the only part of his person he *could* move) to peer at the other in the gloom of their predicament. Lashed to a great wooden cross and suspended over the rim of a pit that went down almost (but unfortunately not) without limit, the Wanderer was not a pretty sight. He never had been, but now he looked particularly ugly.

Eldin was older than Hero's maybe thirty years by at least a dozen; he had a scarred, bearded, quite unhandsome face which yet housed surprisingly clear blue eyes – for all that one of them was now black. Stocky and heavy, but somehow gangly to boot, there was something almost apish about him; yet his every move and gesture (when he was able) hinted of a sensitivity and keen intelligence behind his massive physical strength. Alas, half beaten to death by Gudge's freebooters, that giant strength wasn't much in evidence now, else Eldin's bonds were long since torn asunder. Instead the Wanderer had his time cut out simply forcing words past his broken lips; so that Hero's niggling words and manner were deliberately designed to keep him on his mettle and chipper, as it were. Eldin knew this, knew too that Hero himself had seen better nights. He gloomed back at the younger dreamer, said: 'Well, what about it? Is there a way out of this, or – ?'

'Most likely or,' Hero glumly answered, and when he laid his head back winced from the spasm of pain in the soft spot behind his left ear, where his hair was matted with clotted blood.

Hero was tall, rangily muscled and blond in dreams as he'd once been in the waking world. His eyes were blue like Eldin's, but lighter; they could redden very quickly, however, in a fury, or go a thoughtful, dangerous yellow in a tight spot. They'd been yellow a while now, though nothing had come of it. His nature in fact was usually easy-going: he loved songs a good bit and girls a great deal, but he was also wizard-master of any sword in a fight, and the knuckles of his fists were like crusty knobs of rock. He was very different from Eldin, yes, but they did have several things in common. They shared the same wanderlust, for one, and the same sometimes acid sense of humour for another. The lands of Earth's dreams occasionally make for strange travelling companions.

'Are you saying we should just hang here and wait for the new day?' Eldin seemed surprised. 'Our last day, as it may well turn out to be?'

'Hell, no!' Hero grunted. 'By all means, let's be up and on our way!' He sighed. 'Look, old lad, I don't know about you but I can't hardly move a muscle. I can blink, talk, wriggle my backside, nod my head and wag it too, but that's all. Ergo: knackered! Physically, emotionally, mentally knackered! I haven't completely given up hope, not yet, but at the same time I have to admit that I can't see much future for us. Not if I'm to be truthful about it.'

'Hmm!' said Eldin, gruffly. 'Just as I suspected: you expect me to get us out of it, right? What David Hero can get you into, Eldin the Wanderer can get you out of – just like that!'

However weakly, Hero had to grin. Now Eldin was needling him – deliberately, of course. In fact, neither one of them had been to blame for their untenable situation; their task had been impossible right from square one. And now Hero looked back on how they came to be here ...

... At that same moment but many miles away (the actual distance is conjectural; spans of time and space are deceptive in the land of Earth's dreams) in the resplendent city of Celephais, King Kuranes was echoing Hero's thoughts; except that he did it out loud, for the benefit of friends and visitors from the waking world. For upon reading that brief SOS borne on the leg of a pink temple pigeon, de Marigny

108

had said farewell to Atal, bundled Moreen into the time-clock, travelled at once to the valley of Ooth-Nargai beyond the Tanarian Hills. Since the questers Hero and Eldin were agents of Kuranes, who better to ask of their likely whereabouts – and something perhaps of this Gudge who apparently threatened their lives – than Kuranes himself?

Now, in the King's palace (in fact an ivied manor-house, the very replica of his loftier seat in Serannian), The Searcher and Moreen of Numinos sat at a great table with the king, while whiskered, liveried servants stood in attendance. In his long nightshirt and still not fully awake, Kuranes had put on square-framed spectacles, read the scrap of paper they brought him, turned pale in the steady glow of a pair of antique oil lamps.

'Gudge has them!' he'd gasped then. 'Gudge the pirate, scourge of the Southern Sea and the skies around Zura and Thalarion!'

Kuranes was slightly built but regal in his bearing, grey-bearded yet sprightly and bright-eyed, with nothing of the occasional fuzziness of natural-born dreamlanders (*Homo ephemerans*, as Eldin the Wanderer had long since dubbed the peoples of dream) about him. Quite obviously a man late of the waking world, still he was a powerful force for good in the dreamlands and a long-time enemy of all agencies of horror and nightmare. On reading the note he'd come wide awake in a moment and grasped de Marigny's arm.

'And you came here in your time-clock, that awesome vehicle and weapon I remember so well from your last visit?'

'Oh, yes,' The Searcher had nodded. 'It's out there in the gardens, where your pikemen have placed it under guard.'

'Good!' Kuranes had uttered a huge sigh of relief. 'So perhaps there's a chance for that pair of great-hearted rogues even now.' And then he'd told his visitors all he knew:

'Since the war of the Mad Moon things have been allowed to get a bit lax here in the dreamlands. Our victory was so massive, so decisive, that we've done precious little since but celebrate! A grave, grave error. Atal will have told you of the incidence of unorthodox eclipses? Just so. And did he also read an omen into your presence here at this time?'

'Expertly,' said de Marigny, 'even though Atal had not foreseen just how serious our business here.' And he'd quickly sketched in what he knew of matters: the imminent uprising of the Great Old Ones, as evidenced in the alignment or re-alignment of certain stars; his own presence as a positive necessity now in Elysia, into which place there was still no royal road; Titus Crow's hint that certain clues as to Elysia's whereabouts might be obtained in Earth's dreamlands. Finally: 'And I believe that with the help of Hero and Eldin, I may be able to narrow down my search.'

'Which makes their rescue that much more urgent, indeed entirely imperative!' said Kuranes, slamming down his palms flat upon the table. 'Once more it seems the dreamlands are at risk, and not only the dreamlands but the sanity of the entire universe! Now listen carefully:

'Some six months gone, the Southern Sea and the skies over dreamland were safe and free as never before. With Lathi and Zura defeated in the Mad Moon's war and banished out of the sane lands of dream back to their own dark demesnes – and the Lengites crushed and sorely depleted; and the surly Isharrans subdued, what few of them remained in Sarkomand and points west – honest folk were able at last to go about their businesses and pursuits as is their right, unhindered and unafraid.

'The sky-trade between Serannian, Celephais, Ilek-Vad and Ulthar prospered; sea-trade and -farings between all the ports of the Southern Sea flourished; the Isle of Oriab lost much of its previous insularity and pleasure-seekers flocked to Baharna as before, to enjoy its wonders. Merchantmen had never sailed so close to the shores of infamous Thalarion, or with such small concern past Zura the land – not with guaranteed impunity, anyway – and sightings of black Leng galleys, in both sea and sky, became so few and far between that Captains soon lost the habit of reporting them. It seemed that in the main the horned almost-humans stuck to their forbidden plateau, Lathi to Thalarion, rebuilding her twice-ruined hive, and Zura to her moon-ravaged Charnel Gardens.

'Serannian's guardian sky-armada was expensive to man and maintain; patrols were long and boring for the crews; men were better employed putting to rights the damage rained on the dreamlands in the time of the Mad Moon. All in all, the lands of Earth's dreams were peaceful and prosperous once more, and the memories of dreamlanders are extremely short. Peace, aye, but it was only the lull before the storm . . .

'And so the stage was set for mischief, which came all too quickly in the shape of Gudge and his pirates. Ships began to disappear: on the sea between Oriab and the continental dreamlands, along the coasts of Zura, Thalarion and Dylath-Leen, even in the skies. That's right: even the occasional warship, patrolling out of Serannian, disappearing without trace. And what small pockets of intelligence and information I controlled all pointed in the same direction, arrived at the same conclusion: piracy! Sea-pirates, sky-pirates, probably one and the same! But from where, and under whose black-hearted command and control?

'Oh, I had my suspicions. Zura had built herself a new sky-ship, *Shroud II*, and crewed it with zombies – a "skele-ton crew" – hah! Lathi was rumoured to have repaired and fortified her previously flimsy *Chrysalis*, and brooded aboard while her ter-men and -maids fashioned a new

Thalarion of their extruded paper-paste wastes. But how could Zura be the miscreant? What use to her the spoils of piracy? Anyway, *Shroud II* was only ever spied over the Charnel Gardens sails furled, a kraken-prowed corpse of a ship and gloomy as a menhir. And as for Lathi: her wispy *Chrysalis* could scarce be considered a threat – certainly not to the practised gunners of a warship of Serannian! Cannon-shot would pass right through her, aye, but a fire-rocket would burn her to a crisp. So much we'd learned in the war of the Mad Moon.

'I increased patrols over suspect areas, issued harsh punitive instructions, incurred heavier losses. And I began to lose patience and a deal of complacency. Obviously the problem was greater than I'd suspected; nor could I retaliate until I knew my enemy and his base of operations; patently I must now employ as much cunning as that unknown enemy himself. But then, some real information at last!

'But first ... have you heard of Gytherik Imniss?' Kuranes raised a questioning eyebrow to peer keenly at de Marigny. 'No? Well, I'm not surprised; you've been away for quite some time and he's fairly new on the scene, and something of a novelty to boot. He's a lad from Nir and commands a singular power – a power over night-gaunts! In fact he's dreamland's first gaunt-master, with the freedom of all the skies of dream.'

De Marigny curled his lip in disgust and drew back aghast. 'What a menace!' he said.

'Eh?' Kuranes looked puzzled for a moment, then shook his head. 'No, no, you misunderstand: I myself conferred his freedom of the skies. What's more, his grim won medals in the battle for the Bay of Serannian!'

'Grim?'

'Collective noun for a gathering of the rubbery horrors,' Kuranes explained.

'Very appropriate, too!' said de Marigny, making no

112

effort to hide his astonishment. He shook his head. 'Things have really changed. I mean, am I to believe in beneficent gaunts?'

'It depends who's controlling them,' Kuranes answered. 'But you're perfectly correct: old fears and legends die hard, and gaunts have a very bad reputation. Even now there's a saying in the dreamlands: that the only good gaunt's a dead 'un! Except Gytherik's grim would seem to be the odd-grim-out, the exception that proves the rule. Anyway, back to my tale:

'I was in Serannian pondering my next move, when who should drop in on me but Gytherik and a handful of his gaunts. It was somewhat into the morning and the gaunts were looking a bit grim – if you'll excuse the pun – and not alone from the sunlight, which they don't much care for at the best of times. Two of them at least had jagged tears in their rubbery hides and limbs, which seeped a bit so that Gytherik had to tend them. Afterwards, I·put them up (or down) in a dungeon for their comfort while we talked.

'It came out how he'd been to the mountain Ngranek, letting his gaunts do some socializing there; you know how night-gaunts guard or haunt the entranceways to dream-land's underworld, and how there's one such gateway under Ngranek? Yes – well, the lad's solicitous of the beasts in his charge, you see. Anyway, on his way back to the mainland, flying on the back of a huge brute of a gaunt and with the rest of the grim all about him, he spied below the lights of a merchantman out of Serannian on course for the Isle of Oriab. She was venting flotation essence and settling to the sea for the second half of her trip; Baharna, Oriab's chief port, being a pretty perpendicular place, hasn't much in the way of level mooring for sky-ships, which are obliged to use the harbour like purely mundane vessels. So there she was, this ship, settling down to the sea, when out of the sky like vultures fell three black galleys in a spiral, closing her in!

'Gytherik sent his gaunts winging down through the night to see what the matter was; and there in the darkness he saw these three black ships, showing never a light, set upon the unsuspecting merchantman and pound her to matchwood! Pirates they were, beyond a doubt, who swarmed aboard the doomed, foundering vessel in a trice, putting down all but the Captain and several paying passengers, whom they took off from the sinking ship. As for the crew of that stricken vessel: horrible! There were guttings, hangings and plank-walkings; until Gytherik, watching from on high, was sick from the vileness of it all.

'Now the gaunt-master was just one man, more properly a youth, and unarmed. Likewise his gaunts: they had only their paws to fight with and their wings with which to buffet. Nevertheless he set the grim to diving into the rigging of the black ships and doing whatever damage they could. Alas, the pirates were ready for Gytherik, for they had seen his grim flitting against the disc of the moon. Now that's a strange thing in itself – the *preparedness* of these black buccaneers for the likes of Gytherik and his gaunts – which I'll get to in a minute. Anyway, seeing what he was about, the pirates dragged out hurling devices from under tarpaulins, loading them with tangles of netting armed with razor-sharp barbed hooks! And as the grim swooped and tore at the topmost sails and rigging of the black galleys, so these weird ballistae were fired up into the night! Hooked, maimed, net-entangled, many a gaunt fell into the sea and drowned, victims of the first salvo; others were slashed by hooks, or had the membraneous webs of their wings pierced; so that Gytherik feared he'd soon lose the entire grim.

'Naturally he quickly stood off – there was little more he could do – and there under the moon and stars the pirates hailed him, calling:

'Hey, gaunt-master! You, Gytherik! Let this be a lesson! You're not alone in your freedom of the skies. Let it be known that henceforth Gudge the pirate claims sovereignty over the sea between Oriab and the mainland, also over the skies and shores and hinterlands of Zura and Thalarion!'

'And they set up a great concerted shouting: "Gudge – Gudge – Gudge the Merciless!"'

'And out from his cabin on one of those barbarous black vessels came the leader of that terrible band: Gudge himself!

'It was dark, remember – the dead of night – and Gytherik wasn't able to see as well as he'd like. Also, his viewpoint was aerial: he looked down on things from on high. But still it seemed to him that these pirates were a queer bunch. There was that in their voices which he couldn't quite place: a nasal, guttural quality, if "quality" is the right word. Also, they all wore turbans or tricorns – to a man, that is – and seemed uniformly short or squat for the barrel-chested, bow-legged brigands you might expect. Still, they did carry cutlasses, and some had eye-patches, and all were attired in gaudy rags and striped pants and so on; so what else could they be but pirates?

'But if the motley crews of the black ships were a bit strange, what of their pirate chief? For in answer to the call of his bully-boys he'd fired a brand and tossed it aboard the doomed merchantman; and in the bright glare of that burning vessel, at last Gytherik should be able to get a good look at him. So thought the gaunt-master, but –

'Gudge, whoever he is, was covered head to toe, cowled too, in such voluminous, bulging, billowing robes that Gytherik caught never a glimpse of his actual form or features; and the monster might as well be dumb, too, for all he uttered by way of words or sounds where he stood on the deck of his black command vessel, adored by his terrible crew. And not once did he lift his cowled face to the skies where Gytherik flew; so that the gaunt-master supposed he'd seen and learned all that he might of these

115

pirates and their master at this time; and so, being concerned over his much-depleted grim, that handful of sorely wounded gaunts which remained to him, finally he turned away and limped for Serannian. Which was how he came to me in the morning of the next day.

'But to go back a bit: there's this matter of the pirates expecting or anticipating a gaunt-attack, and their knowing the gaunt-master's name and reputation. Now Gytherik was a veteran and hero of the wars against Zura and the Mad Moon, where he'd used his gaunts to great advantage. Aye, for then there'd been little in the way of defence against gaunt tactics. Also, he'd worked for me, right alongside Hero and Eldin; so maybe these pirates had expected *me* to send him out on patrol. If so, did that give me a clue as to who they might be? Had they perhaps experienced his sort of warfare before? Well, I have my suspicions but I'll keep them to myself for now; but be sure I'd dearly love to know who – or what – it is that keeps itself hidden in that voluminous robe and under that cowl, and sinks the fair ships of dreamland and murders their crews for no sane reason that I can see. For this is the hell of it:

'In all Gytherik told me he never mentioned seeing those dogs take any booty; but he *did* see them cutting down the bodies of those they'd hanged, and gathering the lifeless corpses of those they'd gutted!' And here Kuranes paused and shuddered, and pushed away the plate of cold meat that one of his retainers had placed before him.

'Now,' he eventually continued, 'I thanked Gytherik for his invaluable information and gave him the run of my place until his gaunts were well enough to fly; and in the course of a few days off he went again, bent on recruiting more gaunts to strengthen his grim. For there was little he could do with such a sorry bunch as he now commanded. But he swore he'd be back as soon as he'd beefed up his band a bit.

'And meanwhile ... meanwhile I'd sent out messengers into all parts of the dreamlands to find and bring back to me Hero and Eldin, my agents extraordinary!

'They were found prospecting in the Great Bleak Mountains, grimy as gargoyles and loaded down with their own weight in "simpleton's sapphires" – that is to say a great pile of blue stones, sapphires that weren't. Like "fool's gold", you know? They'd been digging them up for weeks apparently!' Kuranes grinned despite his sombre mood and shook his head. 'How does a man weigh up two such as these?' he asked of no one in particular.

'Anyway, they were penniless, lean and hungry – and completely demoralized that they'd been shovelling pretty pebbles and not fabulous gems – and so ripe for a real quest. So they shipped back to Serannian where I dined them royally for a week, promising them their own sky-yacht and a house by the harbour with a white-walled courtyard, if only – '

'If only they'd go into the badlands along the eastern coast and seek out the lair of the pirates!' de Marigny finished the tale for him.

Kuranes nodded. 'Correct. So they fitted themselves up with a fancy wardrobe: eye-patches, a moppish great wig for Hero (Eldin shaved his head shiny bald!), black leather belts and notched cutlasses, calf-boots to tuck their striped pants into and the like, and off they went one night aboard one of Serannian's galleys, all painted black for this one trip. They were dropped this side of Zura the land, where the Southern Sea meets a craggy shore, and that's the last I've heard of them – till now.'

De Marigny pursed his lips. 'And now they're captives of Gudge, doomed to die at dawn, and the night already two-thirds flown.'

'Dead men, aye,' Kuranes gloomily replied. 'Unless you can find them in time and get them out!'

'Right,' said de Marigny. 'Then here's what I'd like you

to do for me – and it must be done swiftly, so that I can be on my way in less than an hour. First – '

'We,' Moreen cut him off, sweetly but surely.

'Eh?' said de Marigny and Kuranes together.

'So that "we" can be on "our" way,' she repeated. 'You don't think I'm going to let you go off adventuring in the dreamlands on your own, do you, Henri? Oh, I know: you're "The Searcher", not I. But if I were to lose you . . . should I, too, spend the rest of my life searching?' And there was that in her voice which told him there'd be little to gain from arguing . . .

Hero, thinking back on precisely those things Kuranes had related to Moreen and de Marigny, had recalled one certain ludicrous aspect of his and Eldin's 'kitting-up': the choosing of their piratical wardrobes and props. 'Madness!' he sighed now, shaking his head weakly, suspended on his cross over that black pit that went down to dreamland's core.

Eldin had been quiet for some little time, lost in his own thoughts, but now he dragged his head round to peer at Hero through the gloom. 'Eh? What is?' he rumbled, his voice echoing. 'Are you finally admitting it was madness to accept this damned quest in the first place? If so I wholeheartedly agree – you should never have taken it on!'

'*We* took it on,' Hero reminded. 'I clearly recall you drooling over Kuranes' promise of a sky-yacht. "We'll sail off to Oriab," you said, "and look up Ula and Una. We'll drop anchor on some jewel isle and spend a whole month just fishing and fondling." That's what you said.'

'And you were all for lazing in the sun in your own courtyard,' Eldin countered. ' "I'll sit on the wall with a spyglass," you said, "and watch the ships rising out of Celephais to where the sea meets the sky. And I'll spy down on all the pretty girls in the gardens of the villages along the coast." That's what *you* said – lecherous little devil!'

'The specific madness I refer to,' said Hero, 'is the business of the pigeon.'

Eldin gave a groan. 'Not *that* again!'

'See,' Hero growled, 'pirates have parrots, not pigeons. And certainly not pink pigeons! That was a dead giveaway. I mean, fancy tying a damn pigeon to your shoulder, and squawking "pieces of eight" out the corner of your mouth every five minutes! Madness – not to mention messy!'

'But it came in handy in the end, you have to admit,' Eldin justified the thing. 'Before they tied us on these crosses we managed to get a note off to old Atal. By now all Ulthar will know the pickle we're in.'

'Fat lot of good that will do us,' Hero was quieter now. 'Like screaming after you fall off a mountain. Different if we had another two or three days ...'

Eldin knew what he meant: pigeons are pretty speedy creatures, but sky-ships and rescue missions take a lot longer. 'Gytherik and his gaunts could manage it,' he said, with something of desperation beginning to show in his gruff voice.

Hero grunted. 'If we had some bacon,' he shrewdly replied, 'we could have bacon and eggs – if we had some eggs.'

'Eh?'

'It's wishful thinking, old lad,' the younger quester explained. 'Hoping that Gytherik'll be along, I mean. But you're right anyway: remote as the chance is, still it looks like the only one that's left to us ...'

3

Zura of Zura

In fact Hero was wrong, but could hardly be expected to know it. In the night skies of dreamland, at this very moment, there was a second chance. Shaped like a coffin – but yet reminiscent of some weird grandfather clock – it moved at incredible velocity toward Zura the land, where the foetor of rotting flesh hung forever like a mouldering cerecloth over that domain of death.

And in a little while, slowing the time-clock's speed to a crawl, indeed de Marigny knew that he had crossed the borders of sanity into a region of nightmare. For there below, stretching mile on endless mile, lay that monstrous plain of leaning, mouldy menhirs known as the Charnel Gardens, a colossal graveyard where the diseased earth within each and every plot had been pushed up from below! Oh, yes, this was surely that land where graves and corpses are uniformly unquiet, but de Marigny's interest was centred rather in Zura the woman than Zura the land itself.

'And where to find her?' The Searcher wondered out loud.

'Lying in some grave,' Moreen shuddered and crept into his arms, 'with some poor corpse, if what you've said of her is true.'

'All hearsay,' answered de Marigny. 'I've told only what I've had from others. But those who've actually met her in the flesh are few and far between – who lived to tell of it, anyway. She's the sovereign of dreamland's zombies, Mistress of the Living Dead. All those who die cruel or monstrous deaths must go to Zura in the end, to do her bidding in the Charnel Gardens . . .'

'Dawn is only an hour or two away,' Moreen stated the obvious.

'And Zura the land is deep and wide,' de Marigny nodded. 'I know. But Kuranes said she had a sky-ship, *Shroud II*, this awful princess. So maybe that's where we'll find her, aboard her corpse-crewed vessel. For if Hero and Eldin went missing here, in Zura the land, who better to ask of their present whereabouts than Zura the Princess, eh?'

Moreen was at the scanners, widening their scope as she scanned afar, toward Zura's heartland. And in another moment she drew breath in a sharp hiss. Then:

'Oh, yes,' she said. 'That'll be Zura's ship, all right. And very aptly named, too. Why, it's the same shape as the time-clock – except where we stand on end, *Shroud II* lies horizontal, like a great black floating coffin! There she is, moored centrally over that direful city there.'

De Marigny applied his senses to the time-clock's scanners, saw what Moreen had seen: a horizon of mega-lithic mausoleums whose gaunt grey facades reared high and formed the ramparts of the city Zura itself. 'Zura,' he nodded then. 'And you're right: that coffin-ship with its squid figurehead can only be *Shroud II*.'

Now The Searcher scanned the eastern horizon, where he fancied a faint nimbus of grey light made a wash on dreamland's rim. And:

'No more time to waste,' he said then, his voice grim and urgent. 'So ... let's see if Zura's aboard, shall we?'

Zura was indeed aboard, and in an especially black humour.

She stood frowning in the prow of her vessel, behind the blood-eyed figurehead, wide-legged and arms folded across her bosom. A princess of all she surveyed, of bones and mummies and dust, and crumbling sarcophagi.

Tall and long of leg, Zura wore a single black garment

121

which sufficed to cover her arms, back, belly and thighs but left the rest of her quite naked. Golden sandals accentuated the scarlet of her toenails, while wide golden bands on her wrists gave something of a balance to her slender hands and pink nails. Her lips were full and red as her painted toes – too full, perhaps, too red – and they pouted a little as her sensitive nostrils flared in the reek drifting up from the city of the dead beneath the keel of her coffin-ship. A thin film of heavily perfumed oil covered her body, giving her breasts a milky sheen where they stood proud and high and tipped with dark-brown buds.

And seen like that, at a glance – like some strange lewd statue under the moon with its yellow glimmer upon her – Zura was very beautiful, incredibly so. Yet hers was a tainted beauty, like that of the man-eating flowers of jungled Kled, whose tendrils are suckered and pollens lethal. An almost visible aura of evil seemed to surround her, issuing waves of near-tangible terror. Her huge, black, slanting eyes that shone and missed nothing, seemed imbued with the hypnotic gaze of serpents; snaky-sinuous, too, the ropes of shining black hair which fell about her alabaster shoulders.

This then was Zura of Zura, smouldering and silent, and her crew knowing enough of her moods to keep well out of her way this night; so that it might seem she was alone aboard her gaunt, leprous grey vessel. She was not alone, however, not for all the stillness and the quiet; her zombies would stand still just as long as she'd let them, and corpses are mostly silent creatures anyway, especially when their tongues have rotted to slime in their mouths . . .

And: 'Damn!' said Zura of Zura. 'Damn! Damn! *Damn!*' She breathed the words into the night like four grey ghosts, fleeing from between her clenched teeth. 'Damn Gudge and his so-called "pirates", and damn the pact I made with them! They've robbed me of what was rightly mine, and nothing to be done about it.'

She thought back on the hand that fate had dealt her since the war of the Mad Moon:

First her return to Zura the land, under threat of banishment to the alien and utterly horrible – even to her – dreamlands of other worlds if ever again she should set foot outside her own boundaries. That had been disappointment enough: to see her dream within dreams of turning all the dreamlands into one gigantic nightmare of death themselves turned to dust. But then ... to discover Zura the land empty, even deathless! For Mnomquah, the lunatic god of a Mad Moon had drawn all her zombie minions up to the moon on a beam of powerful attraction, and not a single dead creature remained in all Zura the land. Even the foetor of that unthinkable place had been much reduced.

But the worm will have his way, and death conquers all in the end. A quarrier was crushed by a rock-fall in Nir, and his corpse came to Zura one night, shattered ribs and trunk and all. A pair of prospectors in the uplands, stung by a pack of six-legged spider-hounds, arrived all puffed up and bloated with poison. A great ceremonial canoe out of Parg, carrying a bride-to-be and her entourage from Parg to the isle where she'd wed her lover, struck a reef and sank. All were chewed by sharks, and swam to the shores of Zura. And close behind came the bereaved lover, who jumped from a cliff to the sea and the rocks. And so Zura was back in business again.

In a little while a boat-builder came to her, crushed between ship and wharf, and Zura commanded the building of *Shroud II*. But he was an ex-waking worlder, and his previous occupations had included mortician and coffin-maker – which perhaps accounted for the shape and style of Zura's ship. All to the good where she was concerned (the sails were of cerecloth, with ligament rigging and bones for the rungs of ladders).

And soon, once again as before, a ripe miasma of rot

hung over Zura the land, and once again the Princess Zura commanded her legions of the morbidly dead. But corpses disintegrate all too quickly, and suitable lovers are rare in the ranks of the direfully dead and last only a little while. So Zura dreamed dreams within dreams of a great disaster, which would send dreamland's peoples to her in their thousands, and a war where they would slaughter each other mindlessly – but no disaster came, and the peoples of dream war hardly at all. And so her frustration grew . . .

Then –

– Then came Gudge and his 'pirates'! Oh, that peculiar band of supposed buccaneers fooled her not at all; she knew who and what they were, if not what they were about. They'd be up to no good, be sure, but fell motives were not Zura's concern.

What they offered was this: that if Zura step aside and give them free run of the skies over Zura and lands adjacent, and if she make no report of them or their presence here – in other words, ignore them entirely and let them get on with their dubious business – then they'd send her the poor doomed remains of crews and passengers of all the vessels they intended to sack over and around Zura the land, Thalarion, and the Southern Sea. For ostensibly they were to be pirates, and where pirates sail death is a frequent occurrence and corpses very common-place. Lathi of Thalarion had been likewise approached, though in her case (because she had no interest in cadavers) the pressure applied had been that of sheer threat un-disguised: if she failed to accept the presence of the pirates or created any sort of difficulty for them, then they'd simply fire-bomb Thalarion the hive; which the eidolon Lathi knew all too well would prove a very harrowing and possibly fatal experience!

Zura had considered, and it had seemed to her that she was getting the better of the bargain; Gudge, as he called himself, had not even requested harbour or mooring for his ship in Zura (oh, yes, for there had been only one black pirate vessel in the beginning) but had settled for an extinct volcano in the mountains between Zura and Leng for his headquarters. And there, in that dead cone and in the tunnels formed of ancient lava ruins, he had made his home and garrisoned his crew.

Things had gone well at the start; Zura reaped the rewards of her passive assistance; her zombie legion grew apace. But then things started to change, however marginally at first. Numbers of zombie recruits, initially high, began to drop off; Zura complained and the pirates offered her booty rather than bodies, for which she had little use. Then, periodically, the 'extinct' volcano would throw up smoke rings in the hinterland, which might or might not be responsible for certain strange and unforeseen eclipses of the moon; also, there were at times dull rumblings underfoot – like the evenly-paced pounding of mighty hammers or subterranean engines – whose epi-centre would seem to be the root of that self-same ex-volcanic mountain. And then one day Zura's zombie spies reported that instead of one pirate ship there were now three, and that plunderings (or at least sinkings) of dream-land's innocent vessels had increased dramatically – at which Zura had flown into a raging fury!

She'd summoned Gudge to attend her in Zura the mausoleum city, but only the Captain of one of his two surplus vessels came; and when she'd put to that squat, offensive, eye-patched and tricorn-hatted – person? – cer-tain questions, then he'd only laughed unpleasantly. Where were all the freshly dead going? (Zura had wanted to know), for they certainly weren't entering Zura the land. Indeed she was lucky if she saw more than two or three corpses from each ship sacked! Did her pact with Gudge count for nothing at all, and should she now treat it with a similar lack of respect? And anyway, what was that silent, cowled, voluminously-robed creature up to in the mountains, that a dead volcano should suddenly belch itself back into life, however sporadic? Was it the pirate leader's intention to submerge the Charnel Gardens under a lava lake? These were the questions she had put to the wide-mouthed Captain-messenger.

'Cause trouble,' she'd been informed then, gutturally and with many a sneer, 'and Gudge will blow your worm-eaten shell of a ship right out of the sky, reduce your bony bully-boys to glue, put mausoleum Zura to the cannon and the torch, and spray perfumes of Kled over all Zura the land until it may never stink so badly again!' And laughing even more unpleasantly than before, Gudge's man had gone off and left her in a shocked condition bordering on trauma!

Even now she had not fully recovered, so that when the lookout attempted to croak something down to her from *Shroud*'s carrion-crow's nest she almost failed to hear or heed him. But the disturbance was such an uncommon event in itself (so few of the crew having tongues at all) that finally the lookout's harshly gabbled, clotted message got through to her:

'Something approaches from the West, O Princess.'

'Something? Something?' she hissed up at him then, half in astonishment. Had his brain rotted away entirely? 'A sky-ship, d'you mean?'

'If so, a very small one,' came the gurgled, hesitant answer. 'And no sails whatever, and fast as cannon-shot to boot!'

Snatching up a glass, Zura scanned the night sky to the west – then caught her breath as, in the next moment, the time-clock rushed in on her and slowed to a halt, hovering no more than a sword's reach beyond *Shroud*'s octopus prow. And:

'Ahoy, Zura!' came a ringing cry from the curious vessel (de Marigny's voice, amplified by the time-clock's systems).

'Permission to come aboard, if you please.'

She narrowed her slanty eyes and peered hard. 'Ahoy . . . whatever! Who is it approaches Zura of Zura so bold, taking liberties with the sky-space I alone control?'

'That's not what I've heard!' de Marigny contradicted, and the time-clock rose above the rail, came forward and slowly settled to the deck. He opened the door and stepped out – alone. 'As for my name,' his voice was normal, quieter now, 'it's de Marigny – Henri-Laurent de Marigny – The Searcher to some.'

'The Searcher, you say?' and her eyebrows narrowed in a frown. 'Never heard of you!' She backed away, putting distance between herself and the time-clock, whose interior was invisible in the purple glow spilling out onto the ship's deck. This retreat was not fear on Zura's part; she merely wished to draw de Marigny forward, separate him from his vessel; and all along the ship's sides her zombie crew stealthily closed in.

De Marigny could see that worm-ravaged bunch, and certainly he could smell them, but he moved after her anyway. And shrugging, he said: 'I didn't expect you to have heard of me, but you know my surname, certainly; Etienne, my father, is a great friend of King Carter of Ilek-Vad – that is, when he's not exploring in undreamed dimensions.'

By now he'd allowed himself to be lured almost to Zura's cabin door; and there that Princess of death paused, hand on one perfectly fashioned hip, breasts brazenly jutting, her natural pout turning to a languid smile as she noticed just how handsome her visitor was, how tall and strong-seeming. 'Your father, eh?' she said, almost absent-mindedly. 'Aye, I've heard of him. A great dreamer, that one, so I'm told. Well, now . . .'

Behind de Marigny but not unnoticed, Zura's zombie crew ringed the time-clock about. All held rusty cutlasses in white bone and black leather talons.

127

'Bold, I called you,' she said then, her low voice a sin in itself, 'and obviously brave, too, like your father – or utterly foolish. It seems the waking world breeds many brave men these days – and lots of fools, too.'

'Zura,' said de Marigny, moving closer still, 'I'm not much of a one for banter, least of all now. As for being a fool: you're probably right. And I'm searching now for two more fools – except they're very worthy ones, whose lives are in jeopardy.'

But an amorous mood was on her and she hardly heard him. Eyes slitted like a great cat's, she licked her lips and reached out to trace the strong curve of his chin, the column of his neck, the broad reach of his shoulders. Behind him, zombies closed in and placed their swords at his back, where he could feel their points just pricking him. And finally:

'Well, Searcher,' Zura sighed seductively, 'it seems you've come searching in one place too many. Anyway, what could you possibly have hoped to find here? Did no one tell you that Zura is the Land of Pleasures Unattained and Desires Unrealized – except the pleasures and desires of Zura of Zura?' And she laughed however coarsely and arched her body against his, so close that he could smell something of the reek beneath her perfume and oils.

De Marigny only smiled – even a little sardonically, perhaps – and continued to watch her keenly; which Zura noted, mistook for appreciation, and silently approved.

And while her thoughts were on other, more intimate things, still she forced herself to carry the line of the conversation, playing it like a lover's game: 'Why don't we talk some more in the privacy of my cabin?' she purred. 'And anyway, who are these men you seek, these "worthy fools" of yours?'

'Ex-waking worlders,' he answered at once, still smiling, 'and I'm told you know them well. They are called David Hero and Eldin the Wanderer.'

Zura's manner changed on the instant. She snapped erect, nostrils flaring. 'Hero? Eldin? You search for them? For what reason? Anyway, too late, for Gudge has them. Hero will go a-heroing no more, and Eldin's wandering days have meandered to a close.' Now, relaxing a little, her tone grew less sharp than sour. 'Aye, Gudge the so-called "pirate chief" – he robbed them away from me, as he'd doubtless try to rob you away, if he knew you were here.'

'Where's he taken them?' de Marigny's expression had also changed; his words were hard-edged and issued from behind teeth very nearly clenched. Suddenly taut as a bow-string, he was visibly eager – but not for anything of Zura's.

She felt spurned, drew herself once more erect, stood regal and smouldering and quite the most beautiful – the most *evilly* beautiful – creature de Marigny had ever seen. 'You can't help them!' she snapped then, her mouth writhing. 'You're only one man, so how could you? And I can't help them, not even if I would, for I've only one ship. No one can help them – so forget them!' She caught his hand, adopted a pose less seductive than threatening, said: 'And now come and make love to me – love me like you've never loved before, and like you'll never love again – or I give you to my zombies here and now! The choice is yours: you can love me alive or love me freshly dead. For that's how it will be in the end, be sure.'

'Be not so sure!' came the cry of a sweet, angry, infinitely female voice.

'*What?*' Zura's gasp was one of instant rage and astonishment combined. 'You brought – you dared to bring – another woman here? A *living* woman? In that – ?' She pointed a trembling hand at the time-clock. 'Then damn you, Searcher! Your life is forfeit, and then I'll have you anyway!' De Marigny felt the dead men behind him draw back their swords for thrusting. 'And as for your woman, hiding behind that purple haze – some slut of the waking world, no doubt – this is one dream she'll not be waking up from. Instead my zombies – '

But what her zombies would do was never learned.

Twin beams of light, pencil slim but so pure and bright that the eye could scarce discern their colour, leapt from the time-clock's dial and touched, oh so briefly, the undead corpses at de Marigny's back, where even now they would drive their swords home. And where those creaking cadavers had stood ... motes of mummy dust danced in the light of the moon; bones crumbled to chalk in mid-air and rags of clothing fluttered, suspended momentarily; and as twin cutlasses clattered to the deck, so their owners gained merciful release.

And now from the open door of the time-clock, pouring out of the throbbing purple interior, a full ship's complement of sky-sailors, bright steel flashing as they swept aside Zura's zombie crew like so much chaff blown on the wind, toppling their mouldering remains over the rails. For these were Kuranes' veterans of the bloodiest sky-battles, not to be denied by a handful of liquefying flesh and brittle bones.

It was all done in a minute, almost before the mortified (or mortifying) Doyenne of Death could draw breath. But not before she could draw her knife.

'I don't know what sort of vessel or weapon that damned coffin is – ' she hissed then, placing the cutting edge of her steel against de Marigny's neck, ' – and I shall never understand how it is bigger inside than out, but if it issues one more threat – '

Which, at that precise moment, it did. 'Put down your knife, Zura,' came that sweet, angry, amplified voice a second time; and again a pencil beam struck forth. For the merest moment the blinding ray passed between Zura's neck and shoulder, and ropes of shining black hair fell loose, smouldering; and behind her, where the beam touched wood, the timber of her cabin door turned black and issued smoke.

Zura did not fear death for he was her fondest companion, but she did fear burning, utter disintegration and unbeing. And slowly she put down her knife.

Kuranes' men were at de Marigny's side; one of them took Zura's knife and tossed it down to the deck, looked to The Searcher for instructions. 'Ready the ship for sailing,' said de Marigny; and to Zura: 'I'll ask you again, O Princess – where has Gudge got Hero and Eldin?'

By now Moreen had come from the clock. Zura saw her and sniffed haughtily, said: 'Well, at least this explains something of your reluctance. She's pretty, I'll grant you – for a live one, anyway.' And then she turned away, for Zura could not bear the sight of living beauty, not in her domain of death.

De Marigny caught her arm and turned her back to face him. 'I'll ask it just one more time, then take you back to face Kuranes' justice. The dreamlands beyond Hali are hellish, I'm told.'

Zura, pale as death, went paler still. For a moment she slumped, then tossed her head and straightened up. 'Kuranes? Why should I fear the justice of Kuranes? He gave me warning, aye, and set a certain stricture: that I should never more fare forth beyond the borders of Zura the land. Well, nor have I. How then may you illegally abduct me from my own Charnel Gardens, and Kuranes punish me? For what?'

De Marigny was growing desperate. A pale stain was spreading itself over the entire horizon, brightening, sending tenuous streamers of mauve light westward. 'Zura, it's almost dawn. They die at dawn, as I'm sure you know. Now you'll tell me where, and why, and by whose hand. If not . . . then obviously you're in league with the pirates; for which, and for the loss of his finest agents and questers, Kuranes will surely punish you as no one was ever punished before.'

Zura frowned, licked her lips, narrowed her eyes. And

131

slowly she tilted her head a little to one side, nodded, as if to herself, and began to smile. Gudge and his gang owed her one, didn't they? – owed her more than one, for hadn't they also crossed her in the war of the Mad Moon? And in a battle, whichever way things went, lives were bound to be lost and Zura the land enriched. She reached a decision, said: 'If I side with you and supply the answers you seek, and if there's to be fighting – for I warn you now, Gudge has three ships and we have only *Shroud* – will you allow me the captaincy of my vessel, with these fighting men of Celephais and Serannian under my command? This way there'll be no doubt that the pirates are no friends of mine, and Kuranes can apologize if he pleases.'

De Marigny looked at the stern-faced men flanking her, tilted his chin sharply in a gesture of inquiry. 'Well?'

'She's an able Captain,' their spokesman answered. 'Indeed, I cheered her on in the Mad Moon war. And yes, if it will speed matters, we'll accept Zura's orders – lawful orders, that is – for this one night only; for it's a weird ship, this *Shroud*, and who'd know its whims better than its natural, or unnatural, mistress?'

'Zura, O Princess,' came a croak from on high, where at least one member of her crew had been overlooked. 'A ship approaches from the East – Lathi's *Chrysalis*. The grub-Queen pays you a visit!'

'Moreen,' snapped de Marigny at once. 'Into the time-clock, quickly!' But:

'Hold!' said Zura. 'I was expecting Lathi sooner or later. For you see, I'd already decided it was time we did something about Gudge, and so invited the Queen of Thalarion to come a-calling. But tonight of all nights! What a bonus – what an omen!'

The eidolon Lathi's paper ship was closer now; she gusted along at a good pace under her varnished paper sails, leprous decks sickly agleam in starlight and the glimmer of a sun not yet quite risen. And soon:

132

'Ahoy, Zura!' hailed a voice strange and honeyed, while *Chrysalis* came alongside and dropped anchor on Zura the land.

Zura, Moreen, de Marigny and the spokesman for Kuranes' men went to the rail and stared across at the paper ship and her mistress, the beautiful ter-Queen, Lathi of Thalarion.

Where Zura was dark and oil-gleamy, Lathi was all golden and blonde and green-eyed. Young as a girl she looked, and lovely as a rose in full bloom. Except –

She sat (or seemed to sit) upon a bench-like seat beneath a canopy of pink-hued paper; paper curtains hung behind her, extending to the sides. Attended by handmaidens – beautiful-seeming, scantily-clad girls who sprawled at her feet – she was naked from the waist up, but from there down was draped in ruffles and fluffs and piles of silky, glossy pink and purple tissues. De Marigny, who knew almost nothing about Lathi, found her astonishingly attractive; and yet, paradoxically, at the same time he felt inexplicably repulsed.

In a quiet aside to Moreen, The Searcher said: 'Something fishy about this one. Indeed, almost as fishy as Zura.'

'You're right,' she answered. 'Her handmaidens, too. Lathi *looks* real and human enough, but those handmaidens ... their nipples are painted on, Henri, unreal!'

'I've noticed,' de Marigny felt obliged to admit. 'But Lathi's not all she seems either. 'The word "eidolon", after all, is often used to describe a confusing image or reflection – something other than what is seen. Perhaps, under all those paper frills, there's a lot we *can't* see.'

'And a good thing too!' whispered Moreen. 'Are all dreamland's females so brazen?'

De Marigny frowned, left Moreen's question unanswered. He couldn't know it, but he had hit upon the truth: behind the curtains, hidden from view, more of Lathi's termaids were at work even now, massaging and smoothing soft oils into her monstrous lower body – which was nothing less than the vastly pulsating cylinder of a termite Queen! But if her grub-body was monstrous, what of her *appetites*? De Marigny knew nothing of them – the fact that she took her termen whole, and occasionally the men of other races – which was probably just as well; otherwise he might not have been so ready to accept the alliance which Zura even now proposed:

'Lathi,' the Princess of Death called out. 'This is The Searcher, de Marigny; you may or may not have heard of him.' And (though less enthusiastically), 'And this is his woman, Moreen. The men are Kuranes' lot, but I can't deny they're brave fighters for all that. Your ship and mine make two, and with these men and your termen to crew them – and with The Searcher's vessel, small and curious but carrying an awesome weapon – we plan to give Gudge's gang a well deserved clout. What say you? Have you had enough of Gudge and his so-called "pirates" over and around Thalarion?'

The termen Zura had mentioned were tall for dream-beings, handsome and bronzed, with a light yellowish tinge to their skins like sick gold. They were also like as peas in a pod and uniformly vacant-looking where they stood at the rail of the paper ship, their arms crossed on their deep chests. Blank-faced they stood there, dressed only in loin-cloths, like so many mental eunuchs. And if de Marigny could have seen beneath those square flaps of garments, then he would have known the real extent of their 'vacancy'. For all their robotic attitude, however, the termen were well-muscled and carried scythe-like weapons in sheaths strapped underarm. These were Lathi's 'soldiers', her workers, and if they had one purpose in life it was this: to do their Queen's bidding whatever, and protect her life with their own to the very death.

'Had enough of Gudge, did you say?' Lathi now called back, a slightly alien ring to her voice, her beautiful face clouding over. 'Too true I have, Zura of Zura! He's threatened the hive Thalarion once too often. When do we sail?'

'Immediately!' cried Zura with a throaty laugh. 'A surprise dawn attack. Haul up your anchor, Lathi, and we're off.' She fired orders at her new crew, then turned to de Marigny and Moreen. 'Quick now, and as we go I'll tell you all you want to know. Then, while you drive on ahead in that queer coffin of yours and try to rescue those great buffoons, we'll follow on behind and ready ourselves for battle!'

4

Engines of Horror!

In the heart of a certain mountain in the range behind Zura
the land, foothills of a mightier, more distant escarpment,
itself a stony prelude to the forbidden Plateau of Leng, a
pair of haggard questers hung on their crosses over the rim
of a black pit and waited for the fast approaching dawn
and the death it would bring. The ex-volcano's tunnels were
like six outwardly radiating spokes or ribs with Hero and
Eldin at the centre; one spoke pointing to each of the four
cardinal points of the compass, one pointing straight up
through the mountain's peak to the skies overhead, and
the last – forming the pit itself – pointing inexorably down.

The tunnels had all been lava runs in the fire-mountain's
heyday, with the vertical shaft serving, of course, as the
main vent. Even now that shaft (certainly its lower reaches,
in the very roots of the dreamlands), while something other
than volcanic, remained no jot less deadly. The tunnel to
the north was more or less level, cathedral-like in its great
height and width, a mile long from the centre to where it
opened facing distant, ill-reputed Leng. There, at the
mouth of that ancient, gigantic blowhole, that was where
Gudge harboured his three black vessels and their crews.

As for the eastern, southern and western tunnels: they
were narrow, low-ceilinged, in places choked with tephra
and solidified lava; home to spiders and cave-lizards and
other small, creeping creatures.

'The hell of it is,' said Eldin rumblingly, breaking a
silence which had lasted for maybe a half-hour; during
which time the pair had performed sombre inward-directed
inspections of their somewhat dubious pasts, perhaps in
anticipation of yet more dubious futures, 'that we still don't

know what it's all about! I mean, *why* are Gudge and Co. masquerading as pirates? What evil is it they're hiding, or doing, or brewing here? Apart from the sinking of innocent ships, that is, and the eating of their crews. Oh, it has to be something big, be sure – else no rhyme or reason to all the scheming – but what?'

As the echoes of his voice died away in that grim place, Hero tried to shrug and couldn't, so simply answered: 'Beats me. Except . . .'

'Yes?'

'Except I keep thinking we'll be finding out soon enough. Too soon, if you take my meaning. For it has to do, I think, with this volcano – or rather, this ex-volcano.'

Even as he spoke there came echoing up from below a dull, distant booming or pounding, as if some Colossus of inner earth had chosen that precise moment to commence banging away on demon drums. The reverberations from unguessed abysses caused the air to vibrate, brought down rills of dust and pumice from crevices and small ledges; and slowly the pounding took up a steady rhythm, like that of some huge and nameless engine throbbing away in bowels of nether earth.

'Umm!' said Eldin thoughtfully. 'I take it that's what you were talking about, eh?'

'Well it's hardly volcanic activity, now is it?' Hero returned. 'Which in turn begs the question: just what the hell *is* it? I mean, it must go down deeper than Pnoth, this great black flue, and yet something's alive down there . . .'

'Like Oorn in her pit, you mean? That horrible gastropod mate of Mnomquah's, where we sealed her under Sarkomand at the end of the Mad Moon war?'

'Maybe even worse than Oorn,' replied Hero, darkly.

'Worse than Oorn?' the Wanderer grimaced. 'That's a hell of an imagination you've got there, lad! But I know what you mean: if not real life down there, pseudo-life – right?'

'Real, pseudo, whatever!' said Hero. 'Nasty-life, anyway. And –'

'Hold your breath!' Eldin cut him short.

Hero heeded the older dreamer's warning at once. This subterranean pounding wasn't new to them; so far they'd hung here for an afternoon and a night, and this was the third time that ominous thundering had rumbled up from below. By now they were well acquainted with what came with it. First the smell:

'*Yurghhh!*' said Eldin, screwing his eyes shut, clamping his lips together, even trying to pinch his nostrils in upon themselves against a reek that would make the Charnel Gardens smell good. And then:

'*Arghhh!*' agreed Hero, likewise suppressing his sensory tackle, as a hot, stinking black smoke ring came whooshing up from dreamland's core. It clung to the wall of the pit, that rolling ring of noxious steam and smoke and lord-knows-what, billowing over the questers, enveloping them, and hurtling on up the shaft in the mountain's heart to the skies above. Overhead the glimmer of stars fading in the coming dawn was shut out as the smoke ring eclipsed them; while down below the pounding continued its driving, maddening beat, accompanied by subterranean shuddering.

The pair opened their stinging eyes, breathed tentatively at first, then gulped with their mouths at the still foetid air, gradually relaxing the pressure on their nostrils. Eldin was first to speak. 'Lord, what I'd give right now for a clothes peg!' he moaned.

'Save your breath,' Hero gasped. 'You need it, for as we've seen before this is likely to go on for some little time.'

But the Wanderer wasn't listening; instead he was frowning down into the gulf, his chin jutting forward onto his broad chest. 'You'd think there were machines down there,' he said. 'And this the chimney of some monstrous mill, some foul factory of hell!'

138

'That's rather poetic,' said Hero, who had a good ear for such. But he had a fairly decent memory, too, and now his eyes narrowed. 'What's more, it's rather reminiscent of something I've heard before.'

'Oh? And what's that?' queried Eldin – but before Hero could answer: 'Watch it – here we go again!'

Another smoke ring whooshing past, grimy and slimy and yet hot as the breath of some dragon of darkness. And in its wake, as Hero coughed and spluttered and blinked his eyes open:

'Old lad, is it my –' (cough!) ' – imagination, or is it –' (cough!) ' – suddenly a bit lighter around here?'

'Not your imagination, no,' Eldin choked back. 'Before these damned smoke rings started up I'd been lying back my head and staring up at the stars. Of course, from down here there'll always be stars up there – even when it's daylight outside – but for a fact they've been getting dimmer this last hour. It's the dawn, that's what you're seeing: the cold light of dawn come a-creeping down this funnel and along these tunnels of rock. Can't you feel it in your bones? I can, even now: the sun, lifting his golden rim up over the edge of the dreamlands. The sun we'll likely never see again . . .'

'Whoah, there! Hang on, old lad!' Hero cried. 'What's all this then? The sun we'll likely never see again? Where's that old indefatigable Eldin gone to – the never-say-die spirit, the stiff upper lip?'

'As for that last,' said Eldin, 'it's a lip and a bit above this weak wobbly chin! Anyway, you were about to tell me what I'd reminded you of – you know, "foul factories of hell", and such?'

'Ah yes, that!' said Hero. 'It was Kuranes, I think, or maybe old King Carter himself in Ilek-Vad – can't remember for sure. It was at a banquet or some such, and I'd had a bit to drink. I was on muth-dew and you were on your back somewhere or other. But I do recall the subject.

It seems that scattered about in certain of dreamland's darker regions, there are these pits of nightmare that go down into unfathomed depths of madness. And I quote: "down there in the burrows at the bottom of these pits, engines of horror pound, where the souls of lost dreamers feed the blackest dreams of the Great Old Ones and fuel the nightmares which *They* send to plague human dreamers!'

Eldin's voice was much subdued when finally, after a short silence, he said: 'And you think this is one such pit, eh?'

Hero chewed his lip. 'Well, we'll not be the first Gudge has dropped down into darkness, will we? And knowing his lot – their feeding habits, that is – surely that would seem to constitute one hell of a waste of good meat. Unless the pit's needs are greater, more important.'

'Engines of horror, eh?' Eldin mumbled, licking lips grown suddenly dry. And: 'Oh, oh! Here comes an – '

– other smoke ring, he would have finished, except the stench and steam and smoke shut him off as the ring of foul vapour rolled over the questers and hissed up toward the new day. And with that third monstrous exhalation of unknown earth, sudden as it had started up, so the subterranean pounding faltered and shut down; and silence reigned once more in that gloomy, reeking place. But only for a little while. Then –

'You hear that?' said Hero. 'Footsteps! A good many of them, and coming this way.'

'From the north tunnel,' said Eldin. 'Aye, and growing louder by the minute. Gudge and his gang coming to send us to hell. Or to dreamland's black core, to fuel Cthulhu's machineries of nightmare!'

'Eldin, I – ' Hero struggled to find words. 'I just wanted to say – I mean . . .'

'Yes, yes – I know, I know,' the Wanderer's voice was gruff. 'It's all right – I forgive you.'

'What I'm trying to say is ... what?' Hero couldn't conceal the surprise in his voice. 'Forgive me? For what?'

'For all the bad turns you've done me, bad thoughts you've thought about me, bad things you've said to me. I forgive you for all of them.'

For long moments Hero was struck dumb. But then he began to grate: 'Well that's damn big of you – you blustering, beer-swilling, black-hearted, quirky old ...'

'... Including *that* one,' said Eldin, unruffled. 'And not so much of the "old", if you don't mind.' And before Hero could explode: 'Now then, d'you know any half-decent gods we might try praying to? If so trot 'em out, for it looks like that's all that's left to us now ...'

'Horned ones, aye, what else?' said Zura of Zura to Moreen and de Marigny aboard *Shroud II*. 'One of their black ships spotted Hero and Eldin wandering afoot along Zura the land's western border toward the hinterlands. They hoisted the Jolly Roger, dropped down out of the sky, picked 'em up. Now that's doubtless as the questers wished it – to get in with the pirates, find out about them, possibly arrange a bit of sabotage – but as soon as they were aboard they must have seen what they were up against. Lengites! Their squat little bodies would have given the almost-humans away: their wide shoes hiding cloven hooves, their too-wide mouths, the tricorn hats concealing their horns. But no way out of it: too many of them to fight and nowhere to flee, and the black ship already gaining altitude and heading for Gudge's volcano. A-ha! – and the horned ones playing along with the game, pretending Hero and Eldin were welcome aboard (which they were, of course, but not as pirates!) and the questers yo-ho-hoing and acting all piratical – but all of them knowing it for a sinister charade, which must come to an abrupt end as soon as they reached their destination ...

'Anyway, as fate would have it I was aboard *Shroud* that

141

evening and spied them a-sailing. I closed in and hailed them, and spotted that pair of great clowns on the black ship's deck. I called them by name – but the Lengites already had a good idea who they were, I'm sure. And then I demanded that they be handed over to me. Oh, yes, for I had scores to settle with those two!

'But the almost-humans wouldn't hear of it, not now that they knew for certain who their new "recruits" were; Gudge would want to see them, and he'd doubtless have plans of his own for them. And that was that. I should scarper, they said, and stop "interfering" – and never so much as a "by your leave, O Princess!" Well, I had only the crew aboard and no fighters to speak of; the Lengites held all the cards; I could only let them go.'

'Where exactly is this volcano, Gudge's hideout?' de Marigny was eager to be off, desperately afraid that he was already too late.

'Why, it's right . . . *there!*' said Zura, pointing. 'See?'

It was dawn. The sun was one third up and the dreamlands were turning golden – except Zura the land far below, which was gloomy as ever in the shade of misted, moss-grown, leaning tombstones. But far away to the north where Zura pointed, there the hazy peaks of mountains stood faintly purple over a sea of grey mist; and even now one of those peaks shot up a curling black smoke ring toward dreamland's last stars. Also, on the north-western horizon, a pale moon was suddenly blotted out by something near-invisible, some alien cloud that writhed and put out feelers to draw itself down across the sky toward that same range of mountains.

And now de Marigny began to understand. His eyes widened; he grasped Moreen's hand and hastened her toward the time-clock. Only as they entered into that weird vessel did he think to call back: 'Good luck, Zura. Give 'em hell!'

'Luck to you, Searcher,' she called back, nodding. 'And

my regards to that pair of scoundrels when you see them – *if* you're in time!'

De Marigny simply pointed his strange vehicle at the distant volcano and 'went there'. In a vessel like the time-clock, that was perfectly feasible: to be able to see your goal was to make that goal almost instantly accessible. He got there as the third and last black smoke ring was on its way up the mountain's ancient funnel, came to a hovering halt directly over the crater as that expanding vapour-ring whooshed up, briefly encompassed the clock, headed for the sky. And he knew now for a fact exactly what lay below, down in the dead volcano's heart.

'The last time I was in the dreamlands,' he told Moreen, 'Titus Crow was in much the same fix as Hero and Eldin, I fancy. He and Tiania were scheduled to suffer Nyarlathotep's inquisition before being fed into the engines of horror where the Great Old Ones fashion mankind's worst nightmares. And this volcano, which it undoubtedly once was, must now be the exhaust vent of just such engines. Once you've seen those evil black smoke rings you can never mistake them for anything else. Last time it was a pit in the underworld, in a fantastic underground cavern where few dreamers had ever ventured; this time it's here on the surface, and so its gases must have been disguised as the uneasy stirrings of a long-slumbering volcano.'

'And that strange eclipse we saw?' Moreen's excitement was growing. 'Didn't Atal also mention this Nyarlathotep, the Great Messenger?'

De Marigny nodded. 'The massed telepathic mind of the Great Old Ones. They're invading the dreams of men again, in preparation for that same uprising which threatens Elysia! Hero and Eldin are special, important dreamers; Cthulhu will learn what he can from them, through

Nyarlathotep, before grinding them to pulp in his night-mare machines. Look!'

Enlarged by the time-clock's scanners, the lower slopes of the mountain to the west seemed suddenly enveloped by a sickly, crawling mist. Except this mist writhed and put out feelers, then drew itself into the mountain via the extinct, half-choked lava run which opened on that side. 'Nyarlathotep, in just one of his "thousand forms"!' de Marigny rasped. 'Well he hasn't come here for nothing, and so there has to be time yet.'

Then, without further pause, The Searcher dropped the time-clock vertically down the shaft, at the same time scanning the darkness below as the crusted lava walls rushed upwards at a terrific pace and dawn's natural light narrowed to a pallid circle receding high overhead ...

'Well then, what are you waiting for?' Eldin roared up at the massed ranks of wide-mouthed faces leering down on Hero and himself. 'On you go, hack away! Or better still let me up off this cross, give me a sword and *I'll* hack away – but not at any ropes, be sure! *Ha!* Scummy sons of Leng – your fathers were spawned in moonlit mud and your mothers went on all fours! You weren't born but spawned! And when you die – which you all will, and soon if there's any justice – why, not even Zura would welcome such as you to the Charnel Gardens! What? I've seen handsomer night-gaunts!'

'Much handsomer – ' agreed Hero, if a bit less boister-ously, and not a little envious of Eldin's inspired taunting, ' – and they've no faces at all!'

Their comments bothered the almost-humans not one bit, but Gudge, on the opposite side of the pit from where they were hanging, now pushed wobblingly forward. As he neared the rim, so the Lengites hastily made room. Hero and Eldin had met Gudge when the black ship brought them here in the first place. He hadn't fooled them then and made no attempt to do so now.

Robed in red silk, but loosely – for there was no longer any need to conceal himself, not down here under the volcano – Gudge was far less than human. As Eldin had once long-since pointed out: 'Whoever dreamed a thing such as that must have been a madman!' And only half-hidden behind the shuddering folds of his robes, Gudge was indeed a leprous white anomaly; vaguely toadish yet able, within limits, to contract or expand his jellyish body at will; eyeless, yet obviously very clearly sighted; with a blunt snout that sprouted a vibrating mass of short pink tentacles in twin bunches, whose purpose was purely conjectural. Or perhaps not; for certainly the thing's hood, thrown back now, was equipped with wide-spaced eye-holes. So perhaps the pink tentacles served as 'eyes' of a sort. But voiceless beyond any doubt, Gudge conversed by means of a whining ivory flute which he carried in a mushy paw. His interpreter as he played or 'spoke' was one of the Lengites, a more than usually puffy horned one whose position puffed him up more yet.

'Questers,' he translated now, while the torches of his massed brothers flared up evilly all around, ' – you, Hero of Dreams and Eldin the Wanderer – Gudge wishes you to know that you are singularly honoured. Nyarlathotep himself comes to examine you. Even the Great Messenger of *Them* Gudge is pledged to serve! How say you? Are you not overwhelmed?'

'I vomit on Nyarlathotep!' cried Eldin. 'If he smells and looks half as disgusting as Gudge, I vomit twice on him! Even Hero vomits on him, and he's not as fussy as me!'

'In short,' Hero added, 'we're not impressed.'

The cloven-hooved interpreter tootled their comments back to Gudge, whose form at once commenced a rapid shrinking and swelling and fluttering which the questers took for an expression of some fury. And before he could bring himself properly under control –

'Not impressed?' came a new voice, and all heads turned toward the mouth of the west-facing lava run, from which poured a sickly mist that lapped like sour milk and pulsed with a life of its own. The voice – a young voice, whose tones were rippling and mellow, so languorous as to be almost hypnotic – had issued from this bank of seemingly sentient mist. And as the Lengites drew back toward the east- and north-facing tunnels, so the mist began to thicken – or to be *sucked in* toward a focal point, to form –

The shape of Nyarlathotep!

Tall and slim, clad in bright cloth of gold and crowned with a luminous pschent, the human-seeming figure became more solid as the mist merged into it. He was (or appeared to be) a man with the proud face of a young Pharaoh of ancient Khem – but his eyes were those of a Dark God, full of a languid, mercilessly mordant humour.

'So, questers,' he stepped forward a pace or two, causing Gudge himself to draw back in wobbly alarm, 'you are not impressed . . .' And he smiled a very awful smile. 'But you soon will be, believe me.'

For once Eldin was lost for words. Head level with the floor of that central cavern, where the crosses were roped with their tops projecting, he tried to speak but the words stuck in his throat. For there was that about the sinister newcomer, quite apart from his method of arrival, which was infinitely more frightening than Gudge and his horned ones could ever be. It was an alien something which Eldin didn't quite know how to handle.

Hero, who hadn't done so much shouting and whose spit was still comparatively fresh, stepped into the breach:

'Nyarlathotep, who or whatever you are, I don't know why you're so interested in us, but you'll get nothing out of us while we're hanging here. Have us hauled up and cut down from these crosses, and then we'll consider chatting to –'

'*Be quiet!*' the Pharaoh-figure hissed, his lacquered

146

eyebrows arching in a scowl. Gudge and his pirates drew back farther yet, and now Nyarlathotep approached to the very rim of the pit, from where he glared across at the two helpless dreamers. 'You dare to attempt to bargain with me? I am the very *mind* of Cthulhu! I carry the seething thoughts of Yogg-Sothoth! I speak with the tongue of Ithaqua the Wind-Walker, and thus know all the secrets of the winds that howl between the worlds! I *am* Yibb-Tstll, Atlach-Nacha, Tsathoggua the toad-thing, Nyogtha and Shudde-M'ell! My mind is *Their* mind, acrawl with *Their* thoughts. I am Nyarlathotep, the Crawling Chaos!'

Now Eldin found his voice, however croaky. 'Well said,' he nodded his approval. 'A bit theatrical, perhaps, but – '

'*Silence!*' howled Nyarlathotep. And more quietly: 'Silence, and live a little longer. Soon enough the engines of horror shall have you, and the essence of your crushed, terrified souls sent to start dreamers madly awake and raving forever – or would you go down to the pits of nightmare right now, on the instant, without more ado? For the longer you talk to me the longer you live, and when you stop – '

'Then make an end of it,' Hero blurted. 'If we're to die anyway let's have it now, rather than hang here passing the time with the source of all nightmares!'

'Make an end of it?' the Pharaoh-figure was obviously taken aback; but he smiled his monstrous smile to cover his confusion, and when he spoke again his voice was once more languid: 'Is that really your preference? But that implies a choice, and you have no choice.'

And now the questers knew the worst: that indeed there would be no resisting Nyarlathotep, for he commanded – he *was* – all the telepathic power of the Great Old Ones, who read the minds of men like men read open books. A creeping numbless settled over their brains, an iciness as of outer space invaded their staggering minds. And *knowing* he would be answered, Nyarlathotep began his inquisition:

'Dreamers, you have grown learned in the ways of the dreamlands and fast grow into legends. At least, *I* shall make legends of you – when I send you to be pulped in the grinding cogs of nightmare. But you two have talked with that old fool Atal, who in reality is no one's fool, and dined and chatted in company with triple-cursed Kuranes, even conversed with Randolph Carter himself. You are accepted in dreamland's highest echelons, and yet have plumbed the lower levels with equal flair. Lathi knows you, and Zura of Zura. Indeed it is your panache, your talent, that dooms you; too many powerful dreamers control man's subconscious mind in these times, which is not in acordance with *Their* plans. Especially not at this time. Which is why, when I am done with you, you are to be stopped . . .

'Ah! But where Kuranes and Carter and Atal have learned how to close their thoughts to me – to *us* – your minds are like open doors as yet! You may not deny me access. Now know you:

'The stars are very nearly right! The Great Old Ones are coming to claim what is rightly Theirs, in the dreamlands, the waking world, throughout all the worlds of space and time, and all the super- and sub-strata of endless dimensions. This *will* be! The multiverse *will* dissolve to chaos when Cthulhu comes. But there yet remains one great obstacle, one first and final goal which *They* must achieve: the discovery and destruction of Elysia!

'The way to Elysia, however, is a hidden way. The so-called "Elder Gods" hide there; they hide from Cthulhu's wrath, who has sworn vengeance on them that bound him in immemorial aeons. But you two – ex-mortals, men late of the waking world – perhaps you two may know something of Elysia, of the way to that place of the Elder Gods. Incredible, that perhaps you have knowledge of that which Great Cthulhu himself has not yet discovered! And yet I am reliably informed that even now One has come into the dreamlands to seek you out; aye, and he too searches for Elysia. Perhaps he has already found you, talked to you, learned from you … ? I, too, would learn from you – if you have anything to teach me – so now I command you: open up your minds to me, let me see all!'

Twin tendrils of mist reached out from Nyarlathotep's dark eyes, flowed writhingly through the air across the pit, fastened like lampreys to the foreheads of the questers where they fought a last desperate mental fight to keep their minds to themselves. Their brains felt like onions, being peeled layer by layer as Nyarlathotep commenced his 'examination' – but only for a moment.

All eyes were on the tableau formed by Nyarlathotep and the questers, all concentration centred there, so that none had seen the fractionally slow lowering of the time-clock down from the flue of the central vent. The first the horned ones, Gudge, Nyarlathotep, questers and all knew of it was when de Marigny's amplified voice boomed out in the confines of the cavern junction:

'Am I this "One" you seek, Nyarlathotep? If so, why not speak to me directly? For these questers know nothing of me.'

Now all eyes gazed upward; simultaneously, as the silently hovering time-clock was spied there, a concerted gasp broke out from all ranks. But de Marigny had confronted Nyarlathotep before and knew the danger; he had the advantage here and must be careful not to lose it.

'*You!*' the Pharaoh-figure's voice was now a croaking bass belch of sound. 'You, The Searcher, de Marigny!'

'We meet again,' said de Marigny – and he triggered the time-clock's weapon.

A pencil beam of incredible light sizzled down from the clock's dial, drove back the flickering shadows and put the torches of the petrified almost-humans to shame, cut through the tenuous tendril of mental mist stretched between Nyarlathotep and the questers. The connection was severed; but more than that, the shock of the severance was felt throughout the multiverse!

Yogg-Sothoth in his prison dimension beyond chaos reeled as his telepathic polyp mind felt that hot, cleansing breath of Eld; Cthulhu, dreaming mad dreams of universal conquest in R'lyeh, started fitfully, lashed out with terrific tentacles and crushed several aquatic shoggoth guards, who instantly re-formed and backed off; Shudde-M'ell convulsed deep under Earth's mantle, then dived down through salving lava as he felt even his mind singed by that pure, clean fire.

And Nyarlathotep, staggering back from the pit's rim, clapped his manicured hands to his head and croaked: 'Gudge, the questers – *send them to hell!*' And before de Marigny could trigger his weapon again, the Crawling Chaos dissolved into dank mist which writhed away into the crevices of the west-leading tunnel and was gone.

The horned ones were fleeing, stampeding down the north-leading tunnel toward their black ships of Leng, hastened by a salvo of fire from the time-clock; but Gudge, commanded by Nyarlathotep, was forbidden to flee. He took up a fallen sword and flopped wobblingly toward Hero and Eldin – toward the ropes which alone held their crosses in position over the pit's rim. Now that sword was lifted on high, and now it flashed down in an arc which would find both ropes at once where they were made fast to a projecting knob of lava. But –

That arc of bright steel was never completed. Caught by a pencil-beam from the time-clock in mid-sweep, Gudge's sword shivered into shards and took his arm, or whatever he had that passed for an arm, with it! A second stabbing beam struck him full-face, ate into his frantically scrabbling snout-tentacles, the leprous jelly face behind them, and finally the brain or ganglion behind the face. And voiceless though he was, still that creature uttered his first – and last

– shriek, like a jet of steam escaping under pressure, as he floundered to the edge of the pit, flopped to and fro there, toppled into nightmare. A shower of lava-dust and other cavern debris went with him, missing the dumbstruck, delirious dreamers on their crosses by inches.

Then . . .

. . . In a very little while de Marigny had set the time-clock down close to the pit, and not long after that the dazed questers were freed and stumbling about in the purple glow of the clock's open door, flailing and stamping life back into their numb arms and legs. But when de Marigny and Moreen would have led them inside the time-clock:

'Hold!' growled Eldin, stepping back a pace. He looked at Hero and cocked a querying eyebrow. 'Out of the frying pan . . . ?' he asked.

Hero shook his head, said: 'Shouldn't think so, old lad.' And to The Searcher, 'Didn't I hear a certain ex-moon-beast call you de Marigny?'

De Marigny grinned. 'You're probably thinking of my father,' he said. 'But don't worry, for I'm cut of much the same cloth as him – else I'd not be here.'

Eldin seemed somewhat mollified. Grudgingly he agreed: 'Aye, and I remember you now. A banquet in Ulthar – in your honour, too! Henri-Laurent de Marigny, and Titus Crow. It was toward the end of the Bad Days, in which you'd played quite a hand.' Then he looked again at the time-clock. 'Still, that's a damned weird threshold you're inviting us over. And I can't see how we'd manage it anyway. I mean, I'm hardly a stripling, now am I? You and the girl must be stifled in there, let alone asking two such as us in with you!'

Now de Marigny laughed out loud. 'The time-clock is bigger inside than out, Wanderer,' he said.

'Come on in,' said Moreen, 'and see for yourselves.'

And as a further inducement, de Marigny added: 'If we

151

hurry, we might just be in time to see those three "pirate" ships blown out of dreamland's skies by the eidolon Lathi and Zura of Zura.' Which finally did the trick; for *that* was a thought – and a promised delight – which Eldin couldn't resist for the world!

Deep down below in black bowels of earth, a horribly familiar, monstrous throbbing had started up again, like the thundering of vast subterranean hammers. And as Hero and Eldin at last accepted de Marigny's invitation and boarded the time-clock, and as that fantastic vessel lifted off and soared straight up the volcano's vent toward open skies, so, far behind, a hot black smoke ring was formed and billowed toward the surface.

It was an especially black, especially oily smoke ring: Gudge, of course, on his way to where he'd disperse in dreamland's high, clean upper atmosphere ...

5

Shrub Sapiens

As de Marigny had promised, they were in time to see Zura and Lathi's revenge on the horned ones. For as the time-clock rose up into the full dawn light, away down below on the northern slope of the volcano the three black ships of Leng were only just emerging from their vast keep and rising into the sky. Dangerously close together, they were, in a very tight formation, and it was plain that confusion reigned aboard. Each of the three captains had just one thought in mind: to get as far and as fast away as almost-humanly possible. Gudge was no more; a terrible destructive device was on the loose, one the Lengites had known before, which in Dylath-Leen and other places had spelled disaster for them; their moonbeast masters, of which Gudge had been only one, would be most unhappy about things, and someone – perhaps many someones – would be called to pay the price of failure. Horned heads would roll, wherefore . . . now was definitely a good time to run for home and quietly disappear into the less hazardous (for almost-humans) encampments of mist-shrouded Leng.

So that the advent of Lathi's *Chrysalis* and Zura's *Shroud II* from behind the volcano's flanking crags came as a complete surprise to them. The central 'pirate' got away, however, for it was shielded by the vessels to port and starboard, which took the brunt of Lathi's and Zura's vengeful salvoes. And as those two ships, crippled from the onset, put up what they could of a fight, so the one in the middle, unscathed, rose up higher into the sky and headed north for Leng. Its sails quickly filled as it found a good current of air, whereupon it sped off, leaving its comrades to their fate.

De Marigny let the survivor make a mile or two, then casually aligned the time-clock's weapon and triggered off a hastening beam. The black topsail and Jolly Roger went up in a flash of light and a puff of smoke, and The Searcher nodded and lowered his aim a little. But then, when even the slightest mental pressure would reduce the black ship to so much scorched wreckage, he hesitated.

'Well?' Eldin was on tenterhooks. 'What's holding you? You've got 'em dead!'

But de Marigny shook his head and released his mind's grasp on the trigger. 'No,' he said, 'for that's not my way.'

'You mean you're letting them go?' the Wanderer was beside himself. 'I don't believe it! Well, if you've no stomach for it, you just show *me* how it's done and step aside!'

But Hero said: 'Calm yourself, old friend. De Marigny's right – we're the good fellows, remember?'

'Eh?' Eldin rounded on him. 'Good fellows? You speak for yourself! As for me, where these damned Lengites are concerned I'm all baddie!'

'No you're not,' Hero contradicted with a shake of his head. 'And you know it. If de Marigny squeezed that trigger, it would be sheer slaughter. That sort of thing might be okay for Zura and Lathi, but not for us. Anyway, if we kill 'em all, who'll be left to spread our legend abroad, eh?'

'You mean, these buggers'll go back to Leng and say: "that Hero and Eldin, they got the best of us again", right?'

'Something like that,' Hero nodded.

'*Huh!*' Eldin scowled. And: 'You realize of course that it could easily be one of these very Lengites, one of these fine days, who sticks his sword right through your backbone – or mine?'

'Possibly,' said Hero. 'But not today, eh?'

Still furious, Eldin turned to Moreen. 'What do you say, lass? Are these two daft or not?'

'Maybe they are,' she took one of his great hands in both

of hers, 'and maybe they're not. But if the horned ones –
and all other dark creatures and men – weren't here to do
their bad things, would there be any point in a Hero and
an Eldin, or a de Marigny? What would you *do*, Wanderer,
if there was no longer anything to strive for? No more
questing? No last small danger in all the dreamlands?'

'Me,' said Hero, determined to change the subject, 'I'd
head straight for Serannian, take charge of the sky-yacht
Kuranes owes me, crew her with a couple of likely lasses
out of Baharna, and set sail for a tiny jewel island
somewhere off – '

'Ah, but now you're talking!' said Eldin. 'What? Give
me a sky-yacht, a tiny jewel isle and a likely lass – and you
can keep the yacht and the island for yourself!'

And that was that. As the black ship limped for the grey
northern horizon, the Wanderer watched it go and scowled
a very little. But he made no further comment . . .

Lathi was already heading for Thalarion when de Marigny
set the time-clock down on the deck of *Shroud II*. As he,
Moreen and the questers stepped forth, Zura greeted them
with a curt: 'Ho, Searcher and Co! Success to both sides of
our venture, it appears.' Then, staring straight into de
Marigny's eyes, she added: 'But it seems you came over all
faint-hearted when you might have burned that third black
ship to ashes. I was not so foolish.' And she inclined her
head downward across the rail of her ship. On the volcano's
lower slopes, the ruins of her own and Lathi's conquests
lay scattered amidst sharp lava crags.

'Not faint-hearted, Zura,' growled Eldin at once, before
anyone else could say a word. 'Big-hearted. Not foolish but
compassionate. There's a difference such as you wouldn't
understand. We're not all death's bosom-pals, you know!'

Hero scratched an ostensibly itchy nose, hiding his grin;
he controlled himself and nodded, straight-faced, as Zura
now turned her black-eyed gaze on him. Scowling, she

acknowledged his nod anyway, said: 'All intact, I see. I'd thought by now that the horned ones might have eaten you.'

'Our hides might be a bit tough on their teeth, I fancy,' said Hero. 'Anyway, they weren't after eating us but sending us instead down that volcano's throat, fuel for Cthulhu's engines of horror. And it seems we've you to thank for telling The Searcher where to find us.'

'Oh?' she arched her eyebrows. 'Well, save your thanks, Hero of Dreams. Let's not get too friendly. De Marigny didn't leave me much choice, after all; and anyway, it wasn't your interests I was looking after.'

'Zura,' said Eldin, 'you like to play at being hard, but let's face it: you've had a soft spot for Hero here from the moment you first met him. Now deny that, if you can!'

Zura smiled sweetly, or it might seem so if they didn't know her better. But there were crimson points in her black eyes, doubtless in her black heart, too. 'I've soft spots for him, for you, for all of you live ones,' she said, her words honeyed. But then they came sharper: 'Or more correctly, soft plots! Row upon row of 'em: six foot of damp earth in my Charnel Gardens!'

Death leered out of Zura's soul at them, and as one person Moreen, The Searcher, Hero and Eldin, the entire temporary crew of *Shroud II*, stepped back a pace from her. 'What?' she laughed. 'And what good were you to me, if Gudge sent you down to the machineries of madness? And how might I use you, if the horned ones had chewed on all your tenderest bits? But this way – being foolhardy questers and all – one day you'll come to me on my terms. And with a bit of luck none too badly banged about. Aye, and then we'll talk some more of "soft spots," Eldin the Wanderer . . .'

They sailed Zura's coffin-ship back to a mooring over the Charnel Gardens – one with sufficient elevation as to make

156

the stench endurable – and there left that peculiar squid-prowed vessel in charge of Kuranes' men for the nonce. But now, before returning to Serannian, there was another matter to consider: Thalarion the land bordered close to Zura the land, so close indeed that the time-clock would make very short work of the distance between. And there, somewhere in Thalarion's hinterland, Atal's 'strange thoughts' – possibly having their origin in Elysia – had fallen to earth, had even been answered!

'What do you know of the land behind Thalarion?' de Marigny asked the questers when they were once more airborne in the clock and making their leisurely way eastward.

'There's a swamp there where a whirlpool empties itself from a mighty lake in the Great Bleak Mountains,' said Eldin. 'All marsh and rot and toadstools, and creeping leafy things more animal than plant. Terrible place!' He gave a small shudder. 'Me and Hero, we were there once. But thanks, no, we'd prefer not to go back.'

Moreen turned to Hero. 'But is there nothing pleasant or welcoming or friendly in Thalarion's hinterland? You see' (she began to explain something of their quest), 'we're looking for someone or thing – for an intelligent being, anyway – who receives thoughts from the waking world, maybe even from Elysia. Some unknown one who talks with his mind to someone else far, far away in another world.'

'Talks with his mind, you say?' Hero raised a speculative eyebrow, glanced at Eldin.

'Er, and would this telepathic someone be sort of big and green and lumberlike?' asked the Wanderer.

De Marigny shook his head. 'We've no idea,' he said. Then he frowned. 'Did you say "lumberlike"? And do you know someone who's that way – as you've described, I mean?'

'Fact is,' said Hero, 'we do! And that's not all, for – ' he

157

paused. De Marigny had shown the questers how to tune in to the clock's scanners, and now Hero said: 'But look! There's Lathi's *Chrysalis* dead ahead. Can we hover a bit while I ask a question or three? It all has bearing, I assure you.'

De Marigny hovered the time-clock over Lathi's paper vessel, while Hero called out: 'Lathi, it's Hero here.'

'*And* Eldin,' sang out the Wanderer, glowering at Hero. 'Nice job you did back there on that black Leng "pirate".'

Lathi under her canopy was utterly beautiful – the visible parts, at least. She turned her face indolently up toward the hovering time-clock, said: 'Hero, is that really you in there, who sang me to sleep with your beautiful songs in Thalarion the hive? And you, Eldin, who contrived to burn Thalarion to the ground while that sweet-tongued rogue sang? Then stay safe where you are and come not aboard *Chrysalis*. I have neither forgotten nor forgiven. If we were allies once . . . well, that is over now. And where you two are concerned, my termen have standing orders. Now you are intruders, trespassers over Thalarion the land. Be gone from here.'

'Not so fast, Lathi,' growled Eldin. 'And stop making us out as the villains of the piece. Believe me, we've no great wish to stay in Thalarion. But first tell us this: how fares the Tree?'

'The Tree? The Great Tree? Him? What would I know of him, great shambling forest that he is? My termen are forbidden to go near him! He has roots under Thalarion the new hive, in which he holds firestones, great flints he'd strike if I stole so much as a leaf from him! Aye,' she sighed, 'and his the sweetest, most succulent leaves in all the dreamlands.' Then her voice hardened: 'And who to blame but you, Wanderer, who taught him these . . . these *pyro-technics* in the first place?'

'*Hah!*' Eldin was delighted. 'Is that so? Well, good for

158

him!' he said. 'You threatened him with fire, now he threatens you!'

And Hero added: 'We're on our way to see him right now, Lathi, and doubtless he'll tell us whether you've been giving him a bad time or not. And if you have, be sure it's not just his firestones you'll need to worry about. And if you thought my cradle-songs were sweet, just wait till you hear my warsongs!'

That was that; the time-clock fared north-east; de Marigny turned over in his head all he'd heard. And in a little while he asked: 'Are you saying you're taking us to see a tree?'

'A Great Tree,' Eldin corrected him.

'And as I was about to tell you,' said Hero, 'he has kin in Elysia.'

De Marigny's heart gave a great leap. 'Titus Crow has told me about Elysia's Great Tree!' he exclaimed. 'In the Gardens of Nymarrah: a tree to make a redwood seem the merest sapling!'

'That's our boy,' Eldin nodded. 'Or his cousin, anyway. And by the time we're over that range of hills there, we should be able to see him . . .'

Eldin was right. Just across the hills north-east of Thalarion, a prairie rolled to the horizon. Broken only by receding lines of foothills that would rise ultimately to Leng, the plain was lush, golden and green; and standing there majestically, more than a third of a mile high, the biggest tree de Marigny and Moreen had ever seen.

Superficially, and apart from his massive height and girth, *the* Tree was pretty much like any other; but on closer inspection, magnified in the clock's scanners, de Marigny saw that there were several anomalies. The leaves of the giant, huge to match his other dimensions, were soft-edged and lined with a 'fur' of sensitive cilia. Tough, slender tendrils hung down to festoon the shaded area between the lower branches and the earth; tendrils full of a slow,

159

sentient motion, seeking out dry, dead leaves and carefully removing them, casting them aside. A haze of pollens (though no flowers were visible) hung suspended everywhere, dust-motes in the sunlight, giving the Tree a shimmer almost like that of a mirage. But he was no mirage. And then there was that wide ashen swath – the Tree's 'track', the way he had come, inch by gradual inch, since all those years ago when first he took root here – leading off to the north, where the earth was no longer green but dry and crumbly. For Great Trees need a lot of nourishment.

Not knowing how the Tree would react to the time-clock, de Marigny carefully set his strange craft down just outside the three-hundred-foot radius of his branches. There The Searcher, Moreen, and their passengers disembarked; but while the three men approached with some caution, Moreen at once ran through the calf-length grass and into the Tree's shade. In Numinos all creatures had loved Moreen; she had even charmed Ithaqua the Wind-Walker – to an extent. She was the veriest child of Nature and loved all Nature's creatures. But an intelligent, indeed telepathic, Tree? – she could scarcely control her excitement.

Small roots underfoot felt her weight, her motion; the under-leaves 'smelled' or 'tasted' her texture, translated these impressions, recognized her type; the Tree felt her excitement, her wonder, and knew she was a friend. Instantly long, supple tendrils uncoiled from on high, looped down, caught her up. She was lifted effortlessly, borne aloft like a tiny child in the arms of a giant. A soughing – no, a vast *sighing* – filled the Tree's branches.

'Moreen!' Alarmed, de Marigny started forward.

'Easy, Searcher!' cautioned Eldin. 'Moreen's safer with the Tree than she'd be with ... why, with Hero here!'

'Oaf!' said Hero. 'But he's probably right: the Tree's the very gentlest soul in all the dreamlands.'

Now the three were in the Tree's shade; cool tendrils

touched them, tasted, quivered; there was an almost magical dusk all around, where the Tree's pollens were honeysuckle sweet.

'Tree,' said Hero, 'it's Hero – '

' – *and* Eldin!' (from the Wanderer.)

' – and we've brought these friends to talk to you.'

'Hero?' answered a throbbing yet ethereal voice from nowhere – from everywhere – as tendrils fell faster and touched all three. 'Eldin! Both of you, yes, and one other; but not a permanent dreamer, this one. No, a *real* man – and a girl, too – from the waking world!'

Moreen was nowhere to be seen, but her glad cry fell from high, high overhead even as the Tree's strong lifting tendrils grasped the three men: 'Henri! Oh, let him bring you up! This place is wonderful! Come see!'

But they were already on their way, wound up like bobbins on threads and passed higher and higher into the Tree's heart. Breathlessly they were whirled aloft, then suspended motionless for a moment until they got their breath back, finally deposited light as feathers in the crotch of great branches a thousand feet above the ground. And: '*Shrub sapiens*,' gasped Eldin. 'Boisterous, isn't he? For such a big 'un!'

But the Tree only chuckled in their minds. 'Hero and Eldin,' he said again. 'My very dearest friends! And de Marigny and Moreen. Well, well! Visitors again, after all this time. Men to talk to – and a real girl!'

'You've heard of us then?' said de Marigny. 'Of she and I?'

Transmitted to de Marigny's mind by touch, coming to him through leaves and cilia and tendrils, there was mental affirmation as the Tree said: 'Oh, I've heard of you, Searcher. Indeed, I've been expecting you!'

De Marigny couldn't contain himself. 'So Atal's alien thoughts from outside did come from Elysia after all,' he burst out. 'And they concerned me?'

161

The Tree read his meaning clearly. 'You and your young woman, yes, and the time-clock, too,' he answered. But now de Marigny detected a certain reluctance – a note of sadness in the Tree's touch – and his heart sank.

'There's nothing you can tell us, is there?' he said. 'If you know I'm The Searcher, then you know what I seek. And your sadness can only mean that you either can't or won't help me.'

'I can't, and I can,' said the Tree. 'I *can't* tell you how to get to Elysia, no – but I *can* help. That is, I can narrow down your search a little.'

'Tree,' Moreen cut in, 'I don't quite understand. If someone – that other Great Tree, maybe? – spoke to you from Elysia, and if you in turn talked to him . . . I mean, he *must* have known where you were, and vice-versa.'

The Tree followed her meaning and his leaves trembled a little as he considered how best to explain. 'A thought is a thought, child,' he said. 'I read yours by touching you. If I couldn't touch you I couldn't talk to you. But I am more attuned to the thoughts of one of my own race. He found me, yes, though not without difficulty, and once the connection was made I could talk back. But as to his location and how one might go there . . .' (a mental shrug).

'Another dead end,' de Marigny's shoulders slumped. But then he lifted his head and gritted his teeth, still unwilling to accept defeat or even consider it. 'A dead end, yes – but there's something very wrong here. I mean, I know there's no royal road into Elysia – that one makes one's own way there or not at all – but is there any sense in their taunting me? The Elder Gods, I mean? I'm given clues that lead nowhere!' He turned a troubled face to Moreen. 'No man knows Titus Crow like I do, and yet even he . . .' He shook his head. 'Something's *wrong*! Titus and Armandra both, they say find Sssss and he may have something for you. We save Sssss from the Hounds of Tindalos, and he's been told to direct us to Earth's

162

dreamlands – *told* to do that by the weird pilot of some other time-clock from Elysia. In the dreamlands we go to see Atal, the very priest of the Temple of the Elder Gods – but even he has been shut out. "Ah! – but maybe Hero and Eldin can help us," he says. So we save the questers from Gudge – '

'Narrowly!' put in Eldin.

' – and in return they bring us to see the Tree. Now the Tree can actually *talk* to his cousin in Elysia, but he can't tell us the way there, and so – '

'Wait!' said the Tree. 'I *could* talk to him – when he sought me out, And perhaps I could have sought *him* out, given time. But not any more. I tried following his thoughts – their essence – back to their source. Not because I wanted to learn his or any other's secrets, simply because I was lonely. But out there in the voids, in the star spaces between the worlds, the thought-trail petered out. And he has not come again. No royal road, you say? No road at all, not now! I'm sorry . . .'

'What about Serannian?' said Moreen. She took de Marigny's hand. 'There's still Curator, in his Museum.'

'Curator?' said Hero, Eldin and the Tree all together, and with almost the same speculative edge to their voices.

'But that's it!' said the Tree, getting in first. 'That's the message Elysia's Tree gave me before he ... closed down. "Tell them to speak to Curator," he said, "in Serannian." '

'Speak to Curator?' Eldin grunted. '*Huh!*'

'What the Wanderer means is no one ever spoke to him,' Hero explained. 'He has a keen mind and he's a nice mover – and his line in weaponry is at least as good, maybe better, than yours, Henri – but where speaking's concerned he's a dummy. Why, I strongly suspect that most of the time he doesn't even know people are there at all!'

'Except when they maybe, er, annoy him,' Eldin added with some feeling, at the same time looking away.

'Moreen might be able to speak to him,' said de Marigny.

She looked doubtful. 'I can talk to all creatures of Nature,' she said. 'Of if they can't talk, at least I can understand them. But a metal man? I'm not sure.'

'Anyway,' de Marigny was determined, 'we have to try. Tree, I'm sorry but I can't stay – not even for a little while.'

'He's right,' said Hero. 'Kuranes will be anxious, waiting for our report – and there are all those lads to be picked up off Zura's coffin-ship, and –'

' – And my mission's more important than all of that,' de Marigny cut in. 'It's not just for myself and Moreen any more. It's for everything. I *have* to get to Elysia!'

'That's good enough for me,' said Hero.

'And me,' agreed Eldin. 'Let's go!'

'Your visit was welcome anyway,' said the Tree. 'I'll always remember you, Searcher, Moreen. And if you should ever be in Earth's dreamlands again ...'

'We'll always come to see you,' Moreen promised, ' – when and if we can.'

They didn't prolong it. Farewells were short. As quickly as he could which was very quickly indeed, de Marigny picked up Kuranes' men from the deck of *Shroud II* and left Zura to brood alone over her Charnel Gardens. Before noon they were all back in Serannian ...

Kuranes met them on Serannian's sky-floating rim, the wharves not far from where the Museum jutted on its vertiginous promontory. And no need to inquire after Kuranes' pleasure at the sight of his men, the questers alive and well, and Moreen and de Marigny as they trooped from the clock; his absolute joy and relief were visible in every word and gesture. As to his gratitude to de Marigny, that was beyond words; but desperately eager though The Searcher was, still the Lord of Ooth-Nargai calmed him and led him and his party to a wharfside tavern where a meal was quickly ordered and almost as quickly made ready. Famished, Hero and Eldin fell at once to their food and drink, but de Marigny was scarcely interested in eating. Instead, and assisted by Moreen, he took the opportunity to tell Kuranes all that he had not yet grasped of his mission, also all that had happened through the previous night and morning.

When he was done Kuranes nodded. 'Pirates they weren't,' he said, 'not in the true sense of the word. Their vile *acts* of piracy were a simple ploy to keep honest men and ships – maybe even explorers and settlers – away from Zura's hinterland; away from that old volcano, which will doubtless be used as a fortress by the Cthulhu spawn when finally they force themselves upon the dreamlands ... If it were allowed to go that far! But that must never be. So, when Admiral Limnar Dass gets back with my armada from the moon, then I'll – '

'Eh?' de Marigny looked puzzled. 'But you told us your ships were plentiful – and it was crewmen you were short of. You said you'd disbanded them all or something, that they'd be better employed repairing dreamland's moon-ravaged cities ...'

'Ah!' Kuranes looked confused, caught out. 'Well, yes, that's what I *said*,' he agreed, 'but not quite the whole truth. In fact, something of a large distortion. You see, if you'd been taken by Gudge and his lot, and if they'd questioned you – perhaps forcefully – about dreamland's defences ...'

'You didn't want us telling them that your ships were engaged in mopping-up operations on the moon, eh?'

'Something like that,' mumbled Kuranes. 'Not a mopping-up operation, exactly. Just a show of force, to let the moonbeasts know we can get at them any time we choose, if they ever decide to go against us in the future.'

'I see,' said de Marigny. 'And while the bulk of your fleet is there, doing whatever it's doing, at least one moonbeast, Gudge, has been here, preparing a stronghold for the Great Old Ones. Well, that's at an end now, anyway.'

'It will be,' Kuranes agreed, 'when Admiral Dass gets back and I have him bomb that shaft and block it forever! Until then ... well, what has all of this shown us, if not how badly you're needed in Elysia, eh?'

'How's that?' de Marigny raised his eyebrows.

'Cthulhu has always been a great influence in men's dreams,' Kuranes stated the obvious. 'Indeed, he's responsible for most of what's nightmarish in them! But not since the Bad Days has he made so bold, attempting to influence the dreamlands – and through them the thinking of men in the waking world – so greatly. In the affair of the Mad Moon, and now in this. The uprising, certainly an attempt at an uprising, must be very close now. He prepares the way for himself in space and time, and in all the parallel worlds. The Crawling Chaos is abroad, the stars are very nearly right, and strange times have come again ...'

'Kuranes,' said de Marigny, 'you can help me. No one knows Curator and his Museum better than you. I need to see him, somehow talk to him.'

Kuranes' turn to raise his eyebrows. 'The grey metal box?' he guessed. 'Did Atal tell you about that? A box with hands like those on your time-clock?'

'It is a time-clock of sorts,' de Marigny nodded. 'I'm sure of it. For some strange reason of their own, the Elder Gods have chosen to lead me a mazy chase into Elysia. Maybe I have to work for what I want – work hard for it – and even though I'm needed there, still they're making me earn my right of passage. Maybe it's that ... and maybe it's something else. I don't know. But I've been told to speak to Curator.'

'Nice trick if you can turn it,' said Kuranes – and he saw de Marigny's face fall. 'It would be no good my holding out false hopes,' he said. 'It's just that I don't know anyone who ever spoke to Curator – and got an answer! What's more, since the advent of the cube, now locked in his chest, he hasn't even been seen. Who can say where he is? He may or may not be somewhere in the Museum. But where? I don't know where he goes. Nor why. Nor how. Sometimes he's not seen for months at a time.'

'Will you come to the Museum with us anyway?' Moreen begged.

'Of course I will, child,' said Kuranes at once. 'But it seems only fair to warn you: if Curator is not there – if we can't find him – then there's no help for it.'

When Kuranes, The Searcher and Moreen left the tavern, Hero and Eldin were hard at it, while the astonished proprietor brought them plate after plate and flagon after flagon . . .

6

Curator and the Dream-clock

At the sea-wall, where the time-clock stood under guard of half-a-dozen pikemen, Kuranes pointed across the harbour to where a great stone circular structure stood on a promontory at the eastern extreme of the sky-island. Beneath the three-tier building the rock of Serannian was a comparatively thin crust less than fifty feet in depth, and beneath that – nothing. 'The Museum,' he informed. 'Only one way in and out: along that narrow causeway over the neck of the promontory – unless you're a bird, that is! Thieves think twice and then some more, before tackling the Museum. And then, when they've seen Curator, they don't even think about it any more. Most thieves, anyway ...' And he glanced back the way they'd come and smiled a little. 'Hero and Eldin tried it on once – twice in fact – since when they've given Curator and his Museum a wide berth.'

He led the way round the harbour to the causeway, paused before venturing out over that narrow span. 'No place for vertigo sufferers, this,' he commented. 'You've heads for heights, have you?' And as Moreen and de Marigny nodded in unison he led on.

The causeway was low-walled, perhaps thirty yards long, cobbled. Since there was room for only two abreast, the trio had to cross single-file in order to leave the way free for sightseers leaving the Museum. Looking down over the wall as they went, de Marigny and Moreen were able to gaze almost straight down into uncounted fathoms of air – the 'deeps' of the Cerenerian – at all the towns and rivers, shores and oceans of dream, which sprawled in fantastic vistas to all horizons. Far off they could even see Celephais, clearly landmarked where Mount Aran's permanently snow-capped peak stood proud of the gentling Tanarians.

They entered the Museum through a tall stone archway to find themselves in a three-storeyed building whose sealed windows were of unbreakable crystal. Ventilation was through the archway, which had no door, and also through a square aperture in the ocean-facing curve of the wall which was big as a large window but placed much higher. The first and second floors of the Museum contained only those items with which ordinary museums commonly concern themselves; as David Hero had once commented: 'mummies and bones and books', and suchlike. The ground floor, however, was where the Museum's true valuables were housed – of which the quantity and quality were utterly beyond belief.

For here were all sorts of treasures: jewels and precious stones, golden figurines, ivory statuettes, jade miniatures, priceless antiques and bric-a-brac from lands and times forgotten in the mists of ancient dreams, objets d'art which could only have been conceived in the fertile dreams of very special artists and sculptors. In its entirety, the place would be ransom for fifty worlds!

'Curator's collection,' said Kuranes, drawing back de Marigny and Moreen's minds from rapt contemplation, 'of which he's extremely jealous. Oh, yes, for each item has its place – and pity the man who'd try to change it! Myself, I find the upper floors even more awesome.'

The Searcher knew what he meant. He'd seen shrunken heads from immemorial Kled up there; and shrivelled mummies from a caverned mountain in primal Sarkomand; and stone-flowers from some eastern desert at the very edge of dreams, which must be kept bone dry, for a single drop of water would rot them in an instant; and books whose pages glowed with runes written (so Kuranes had it) by mages in antique Theem'hdra at the very dawn of time. And so:

'It is a very wonderful place,' de Marigny agreed, his hushed voice echoing in the now almost entirely vacated Museum, 'and we've seen wonders galore here.'

And reading his mind, Moreen added: 'But nowhere Curator.'

Kuranes sighed. 'I told you, warned you. No man can ever guarantee or govern Curator's comings and goings.'

They left the Museum empty of human life, walked back across the causeway. There, along the curve of the sea wall close to the time-clock, a pair of sated questers leaned, propped up by the wall, gazed out over folded arms at the merchantmen and other vessels riding at anchor on a bank of rose-tinted cloud. Hero looked up as Kuranes and his visitors from the waking world approached. 'No luck?' He read the answer in their faces.

Now Eldin straightened up, patted his belly, uttered a gentle, happy belch. And: 'Ah, well,' the older quester rumbled. 'I'd hoped it wouldn't come to this, but plainly there's little else for it.' Swaying like a sailor – or perhaps swaggering like a pirate – he passed the three by and headed for the Museum. Curious, they turned to watch him as his pace picked up and he determinedly strode toward the causeway over the promontory. And now Hero ambled up and joined them.

'See,' the younger quester explained, 'Curator has a thing about us – especially about Eldin. Damn me, but that old metal man doesn't trust the Wanderer a bit! It has to do with a couple of big rubies we once almost, er, borrowed from the Museum – almost. Curator took umbrage, of course, and stopped us, since when we've steered clear. But now it seems we can use this, er, *aversion* of his to your advantage. Except Curator-taunting's a dodgy business at best – which is why we tossed for it.' He handed de Marigny an antique, much-rubbed triangular golden tond, upon which – on both face and obverse – the same bearded, long-forgotten face remained faintly impressed.

170

De Marigny stared at the coin in his hand, stared harder, and:

'A double-header!' The Searcher exclaimed. 'You tricked him into it!'

Hero looked at de Marigny and narrowed his eyes a little – but only for a moment. Then he smiled and said: 'When you know Eldin and me better, you'll know there's no such thing as cheating or trickery between us. A bit of one-upmanship, maybe, that's all. The gamble was Eldin's suggestion, not mine. The coin's his, too. Oh, and incidentally – he's the one who won!'

De Marigny's embarrassment knew no bounds, but before he could say anything to perhaps make it worse –

'Ahoy there in the Museum!' called Eldin, his great hands cupped to his mouth. Passers-by paused in small groups to stare at him, and seagulls on the wall flapped aloft noisily, shocked by his shouting. 'Ahoy old klanker! Come out, come out wherever you are! An old friend's here to see you, and perhaps sample some of your valuables. And if he *doesn't* see you, he'll *certainly* sample them!'

Hero grinned as he and the other three moved closer to where Eldin stood at the mainland end of the causeway. 'He's just getting warmed up,' he stated. 'He can taunt a lot better than that, believe me.'

'Well then, you metal mute, what's it to be?' roared Eldin. He swaggered forward a few paces onto the walled bridge, cautiously began to cross. But for all his bellowing, his eyes were fixed firmly on the Museum's archway entrance at the other end of the causeway. 'Ho, tin-ribs!' he shouted. 'The Wanderer's back and lusting for loot! So where's the rusty pile of rubble who runs this ruin, eh? Come out, you cowardly can of nuts and bolts!'

Eldin was a third of the way across now and beginning to think that perhaps Curator really was absent. Hand in hand with that thought had come another: if Curator *really* wasn't here, what was there to stop him from implementing his threat? Say one small pigeon's egg-sized ruby? Why, he could be in and out of the Museum's ground floor quick as thought, and not even Hero would guess what he'd done – not until they were well away from here, anyway. Eldin's eyes gleamed. On wealth like that, why, they could live like lords for years!

Now Eldin could have stamped up and down the causeway and bellowed for a month to no avail. Likewise his taunting: it would not have turned the trick. Curator was not attuned to stamping, bellowing or taunting. But he *was* attuned – sensitive to an infinite degree – to all thoughts of thievery, malicious damage, or other fell intent where the Museum was concerned. Such thoughts or intentions would have to be investigated and dealt with no matter what the source, but when that source happened also to be Eldin the Wanderer ...

'Oh-oh!' gasped Hero. 'Do you see what I see?'

Kuranes, de Marigny and Moreen, they all saw. But not Eldin, for he was facing in the wrong direction. In the middle of the causeway he now crept like a cat (remarkable, for one his size and shape), and his bluster had fallen to little more than a whisper: 'Curator? Oh, Curator! Eldin's here to purloin a pearl, or burgle a bauble, or filch a figurine. Or maybe simply rip off a ruby, eh?'

'Eldin!' Hero called out, trying to stay calm. 'I think – '

'*Quiet!*' the Wanderer hissed without turning round. '*Shh!* – I'm concentrating.' Two-thirds of the way across, he could almost taste success.

But at the landward end of the causeway, behind and below him, Curator 'tasted' something else entirely: he tasted the essence of a thief, the scent of a scoundrel, the suspicious spoor of Eldin the Wanderer. And that was a scent he knew all too well.

Dry-mouthed, Kuranes, The Searcher and Moreen could only look on as Curator emerged more fully from *under* the causeway; but Hero was already running forward. 'Eldin, you idiot! You've succeeded, man – only too well! Look behind you!'

Curator was a vaguely manlike thing; tall and spiky yet somehow lumpy looking, with many spindly arms, a metallic sheen, and faceted, glittering crystal eyes that missed nothing. He came up from beneath the causeway like some strange steel spider, making scarcely a sound as he swung his thin legs up over the wall and drew himself erect on the cobbles of the narrow bridge. At which point, hair bristling on the back of his neck, Eldin slowly turned and saw him.

'B'god!' said Eldin, trying to smile and gulp at the same time. 'If it isn't my old pal the estimable Curator!'

Curator's eyes, a glittering icy blue one moment, turned scarlet in the next. At the same time Hero hurled himself at the metal man's back and grabbed hold of the blunt projection which was his head. Which action doubtless saved the Wanderer's life. For as Hero yanked at Curator's head, twin beams of red death lanced out of his eyes, missed Eldin by a fraction and blackened a patch of stonework on the archway behind him. 'He was only joking, you metal monster!' Hero roared, still trying to pull Curator's head off.

'Curator!' Kuranes was shouting. 'Curator, you're making a dreadful mistake.' But Eldin, who knew he wasn't, had already darted inside the Museum and disappeared from view. Now Curator turned his attention on Hero, for after the Museum and its contents, his next priority was himself.

De Marigny yelled, 'Moreen, the clock!' and raced for his time machine. If he could put the time-clock between Curator and the questers, then they would stand something of a chance. The girl, on the other hand – who had no fear of creatures no matter how weird or monstrous – ran the other way, onto the causeway where even now Curator was

173

hauling Hero off his back and holding him at arm's length. There was a split-second of near-instantaneous and yet minute scrutiny, and then Curator pivoted and swung Hero out over the wall. Hero's legs hit the wall and hooked there – clung for dear life – as Curator released him!

Moreen was almost upon the metal man but Curator hadn't seen her yet. Instead his head bent forward and his crystal eyes lit on Hero's legs, bent at the knees over the top of the wall. A metal hand reached out, grasped one ankle, straightened the leg. Another arm stretched its hand toward the other ankle, and –

Moreen was there. Without pause she got between Curator and Hero, reached over the wall and grabbed at one of the quester's flailing arms. And half-turning to Curator she cried: 'How dare you? How *dare* you?! Who are you to murder men for the sake of your stupid Museum? Now you fetch Hero up at once!'

Kuranes arrived puffing and panting. He leaned over the wall and caught at Hero's other hand, began hauling him up. Together, he and Moreen finally dragged the whey-faced quester back to safety – of a sort. But still Curator had not quite released him. Nor had he forgotten Eldin.

Seeing Hero in deadly danger, the Wanderer had come charging from the Museum, fists up, adopting a classic boxing stance. Curator saw him, relinquished his hold on Hero (however reluctantly), stepped clankingly, threateningly, toward Eldin. At which point de Marigny set the time-clock down on the causeway between the two.

Curator saw the time-clock; his scarlet eyes slowly cooled to a still-dangerous orange, burned a fierce yellow for a moment, finally turned blue. They glittered like chips of ice as he took one clanking pace, then another, toward the clock. And inside the time-clock, suddenly de Marigny knew what he must do. Hadn't Atal told him that Curator 'talked' to the grey metal cube by imitating the movements of its four hands – a robotic semaphore? Well, now he must use the time-clock to 'talk' to Curator in the same manner. But how? The time-clock hid many secrets in its intricate being, and this was one of them. Titus Crow had often hinted that the device was half-animate, semi-sentient; but that it should also have this power of mechanical speech . . . And yet why not? Didn't computers 'talk' to each other in the waking world? And why shouldn't time-clocks? Even Crow had never known the real significance of those four, often wildly vacillating hands: the time-clock, calculating, thinking, 'talking' to itself?

De Marigny knew how to use the clock's scanners, its sensors, its voice-amplification and weapon systems. He could drive it through time and space and places between the two. The 'buttons' and 'switches' and 'triggers' were all in his mind. In the clock's mind. In *their* minds, his and the clock's, when their minds were one. He closed his eyes now and felt for those familiar instruments, controls, and found them. And: *I have to talk to Curator*, he told the clock. *Through you. Please, help me talk to Curator.*

In the waking world it might not have worked, but in dreams things are often simpler. This time it was simple: de Marigny felt a door open in his mind, or rather a door *between* his mind and the clock's, and knew he'd found the space-time machine's 'communicator'. And now he could talk to Curator.

Outside on the causeway, Curator came closer still; his crystal eyes seemed full of strange inquiry; he 'stared' expectantly at the hands on the time-clock's dial. And de Marigny didn't keep him waiting.

The change come over the metal man was at once apparent to Kuranes, Moreen and Hero; the change, too, in the time-clock. Its hands, never less than erratic in their movements, now seemed to lose every last vestige of normalcy; they moved insanely, coordination all awry. Or all *together*, coordinated as never before. Not in de Marigny's experience, anyway. And:

'Look!' whispered Kuranes. 'Curator makes hands like those of the time-clock. See, they converse!'

Four of Curator's spindle arms had swivelled round to the front of his canister body. Now they clicked into a central position, retracted or extended themselves into appropriate lengths, commenced to whirl and twitch and jerk in keeping, in rhythm – and yes, in conversation with de Marigny.

'I am The Searcher,' said de Marigny. 'I think you've heard of me.'

'Indeed. I've heard of many things. Of you and Moreen, of the time-clock through which you talk to me, and of Elysia which you would discover. I have heard of a primal land at the dawn of time, and a white wizard named Exior K'mool. I have heard of Lith where the lava lakes boil, while Ardatha Ell sits in his floating manse and measures the pulse of a dying sun which would yet be born again. And I have heard, from many quarters, of a rising up of evil powers, one which threatens the fabric of the multi-verse itself.'

'Then you can surely help me,' said de Marigny. 'Can we talk somewhere, in privacy, in ... comfort?'

'I am comfortable anywhere,' Curator answered, 'but I am most at ease beneath Serannian, clinging to the sky-suspended stone, with all the dreamlands spread below. I perceive, however, that this would never do for you; are you not comfortable in the time-clock?'

'Yes, but – '

' – But you are a human being, and need familiar surroundings, accustomed atmospheres, personal privacies. Well, I understand that. I, too, am a private being. Shall we enter the Museum? But first, there are certain annoyances I must deal with – two of them. One of which hides behind your time-clock even now ...'

De Marigny was quick off the mark with: 'Curator, you must not harm the questers!'

' "Must not?" ' Curator seemed surprised. ' "Harm?" I know the meaning of such words, but fail to see their application here. You have not understood: I merely protect the Museum, in which are stored fragments of the strangest, greatest, most fabulous dreams that men ever dreamed! For here are dreams untold, forgotten by their dreamers when they awoke; and here are nightmares, safely stored, whose release would drive men mad. There are dreams of empire here, and dreams quite beyond avarice – except – '

'Yes?'

'While *I* know the meaning of that last, and while I am sure that *you* know it, still there are two here who do not. Nor could they ever perceive the consequences of inter-fering with this Museum which I protect, and *from* which I must protect the lands of Earth dreams. But you say I must not harm them? Nor would I – but *they* do not know that! So step aside and let me deal with them my way. First him who cowers behind you.'

On Curator's word that he would do the questers no harm, de Marigny lifted the time-clock skyward and re-vealed Eldin who again raised his great hands. 'Come on then, Curator! Just you and me – man to man,' he cried, ' – or whatever!'

Curator's eyes glowed scarlet. Twin beams reached out faster than thought, ignored Eldin's fists, cut through his clothes here and there without so much as scorching a single hair beneath them. And without pause the beam relocated, slicing at this and that, reducing the Wanderer's clothing to ribbons. As fast as Eldin could move his hands, clutching at his rags, so the beams sought other targets. His pockets were sliced, releasing a fistful of large, glittering jewels to fall to the causeway's cobbles – following which Curator went to work with a vengeance!

In mere moments Eldin was almost naked, holding scraps of rag to himself to cover more than his embarrassment.

177

And when all of the Wanderer's bluster had been quite literally cut out of – or off of – him, then Curator turned his attention to Hero.

Kuranes and Moreen at once stepped aside; Eldin had not been hurt – except for his pride, possibly – and therefore Hero should also be safe. As for Hero's feelings:

When first the metal man had 'attacked' Eldin he'd been thoroughly alarmed; but the Wanderer's punishment had seemed only just, so that soon Hero had started to grin, then laugh. But now:

Now Curator's eyes were silver, them and the beams that issued from them. Hero felt those beams tugging at him, held up his hands as if to ward Curator off. 'Now hang fire, tin-shins!' he cried. 'I mean, what did I do?'

But the silver beams had fastened on Hero now, floating him off the cobbles and suspending him in mid-air. Curator inclined his gaze upward, lifting Hero swiftly into the sky over Serannian. The metal man's head tilted back farther yet, until he looked straight up – at which point the beams swiftly extended themselves and rocketed Hero into the clouds overhead and out of sight. Then the beams cut out, were instantly withdrawn. All human viewers of that act held their breath – until Hero came tearing through the clouds, plummeting back into view. And then the beams reached out again, unerringly, to catch and lower him to the wharfside. Breathless and dizzy, Hero staggered and fell on his backside as Curator released him.

And without pause the Museum's keeper again turned, lifted Eldin from the causeway in a like manner, dumped him beside his friend. Now golden beams lanced forth from eyes suddenly yellow. It was that bright yellow with which wasps are banded, and the beams likewise appeared to have the sting of those unpleasant insects. Yelping, leaping, howling whenever the stinging beams struck them – with Eldin doubly tormented where he clutched his rags to cover himself – the two tumbled in the direction of Serannian's mazy alleys where they quickly disappeared from view.

'Harm them?' said Curator again, clanking to where his almost-stolen jewels lay on the cobbles and collecting them up. 'A very little, maybe. If only I could be sure I had deterred them, that would suffice. But where that pair are concerned . . .' And very humanly, he let the sentence hang. And having retrieved all of the gems, he went on into the Museum.

De Marigny followed in the time-clock, and behind him Moreen. As for Kuranes: he went off after the questers. He owed them a small sky-boat – to say nothing of a telling-off – and since they'd soon be a laughing-stock in Serannian (and therefore ripe for many a brawl), it might be best to 'banish' them from the sky-island, for a little while anyway.

In the Museum, Moreen entered the time-clock and de Marigny showed her his discovery: the clock's 'communicator'. Now Curator's 'conversation' reached her also.

'You seek Elysia,' the metal man said. 'Well, it is my understanding that I was made there. I was given form in Elysia, and life here. But I can't tell you how to get there. I know nothing of Elysia, except that the way is long and hard. However, your coming here was anticipated. Before you someone – something – also came into Earth's dreamland to see Curator.'

'The grey metal cube,' said de Marigny. 'Some kind of time-clock. It brought you instructions for me, from Elysia.'

'Say on,' said Curator, impressed. 'Perhaps the dream-clock is not required. Perhaps you already possess the necessary information.'

'Dream-clock?'

'Of course. The grey metal cube is a dream-clock – a monitor working in the subconscious levels of intelligence. No previous need for such a device in Earth's dreams, for I was here. But on this occasion the cube came as a messenger.'

De Marigny frowned, said: 'Titus Crow told me to look in my own dreams, and to carry my search into the past – rather, my past. He mentioned a wizard, just as you have mentioned a wizard: Exior K'mool. The sentient gas Sssss told me much the same things. Well, I've tracked down all possible leads here in the dreamlands, so now it seems the final answer must lie in the remote past. With Exior K'mool in Theem'hdra.'

'Good!' said Curator.

'But the past is more than four billion years vast!' said de Marigny. 'Where in the past – *when* – am I to seek for Theem'hdra? And where *in* Theem'hdra will I find Exior K'mool?'

'Ah!' said Curator. 'But these are questions you must ask of the dream-clock. For he alone has the answers, which were given to him in Elysia.'

Curator's chest opened; panels of shining metal slid back, telescoped, revealed a space. And snug in that cavity, there the grey metal cube rested – but for only a moment longer. Then –

The dream-clock slid from Curator's keeping, hovered free, spun like some strange metal dervish for a few seconds until it located and recognized the time-clock, then commenced to 'talk' in its own voice, the exotic articulations of its four hands. De Marigny 'heard' the opening details of the dream-clock's message, ensured that the clock was recording the spatial-temporal co-ordinates which constituted that singular monologue, then returned his attention to Curator:

'The dream-clock's information means nothing to me personally,' he said. 'I would need the mind of a computer. But the time-clock understands and records all. It is the location of Exior K'mool in primal Theem'hdra, yes. That's my next port of call, and I have you to thank for it, Curator.'

'You owe me nothing,' said Curator. 'But you owe your race, the race of Man, everything. You deserted that race

180

once for a dream, and now you return *to* a dream. And in you, germinating, lie the seeds of that race's continuation. The stars are very nearly right, Searcher, and you still have far to go. You seek a source and the clock now has the route, knows the destination. Waste no more time, but use it!'

The dream-clock's hands had steadied to a less erratic rhythm; it whirled for a brief moment, stopped abruptly and slid home into Curator's chest. The panels closed it in.

'Then it's time to say farewell,' said de Marigny.

'Indeed,' said Curator. 'As for the dream-clock: for the moment he stays here with me, perhaps forever, or for as long as we have. Only if you are successful will he ever return to Elysia. Until then, all Elysia's expatriate children must remain in exile.'

'Why do you say that?' de Marigny asked. 'What do you mean?'

'I have already overstepped myself,' said Curator. He began to turn away. 'Farewell, and good fortune ...' He clanked away into dream's oldest, rarest memories.

De Marigny and Moreen watched him go. Then The Searcher said to the time-clock: 'Very well, you have the co-ordinates. Now take us to Exior K'mool. Take us to Theem'hdra, the primal land at the dawn of time.'

Which without more ado the clock set out to do ...

PART THREE

The End of the Beginning of the End

1

Exior K'mool

Theem'hdra . . .

There had been other 'primal' lands: Hyborea and Hyperborea, Mu, Uthmal, Atlantis and many others; but in Theem'hdra lay the first, the original Age of Man. It *was* Pangaea, but not the Pangaea of modern geographers and geologists and theorists. How long ago exactly is of little concern here; suffice it to say that if the 'popular' Pangaea was last week, then Theem'hdra was probably months ago. Certainly it was an Age of Man which predated the Age of Reptiles, and was dust when they were in their ascendancy. But civilizations wax and wane, they always have and always will, and some are lost forever.

Theem'hdra, whereon a primal Nature experimented and created and did myriad strange and nightmarish things. For Nature herself was in her youth, and where men were concerned . . . she had not yet decided which talents men should have and which should be forbidden, discontinued.

In some men, and in certain women, too, the wild workings of capricious Nature wrought weird wonders, giving them senses and powers additional to the usual five. Often these powers were carried down through many generations; aye, and occasionally such a man would mate with just such a woman and then, eventually, through genealogical patterns and permutations long forgotten to 20th Century scientists, along would come the seventh son of a seventh son, or the ninth daughter of a ninth daughter – and what then?

Mylakhrion the Immortal, who had been less than immortal after all, was the greatest of all Theem'hdra's wizards; and after him, arguably, his far removed descendant, Teh Atht of Klühn. Next would probably be Mylakhrion's one-time apprentice and heir to many of his thaumaturgies, Exior K'mool. And Exior would not be the first magician whose experiments had led him into dire straits ...

Mylakhrion had been dead for one hundred and twenty years, victim of his own magic. Long before that, Exior's first master, Phaithor Ull, had rendered himself as green dust in an ill-conceived conjuration. And where Um-hammer Kark's vast manse had once sprawled its terraces, walls and pavilions on Mount Gatch by the River Luhr, overlooking the Steppes of Hrossa, a great bottomless pit now opened, issuing hissing clouds of mordant yellow steam. Wizards all, and all gone the way of wizards. Who lives by the wand ...

And now:

'My turn,' gloomed Exior K'mool to himself, where he prowled and fretted in his walled palace in the heart of ruined Humquass, once-proud warrior city. Lamias flaunted their buttocks at him as he passed, and succubi rubbed him with their breasts, eager to balm him; but Exior said only. 'Bah!' and brushed them aside, or sent them on meaningless errands to keep them from annoying and pestering him. Did not the idiot creatures know that his doom would be theirs also? And could they not see how close that doom was now?

Exior's hair was short-cropped and grey – as grey as it had turned on the day he first looked in Mylakhrion's great runebook, one hundred and seventy-three years earlier – and his mien, as might well be imagined, was that of an old man heavy-burdened with wisdom and knowledge and some sin; for it's a hard business being a wizard and remaining free of sin. And yet his long slender back was only slightly bent and his limbs still surprisingly spry. Aye, and his yellow eyes undimmed by his nearly two centuries of rune-unriddling, and his mind a crystal, where every thought came sharp as a needle. And for this not entirely misleading simulacrum of vitality he could thank long-gone Mylakhrion, whose fountain of youth and elixir of longevity and wrinkle-reducing unguents had kept the years in large part at bay. Alas that he must also 'thank' that elder mage for his current fix, which in all likelihood were his last.

Exior's palace had a high-walled courtyard before and high-walled gardens behind; in Humquass' heyday, the palace had been the city's tallest edifice, its towers even higher than the king's own palace. Now it was not only the tallest but the *only* building, chiefly because Humquass was no more. But the palace, like Exior himself, had survived wars and famines and all the onslaughts and ravages of nature; aye, and it would survive for many a century yet – or should.

It should, for from its foundations up the place was saturated with magical protections: spells against decay and natural disaster, against insect, fungus and human invasion, against the spells of other sorcerers, but mainly against the incursion of that which even now frothed and seethed on the other side of the walls, seeking a way in. A legacy of Exior's search for immortality. Like Mylakhrion before him, he had sought everlasting life until finally he'd attracted imminent death.

'Exior, Exior!' croaked a black, fanged, half-man, half-insect thing where it scuttled about his feet as he walked in the gardens. 'A doom is upon you, Exior! A great doom is come upon Exior the Mage!'

'Hush!' he scowled, kicking half-heartedly at the creature and missing. He stooped and found a pebble, hurled it at the scurrying, hybrid monstrosity. 'Away with you! And what are you for a familiar anyway? Be sure that if that slime out there gets me, then that it will surely get you also! Bah! I'd find a better familiar among the cockroaches in my kitchen!'

'But you *did* find me there,' croaked that unforgiving creature, ' – half of me, anyway – and welded me to Loxzor of the Hrossaks. I, the Loxzor part, was also a magician, Exior – or had you forgotten?'.

In fact Exior had forgotten; but now he shook a fist at the thing, yelled: 'How could I forget, with your infernal crowing to remind me day and night? 'Twas your own fault, Hrossak – sending your morbid magics against me. Be thankful I didn't give you the habits and lower half of a dung-beetle – and then make you keeper of the palace privy! Indeed, I still might!'

As the Loxzor-thing hastily withdrew, Exior climbed a ladder beside the wall and carefully looked over.

In his life Exior had seen, had even created, shuddersome things; but nothing he had seen or made or imagined was more noxious, poisonous, mordant or morbid than the frothing slime that lapped all about his palace walls and closed them in. At present the walls and his spells combined to hold the stuff at bay, but for how much longer? In extent the slime covered and roiled over all of olden Humquass' ruins, and lay deep as a thick mist all about. But never before a mist like this.

It was mainly yellow, but where it swirled it was bile-green, or in other places red like bad blood in pus. It was a gas or at worst a liquid, but now and then it would thicken up and throw out tendrils or tentacles like a living thing. And indeed Exior knew that it *was* a living thing – and the worst possible sort.

Even now, as he stared at the heaving, sickly mass, so it sensed him and threw up groping green arms. But Exior had spelled a dome of power over the palace, enclosing the entire structure, grounds and all. Now tentacles of slime slapped against that invisible wall mere inches from his face, so that he drew himself back and quickly descended the ladder into the gardens. But not before he'd seen the crumbling and steaming of the walls where the stuff's acid nature was eating into them.

'Shewstone!' muttered Exior then, under his breath. And, stumbling toward the main building: 'Last chance . . . shewstone . . . no spells can help me now . . . but if I can find just *one* possible future for myself . . . and then somehow contrive to *go* there . . . *Hah!* . . . Hopeless . . . Not even Mylakhrion could control time!'

Outside, were it not for the slime, the season would be autumn. In Exior's courtyard, however, it was spring; he controlled the seasons within his own boundaries; but even so, still black clouds were building, and he felt in his bones the nip of winter. The winter of his years, perhaps? His days? His . . . hours? Was that all he had left, who so recently sought immortality, hours?

Grinding his teeth with anxiety, Exior entered his basalt palace, followed the corkscrew stairs of a tower where they wound inexorably upward, finally came to that place which had been his room of repose and was, more recently, his workshop. Here he had worked unceasingly to discover a way to nullify the ever-encroaching slime sea, to no avail. For here, scattered about, were the many appurtenances of his art, all sorts and species of occult apparatus.

Here were the misshapen skulls of an ancient order of sub-man, and the teratologically fabulous remains of things which had never been men; bottles of multi-hued liquids, some bubbling and others quiescent; flutes made of the hollow bones of *pteranodon primus*, capable of notes which would transmute silver into gold and vice-versa; shelf upon shelf of books in black leather and umber skins, at least one of which was tattooed!

Here too were miniature worlds and moons in their orbits, all hanging from the tracked ceiling on mobile ropes of jewelled cowries; and here pentacles of power adorned the mosaic walls and floor, glittering with the fire of gem-chips, from which they were constructed. Sigil-inscribed scrolls of vellum were littered everywhere; but alone in the comparatively tidy centre of the room, there was Exior's showpiece: a great ball of clouded crystal upon its stand of carved chrysolite.

Kicking aside the disordered clutter and muttering, 'Useless, all useless!' he approached the shewstone, seated himself upon a simple cane chair, made passes to command a preview of possible futures. This was not the first time he had scried upon the future (hardly that, for his greatest art lay in oneiromancy: reading the future in dreams, in which he'd excelled even as an apprentice) but it was certainly the first time he'd achieved such dreary results.

He was shown a future where the slime lapped over the palace, devouring it, and himself with it. He saw a time when Humquass was a scar on the land, like a great sore in earth's healthy flesh. He scried upon a stone raised by some thoughtful soul in a shrine built centrally in the blight, which read:

> 'Here lies Exior K'mool, or
> would if alien energies had
> not eaten him entirely away.
> Here his shade abides, anyhow.'

But nowhere, for all his desperate passes, could he find a possible future where Exior K'mool lived. A fact he could scarce credit, for his dreams had foretold otherwise: namely that there *was* a future for him. Indeed he had *seen* himself, in recurrent dreams, dwelling in a manse whose base was a bowl that floated on a lake of lava. And he had known the world or lake where the manse drifted on liquid fire as 'Lith', and he had lived there a while with the white wizard Ardatha Ell, of whom he'd heard nothing except in his dreams. But where was this future, and where Lith? The shewstone displayed nought but dooms! All very disheartening.

Exior sighed and let the crystal grow opaque, turned to

190

his runebook and thumbed disconsolately through its pages. Runes and spells and cantrips galore here, but none to help him escape the slime, not permanently, not in this world or time. The stuff's nature was such as could not *be* avoided, it would pursue him to the end. His end.

And full of despair, at last his eyes lighted upon a spell only three-quarters conceived, borrowed from a fragment Mylakhrion had left behind when long ago he took himself off to his last refuge, the lonely isle of Tharamoon in the north.

At first, staring at the uncompleted page, Exior saw little; but then his eyes widened, his mind began to spark; and finally he read avidly, devouring the rune almost in a glance. A spell to call up the dead, but without necromancy proper. If he could complete the rune, perhaps he could call up some wizard ancestor to his aid. There must surely have been magic in his ancestry, else he himself were not gifted. And what if he erred in completing the thing, and what if it came to nought? Well, and what had he to lose anyway? But if he were to succeed – if indeed he could find and call up some mage ancestor centuries dead – well, even at worst two heads are better than one. And certainly better than none!

He set to work at once.

Using other runebooks, lesser works, slowly he put the finishing touches to the invocation. No time to check his work however, for day crept toward evening, and a grim foreboding told him that the palace walls and his slime-excluding spell could not last out the night. And so, with stylus that shook even as his hand shook, he set down the last glyph and sat back to cast worried, anxious eyes over the completed rune.

Outside the light was beginning to fail. Exior called for Loxzor – ex-cockroach, ex-Hrossak, ex-wizard – and commanded: 'Look upon this rune. What think you? Will it work?'

Loxzor scuttled, drew himself up to Exior's table on chitin legs, glared at the freshly pigmented page with many-faceted eyes. 'Bah!' he harshly clacked. And maliciously: 'What do I know of magic – I'm a cockroach!'

'You refuse to help me?'

'Help yourself, wizard. Your hour is at hand!'

'Beastly creature!' Exior cried. 'Go then, and suffer the slime when it whelms this place! *Begone!*' And he chased Loxhor from the chamber. Then –

– Then it was time to test out the spell. The last rune of Exior K'mool . . .

Far removed from his own era – if he could any longer be said to have one representative or contemporary time – The Searcher hovered the time-clock high over Exior's palace and looked down through the scanners and sensors on the scene below. Beside him, Moreen snuggled close and said: 'Henri, I know we've left Earth's dreamlands far behind – or before us – and that this is the waking world in a time when the Motherworld was in her prime, but looking down there, on that . . .'

'I know,' he answered, grimly. 'You'd swear we were still dreaming, eh? Nightmaring, anyway. It seems Exior K'mool's got himself in deep waters. Also, if that dome of force is anything to go by, he's a wizard of some note.'

To merely human eyes Exior's dome would be invisible, but the clock's sensors and scanners showed it as a pale, vibrating hemisphere, with Exior's palace locked inside like a scene viewed through blue smoke or heat-haze. The scanners also showed the slime, and de Marigny's immediate revulsion told him something of its nature. 'It seems we're to be used yet again,' he commented wryly.

'Used?'

He nodded. 'We were used to rescue Sssss from the Hounds of Tindalos, likewise Hero and Eldin from Gudge, or more properly Nyarlathotep – and now –'

'Exior K'mool from that . . . that filthy stuff? Or is it in fact a filthy thing? I can't tell, but I know it's nothing of nature. Not as I know nature.'

'It's both,' said de Marigny. 'It's a slime, but it gets its form, its purpose, its motive for being from a source which is far worse. Do you know what this stuff is? I do, for I've met it before – or will meet it, in the distant future. In ancient Khem it took, *will* take, the form of a proud young Pharaoh. But by then it will have a thousand other forms, too. Here in the primal land, it too is primal; Cthulhu uses crude means to achieve his ends; no need for sophistication in a mainly unsophisticated age.'

'Nyarlathotep!' the girl shuddered. 'Again?'

'I'm sure of it,' de Marigny nodded again. 'The Crawling Chaos – but formless in this age. A mass, crawling, chaotic. A primal force in a primal land. It's an age of magic and monsters, remember? And certainly this stuff is monstrous. It's the morbid mind-juice of the Cthulhu Cycle Deities, telepathy bordering on teleportation; it's something the Great Old Ones have sent to exact a revenge, or collect a debt. It seems Exior has had business with Cthulhu, which is the same as making a deal with the devil!'

'It's eating at those walls,' said Moreen, 'and it seems to me that Exior's dome grows thinner, weaker, with each passing moment. 'Can we get inside?'

'I think so. The time-clock ignores most barriers. It was designed to breach the greatest of them all: time and space and all the planes and angles between and beyond. We'll soon see . . .'

He located K'mool in his tower workshop, slipped the clock sideways through space-time, emerged in a shimmer of air *within* that marvellous room – where a moment before the wizard had spoken his rune and completed the intricate attendant passes. And:

'By all the Lords of Darkness!' Exior gasped, his jaw falling open. He stumbled back from the time-clock where it hovered inches over the mosaic floor, tripped, flopped backward into his cane chair. 'I called upon a dead ancestor and got him – coffin and all!'

But as de Matigny set the clock down, and he and Moreen stepped out of the open door in a wash of purple, pulsing light: 'Two ancestors!' Exior croaked. 'And solider far than any ghosts I ever say before!'

None of which made any sense to the time-travellers, for it was spoken in an alien – a primal – tongue. 'We'll have to speak to him through the clock,' said de Marigny, turning as if to re-enter the time-clock. But –

'Wait!' Exior cried, this time in English. 'No need for any interpreter. I, Exior K'mool, am a master of runes – and what are languages if not runes expressed as words? Magic or mundane, all is one to me; I understand tongues indeed, I've fathomed yours from the merest sentence.'

'Amazing!' said Moreen, round-eyed. She approached the wizard and he made a bow. 'You heard a few words and learned a language! But you must be the greatest linguist of all time.'

'So I pride myself,' said Exior. 'It is a measure of my magic – with the help of some skill – all of which is in the blood *you* passed down to me, O mother of all my ancestors.'

Moreen laughed, shook her head. 'But I'm not your ancestor,' she protested. 'I won't even be born for millions of years yet – and when I am born, it won't be on this world! We're from the future, Exior, far in the future.'

The wizard was astounded. 'It's true I was less than one hundred per cent sure of the rune,' he gasped. 'But to have got it totally reversed is ... are you saying I've called up *future* dead? Not my ancestors but my descendants? *Hah!* So these lamias and succubi had their uses after all!'

'Ah, that's the other let-down, I'm afraid – ' said de

Marigny, ' – depending on your point of view, of course. We're not dead, Exior, and we're not your descendants. I'm Henri-Laurent de Marigny, called The Searcher, and this is Moreen of Numinos.'

Exior peered at him (very closely, de Marigny thought), then at Moreen. And finally, slowly the wizard shook his head. 'No,' he said, ' – oh, I grant you all else you've said – but not the matter of your lineage. Man, look at you – then look at me. And you tell me I am not your ancestor? In this I am surely not mistaken; apart from our ages, we are like as petals of the same flower, or eyeteeth of the same dog! At least I *cannot* be mistaken when I name you for a magician. In this, and in the matter of your calling, I am surely correct; indeed, for you came in answer to my summons, my rune. Alas, I was in haste with the thing; instead of getting someone out of the past, I got you out of the future.'

Moreen was both embarrassed and sorry for him. 'No, Exior,' she said, softly. 'We aren't here to answer your call or spell or rune. We were looking for you anyway.'

'And through you,' de Marigny added, 'hopefully, we may yet find Elysia.'

'Too much, too much!' Exior cried. He threw up his hands, collapsed again in his cane chair, let his arms and his head flop. 'I have been under great stress,' he mumbled. 'The filth closing in . . . and no escape, no refuge . . . You come from the future, you say? And what good is that to me? I have no future . . .' But then he looked up, narrowed his eyes. 'Unless – '

'Why don't we trade?' de Marigny suggested. 'I can take you out of this, wherever you want to go. In return, perhaps you can tell me about Elysia. I have to find Elysia.'

Exior seemed to ignore him. Eyes gleaming, filled with a strange excitement, he leaped up. 'From the future! But how *far* in the future?'

'Millions of years,' said Moreen, backing away.

'Eons,' said de Marigny.

'Yes, yes – you said that before!' Exior danced feverishly. 'But I scarce heard you – I'm under such pressure, you see? Millions of years, you said, eons. And I scanned mere thousands! I have searched for a future for myself, to no avail. And yet in my dreams, which are oneiromantic, I have *seen* a future: in distant Lith, where I dwelled with Ardatha Ell in his manse, floating on a lake of lava.'

De Marigny's turn to be excited. Goose-flesh crept on his back, set the small hairs erect on the nape of his neck. Curator had mentioned this same Ardatha Ell, these same lava lakes of Lith – and then had gone on to remark how he'd said too much! And the name itself, 'Ardatha Ell', was an echo from something Titus Crow had once told him of Elysia: that he'd met a white wizard there from doomed Pu-Tha – Ardatha Ell, of course! One and the same! So if any man might know where Elysia could be found, surely that man *must* be Ardatha Ell.

'I could take you there,' he told Exior, 'if I knew the way. To Ardatha Ell's house – or manse – in Lith.'

Exior wasn't listening, or barely. Instead he stood before his shewstone, making weird, rapid passes with his hands while the crystal ball as quickly flickered from scene to scene. 'Millions of years,' he muttered to himself. 'Many millions of years. Very well, now I cast my net wide as I can, and – '

Moreen and de Marigny moved to flank him where he stood before the crystal on its pedestal.

' – There!' said Exior K'mool.

In the shewstone, two men sat at an ornate table before a curving window of some glass-like material. Beyond the window, distorted by its propeties, yellow and crimson flames leaped like a scene from hell; but the men at the table showed no discomfort, carried on with their game.

De Marigny saw that it was chess. One of them was clearly Exior K'mool himself, unchanged, the same man as stood here now. The other was tall, incredibly so. Eight feet, de Marigny reckoned him, standing; slender as a reed in his robes of fiery mesh-of-bronze; zombie-like in aspect, this man – if he *was* a man! For his hands each had six digits, with thumbs inside and out, and his features were sharp as blades. He could be none other than Ardatha Ell; little wonder Titus Crow had recalled him so vividly.

'There!' said Exior again. 'See?' And at that precise moment there sounded a low rumble – like a wall collapsing!

Moreen looked up anxiously, hurried out onto a balcony, came back pale and breathless. 'The slime has forced an entry. It's pouring in through a breach in the wall!'

'Exior,' said de Marigny sharply, 'where is this Lith?'

'Watch!' the wizard answered. He made more passes in the air, his practiced fingers building skeins impossible to follow. The picture in the shewstone blurred; the scene switched to outside; de Marigny seemed to look down on the manse where it floated on ·a turgid, red and black, fire-streaked lake of lava.

The place was like two disproportionate hemispheres, with the small one on top like the dome of some observatory. A central pole or axis looked as if it went right through the structure, forming a single antenna on top and (de Marigny supposed) a sort of keel below, giving the manse its lava-worthiness. There would be a heavy blob of material at the sunken end, keeping the place from capsizing.

'Fine,' he said. 'Now I know what Ardatha Ell's manse looks like, but I still don't know where it is. Can you back off some more? If that's a planet I need to know where in space I can find it.' He stepped to the time-clock, leaned head and shoulders inside, made mental adjustments. 'There,' he said, returning to the display, 'now the clock will record this, trace the co-ordinates. But not until we can see that entire world against a background of stars. After that it should be a simple – '

The palace trembled violently, causing the three to stumble. For a moment the scene in the shewstone convulsed, then steadied, as Exior regained control. More yet the picture retracted: it showed not a lake but a veritable sea of lava now, where the floating manse was the merest speck of white in a crusted cauldron of slowly, oh so slowly congealing rock.

Moreen rushed to the head of the stairs, cried: 'Oh, no! The stuff's in the palace – it's coming up the stairs!'

'Moreen, get in the clock!' de Marigny yelled. And to the wizard: 'More yet, Exior – let's see this Lith from space.'

The scene in the crystal drew away; the lava sea became an angry sore on a mighty black disk that floated free in the velvet void; stars showed beyond its rim. 'There,' said Exior K'mool. 'There – a dying sun!'

'More yet,' de Marigny repeated, his voice hoarse.

Something gurgled at the head of the stairs and the tower rocked again. Moreen gave a little shriek, ran to the time-clock, entered into the purple glow beyond its door. Exior sweated, struggled, his eyes stood out in his head. His passes were weird and wonderful: his hands described figures at least as complicated as those of the hands of the clock. De Marigny was struck with the similarity. Magic, or a primal science?

Living slime came slopping through cowrie curtains!

And at that precise moment the scene in the shewstone retreated suddenly and violently. Lith jerked away from the viewers, grew tiny against the vast backdrop of space, became a smouldering smudge of light in a great wheel of stars whose brilliance quickly drowned it. And –

'Andromeda!' de Marigny gasped. And without pause: 'Exior, that's all we needed. Quick, into the clock!'

The tower was sinking down into its own foundations, melting like a sandcastle. Its master stumbled, staggered; the scene in the crystal ball blinked out. 'All done, all gone,' moaned Exior. 'The end of all this. My runebooks, instruments, shewstone –'

The slime was on the move. De Marigny grabbed the wizard, half-pushed, half-dragged him toward the clock. The slime rose up in a stinking great flap of filth like a wave, and –

A pencil-slim beam of purest light lanced out from the time-clock, played on the slime – *and halted its progress not at all!*

De Marigny jammed Exior in through the purple-pulsing door, quickly followed him inside. 'Moreen,' he croaked, 'the weapon isn't working! Here, let me try.'

'Not working?' said Exior. 'A weapon? Of course it's not. Hurtful mechanical magics are forbidden in my palace. So I spelled it when Black Yoppaloth of the Yhemnis sent a squad of onyx automatons against me. They had quicksilver blood and glass scythes for arms, and –'

De Marigny frantically commanded the clock forward in time – and it stood stock still! 'But this is only hurtful to us!' he yelled. 'Now the time-clock is stuck!'

'My protective runes at work!' cried Exior. 'A rune against abduction, which –'

'Man, your runes are going to *kill* us!' de Marigny grated through clenched teeth.

The slime slopped across the mosaic floor, reared before the clock.

'We entered,' shrilled Moreen, clutching at both men, 'and so should be able to leave.'

Exior shook himself free of her hand. 'You entered because I called you,' he insisted. 'Such a fuss! – *there!*' and he made a simple downward-sweeping pass.

The slime hurled tentacles to encircle the clock – but too late by a single instant of time. Side-stepping through space-time, the clock disappeared, re-appeared a mile high over the crumbling, slime-reduced pile which was once Exior's palace. Tapering tentacles of filth lashed skyward after the clock failed, fell seething back to earth . . .

2

Ardatha Ell's Vigil

De Marigny sighed, allowed himself to slump for a moment. 'That's the closest I ever want to come,' he said. 'That Cthulhu mind-stuff – Nyarlathotep, sentient slime, call it what you will – could have entered the clock as easily as the Hounds of Tindalos themselves. But now,' he straightened up, ' – now let's get out of here.'

'Wait!' something clacked harshly where it scuttled about their feet. 'And what of me?'

De Marigny saw the thing, gave a violent start. 'What in the name of all the hells – ?'

'This is Loxzor,' said Moreen. 'He got in while you and Exior were busy.' She looked reproachfully at the wizard. 'And Loxzor's not quite what he seems to be, either. Like Exior, he's something of a linguist – yes, and he's been telling me a few things.'

Exior hastily offered his version, and added: 'But since he's here anyway . . . I suppose we could always take him back to his steppes? If you feel inclined.'

De Marigny flew the time-clock south-west at Exior's direction, brought it to rest on a hill crested with a bleak stone shell. 'My castle,' clacked Loxzor, 'fallen into ruins through these fifteen years of hybridism.' He scuttled out of the door as soon as de Marigny opened it for him, crying: 'Ruined, aye, all ruined – thanks to Exior K'mool!'

'No,' Exior shook his head, 'thanks to your own dark inclinations, Loxzor. However, since I'll no more be here to suffer you as a neighbour, I'll now unspell you.' He pointed a bony finger, uttered a word. It had a strange sound, that word, impossible to remember or repeat, except for Exior. Green lightning lashed from his finger, set the hideous roach-man leaping and shrieking where it covered him in a mesh of emerald fire. There came a puff of smoke, and when it cleared –

Loxzor of the Hrossaks stood there, a whole man again. A pallid, yellowy bronze in his dark cloak and cowl, he stood hunched, scowling. At his feet a cockroach scurried. He spied it, said '*Hah*!' – crushed it with his naked foot.

'And there stands Loxzor,' said Exior in disgust. 'He shared that poor creature's body many a year, and now pulps the life out of it without a moment's thought. Well, farewell, Hrossak mage – but one last piece of advice. 'Ware wizards whose powers are greater than your own, eh, Loxzor?'

Loxzor stared stonily, eyes yellow and unforgiving. The three turned away from him, entered the clock. As the door closed on them, Moreen queried: 'But what's he doing now?'

Exior, during their brief flight to Hrossa, had explored something of the clock's workings; his wizard's mind had quickly discovered the use of most of its 'accessories'. On entering the clock this second time, he had followed Moreen's lead in tuning himself to the scanners. De Marigny, taking the actual controls (as it were), was startled yet again when Exior answered Moreen's query with a cry of warning:

'Hurry, Searcher!' hissed the wizard. 'That's a "follow-him" spell he's weaving! See, he makes his wicked passes, points in the direction of my late palace in Humquass – and now he points directly at us!'

De Marigny saw – saw, too, the thin trail of noxious yellow vapour, like the trail of a meteorite, on the horizon, speeding toward them – and gave the clock its instructions. Wisps of slime, made aerial and lightning-swift by Loxzor's spell, arced down toward the clock ... but the clock was no longer there.

'I think,' said de Marigny with feeling, piloting the clock into the future, 'that if that was Theem'hdra, then I've had all I want of it!'

'What of Loxzor?' asked Moreen.

'Eh?' said Exior. 'But surely you heard me warn him, child? Never a mind so contrary, so warped, as Loxzor's. And never a man so doomed.'

'Oh?' said de Marigny.

Exior nodded. 'The mind-slime has lost us, but Loxzor's spell calls for a victim. Such black magic as he used carried its own retribution. The slime now follows him . . .'

'And no escape?' Moreen was full of pity.

'None,' Exior shook his head. 'It will follow him to the end and take him, just as it would have taken me but for your intervention.'

There was a long silence, then Moreen said: 'I sensed him as a cruel creature, but still he was a man. It seems a monstrous way for a man to die.'

To put the matter in its correct perspective, and also to clear the air, de Marigny said, 'As Exior points out, Loxzor brought it on himself. The best thing to do is forget him. After all, he's already a million years dead.'

And that was that . . .

'How did you get in that mess?' de Marigny asked Exior when they were well underway.

'It's a long story,' said Exior.

'Tell me anyway.'

Exior shrugged. 'As a boy,' he began, 'I was apprenticed under Phaithor Ull. In his dotage, Phaithor sought immortality – we all do – and made himself the subject of several thaumaturgies. One morning when I went to wake him, he was a heaping of green dust on his bed, all spread out in the shape of a man. His rings were in the 'hand' formed of the dust, as was his wand. It, too, fell into dust the moment I took it up.

203

'Later I served Mylakhrion, however briefly. To test my worthiness, he sent me on a quest. I was to find and return to him a long-lost runebook. I succeeded – barely! My reward: Mylakhrion gave me his palace, made me mage to Morgath the then King of Humquass. And off *he* went to seek immortality! Strange how men want to live forever, eh?'

De Marigny smiled, however wryly, and nodded. 'Some men seek to slow time down, yes,' he said. 'Others speed it up!'

'Eh? Oh, yes! Your time-clock, of course. Very droll! But to continue:

'Eventually I, too, began to feel the weight of my years. Humquass was forsaken, except for me. The city fell into decay. Years went fleeting. Naturally – and unnaturally – I too sought immortality. I went to Tharamoon hoping to find Mylakhrion. His potions and ointments and fountain of vitality had held the years back a little, but not entirely. Perhaps by now he'd discovered the secret, maybe he'd even share it with me. So I thought. But in Tharamoon, when I found Mylakhrion's tower, it too was a ruin. Mylakhrion's bones lay broken at its base.

'I searched the place top to bottom, brought back with me all I could of his paraphernalia: books and cyphers, powders, elixirs, unguents and the likes. And I read Mylakhrion's works most carefully. His diary, too . . .

'He had fallen foul of Cthulhu, who sleeps and dreams and makes men mad. Do you know of Cthulhu?'

'Too much!' de Marigny frowned.

'To know his name is too much!' said Exior. 'Mylakhrion had promised to do Cthulhu's bidding in return for immortality. But when that most monstrous of the Great Old Ones ordered that which might free the prisoned demons of his evil order . . . Mylakhrion refused! For which Cthulhu killed him. Mylakhrion had broken the pact – Cthulhu broke Mylakhrion.'

De Marigny nodded. 'That's a familiar pattern,' he said. 'And you fell for it too, eh?'

Exior hung his head. 'Indeed. Foolish old Exior K'mool, who thought himself mightier than Mylakhrion. I made the same pact, for I was sure I could defend myself against Cthulhu's wrath. As you have seen, there was no defence – except this. Flight into the future.'

Something bothered de Marigny. 'But you had made a form of agreement, a contract with Cthulhu. And did you get your immortality? It seems unlikely, for if we hadn't come along in the time-clock you'd be dead. If you can die you're hardly immortal.'

Exior looked up and slowly smiled. A wondering smile, very peculiar. 'But I am not dead,' he pointed out. There was something about his voice . . .

De Marigny said: 'Tell me, just exactly what did Cthulhu tell you about immortality? How were you to make yourself immortal?'

Exior shrugged. 'All a trick!' he snorted. 'The only way I could become immortal was in my children's children. Which is the same for all men, for all creatures, even for the simple flowers of the field. A blade of wheat grows, sheds its seed, dies – and is reborn from its seed. And a man? This was the immortality for which Cthulhu drove so hard a bargain. A man's natural right!'

Moreen had overheard all. 'Then perhaps you've succeeded after all,' she said. 'Or if not immortality, something close to it.'

They looked at her. 'He's right, you know,' she said to de Marigny. 'About how you both look alike. Like two petals of the same flower . . .'

'Ridiculous!' said de Marigny. 'There are eons between us.'

She smiled. 'Then that really would be immortality, wouldn't it?'

De Marigny shook his head, said: 'But – '

' – We *think* we went back into time of our own accord,' she cut him off, determined to make her point, 'but what if he really *did* call us back – to save him? Perhaps Cthulhu didn't cheat him after all, the secret did lie in his children's children. He was saved, made "immortal", by his own descendent – by you, Henri.'

'Her reasoning is sound,' said Exior. 'And with luck, I shall yet make myself truly immortal. You seek Elysia, correct? Yes, and so do I – now! Why, Elysia *is* immortality!'

'That's playing with words,' de Marigny protested – but he remembered that Titus Crow had told him to look in his past. Not *the* past but *his* past. And wasn't there something else Crow had said to him long ago: about a spark in de Marigny carried down all the ages, which would flare up again one day in Elysia?

'We can put the girl's theory to the test,' Exior cut in on his thoughts. 'Wizards often run in unbroken lines of descent. You are a wizard, even though you deny it. Oh, you haven't discovered your full potential yet, but it's there. The proof is this: your father would have been another.'

'My father?' de Marigny almost laughed out loud. 'My father was a 20th Century jazz buff who lived in New Orleans! He – ' But here the smile died on The Searcher's lips and his jaw dropped. For Etienne-Laurent de Marigny had also been New Orleans' premier mystic and occultist – and even now he was a prominent figure in the land of Earth's dreams. In short, a magician. In his lifetime and after it. A wizard!

Wide-eyed, de Marigny gazed at Exior K'mool.

And Exior gazed at him.

And the time-clock sped into the future . . .

'Time travel takes time.' De Marigny grinned and did it again: 'An amazingly accurate alliteration.'

'What's that?' Moreen had been half asleep.

'Nothing,' said de Marigny. 'Sorry I woke you. I was just thinking out loud. About time travel. It takes time.'

Exior approached, his face animated, excited in the clock's soft purple glow. 'Yes, it does,' he agreed, 'if you only use this wonderful device as a conveyance. And of course you must, for the time-clock is vital to you. It has to go where you go.'

'Just what are you getting at?' de Marigny raised an eyebrow. 'And you really shouldn't go wandering about in here on your own. The clock's a death-trap for the unwary. You could end up almost anywhen.'

'Precisely my point. You use it as a conveyance, but it could be used as a gateway!'

De Marigny nodded. 'We know that. Titus Crow has used it that way. As for myself: I don't know how to. I've never had to or even wanted to. In any case, if I did use the clock that way, what if I couldn't find my way back again?'

'Exactly!' Exior answered. 'You depend upon the clock – but I don't. The only place *I* want to be is Ardatha Ell's manse in Lith. And right now I'm wasting time getting there.'

'What?' de Marigny had suddenly realized what Exior was saying. 'Exior, you're out of your mind! I've piloted this ship for more than six years now, and I still don't know half of all there is to know about it. And you're telling me that after a few short hours of travel in the clock you plan to use it as a gateway?'

'Henri,' said Exior patiently, 'I unriddle runes, languages, systems. My mind is built that way. Yours, too, but undeveloped as yet. The time-clock's systems are intricate, yes, but not unfathomable. Your friend Titus Crow has done it, and I'm going to do it too – now.'

'Now?' Moreen gasped.

'I only came back to say goodbye – for now. For of course, I'll see you both again in the lava-floating manse on Lith.'

'But ... right now?' de Marigny still couldn't accept it. 'I mean – how?'

Exior smiled, meshed his mind deeper with the clock, deeper than de Marigny had ever dared to go. 'Like this,' he said. His form wavered, broke down into bright points of light, blinked out.

And de Marigny and Moreen stood alone ...

Exior and Ardatha Ell met over the lava lakes. Below, no manse was anywhere visible. Exior, now an extension of the time-clock, slowed himself down, cruised into the future rather than rocketed. His speed was now only a little faster than true time itself. 'No manse,' he said to the other, deeming introductions unnecessary.

'Indeed,' said Ardatha. 'I had assumed it was your place.'

'And I thought it was yours!'

'No matter, we'll build one.' Ardatha used cohesive magic to draw together a great mass of heat-resistant matter, which formed like a scab on the bubbling lake below. Exior pictured the manse as he had seen it in his shewstone, formed it in two hemispheres, welded them together. The work took moments, but it drained both of them.

'Let's get inside,' said Exior, breaking his connection with the clock and slowing all the way down to normal time. And within the lava-floating manse, after briefly resting, they each constructed rooms to their own tastes. Later still:

'It seems we've known each other for some time,' said Exior, where they sat sipping conjured essence in a room with tinted portals.

'Because we knew it would be, it feels like it has always been,' replied Ardatha Ell. 'In fact, when I explored a little of Lith's future, from Elysia, I was surprised to find your manse – er, this place – floating here. I had intended to come anyway, you see, as an agent for Kthanid. It seems that Lith, in some manner yet unknown to me, will soon become vastly important.'

'Oh? Could that be, I wonder, because the son of my most remote sons, Henri-Laurent de Marigny, called The Searcher, and Moreen are even now en-route here?'

'Ah!' Ardatha was pleased. 'So they've fathomed all clues, overcome all obstacles, have they? Kthanid foresaw it, of course – or at least, that was one of the futures he foresaw. But so many possible futures! Kthanid is incredible! Such computations! Such permutations! But he chose the best future he could, then set about to make it work out that way.'

This conveyed a great deal to Exior's wizard's mind. He drew much more from Ardatha's words than any ordinary man might ever comprehend. 'In my shewstone,' he said after a while, 'I saw that we played a game. It was strange to me. Obviously it had not been invented in my time, though it reminded me of trothy, which is also played on a board.'

'That must have been chess,' Ardatha beamed. 'A favourite of mine!' He conjured a board and pieces. 'Here, let me explain the rules . . .'

They played, and at the same time and for long hours amused themselves with certain matters of cryptical conjecture – hypothetical problems of interest only to magicians – and yet still found time and space to carry on a more nearly normal conversation:

'Your purpose in coming here?' Ardatha eventually asked. 'Apart from carrying out a temporal necessity, of course. That is to say, having seen yourself here – and while obviously you obeyed the omen and came here – was that the only reason?' Wizards seldom have only one motive for their actions.

'I seek immortality,' Exior explained. 'I have done so for years. When de Marigny mentioned his goal, Elysia, I saw the answer at once. For as I said to him: Elysia *is* immortality! And so, since this manse, Lith, and you yourself formed a focal point, a way-station along de Marigny's route . . .'

'Hmm!' Ardatha mused. 'And how will you complete the final stage? From here to Elysia, I mean, when the time comes?'

'In the time-clock, with The Searcher and his woman. Won't you join us? Since you already have a place in Elysia, and Lith being such a boring place and all . . .'

'I think not,' answered Ardatha Ell. 'You see, I don't know how long I may be called upon to stay here – or even *why* I'm here – except that it was Kthanid's wish that I should come. Also, I rode a Great Thought to this place. My shell – my flesh-and-blood body, that is – is still in Elysia. And so when I return it shall be a simple matter of instantaneous transfer. However, I thank you for your – ' He paused abruptly, came stiffly erect in his chair.

'Is there something?' Exior enquired.

Ardatha unfolded his tall, spindly frame, stood up. 'A messenger enters my sky-sphere in Elysia,' he said, his eyes far away. 'I had expected some such. A message from Kthanid. Come, you shall see.'

He quickly loped to his room and Exior followed on behind. There they seated themselves before Ardatha's shewstone, in which a picture had already formed. A Dchi-chi stood at the threshold of Ardatha Ell's inner sanctum in his sky-floating sphere high over Elysia. Ardatha himself – or his body – lay suspended on a gravitic bed of air in the centre of the room. All was silent until the Elysian wizard's Lith facet made a six-fingered pass, and then the scene came alive with conversation:

'I beg to differ,' came a voice from some mechanical source, but clearly Ardatha's voice, or a good imitation. 'The lesser part, surely? For his recumbent shell here is only the flesh of Ardatha Ell. The mind – which is greater by far, which is more truly *me* – that is in Exior K'mool's manse in Andromeda.' And so the conversation continued, as we have previously seen, while in Lith Exior and Ardatha looked on. Until finally the Dchi-chi passed his message.

In Lith Ardatha absorbed that message, reeled for a moment, then frowned mightily. And from the shewstone he heard himself say: 'There, all done. Aye, and this is an important task Kthanid has set me. You should have said so before now, little bird, instead of posing and parroting.'

There followed the matter of the Dchi-chi's exit from Ardatha's sphere – his hasty, somewhat fearful exit – after which, chuckling good-naturedly, the wizards in Lith returned to their game of chess.

And in a little while: 'What was Kthanid's message?' Exior asked.

'It contained the reason for my being here,' Ardatha answered. 'Which is this: that I keep a vigil.' He won the game in three moves, produced a wand which elongated into a rod six feet long, stuck its ferrule in the floor and bent his ear to the silver handle. He seemed to listen to something for a moment, straightened up, smiled grimly. 'A vigil, aye,' he repeated.

And then he explained in greater detail ...

In Elysia all was ready, all preparations made. Kthanid – *only* Kthanid – had retained a measure of surveillance on the outside multiverse, and now even he was 'blind' to occurrences beyond Elysia's boundaries. Nothing physical or mental departed from or entered into Elysia. No Great Thoughts went out, no travellers returned; no telepathic transmissions were sent or received; no time-clocks plied the limitless oceans of time and space. Elysia lay silent, hidden, secret, more mythical than ever before ...

And yet, because Kthanid himself was of the flesh and the mind of the Great Old Ones, he was not entirely closed off, not totally insulated from their activity. In his own incredible dreams he heard echoes from outside. The massed mind of the Great Old Ones – their use of telepathy, their 'Great Messenger', Nyarlathotep, which carried their thoughts between them in their various prison environs – would occasionally impinge upon Kthanid's mind; and then, in snatches however brief, he would learn what they were about.

When de Marigny and Moreen had left Borea in the time-clock – and when Ithaqua had tormented certain minds to extract information from them, which was then passed on to the rest of the Great Old Ones, particularly Cthulhu – Kthanid had known it. He had known, too, of the loss of countless Tind'losi Hounds in a black hole, and of the saving of Sssss. From Earth's dreamlands, echoes had reached him of damage inflicted on Cthulhu's plans to further his infiltration of Man's subconscious mind, and one shriek of mental fury and frustration had signalled a strike against Nyarlathotep 'himself'.

Most of which had been anticipated . . .

And between times:

In the Vale of Dreams the gigantic N'hlathi had emerged from their immemorial burrows to graze on the seeds of great poppies, and even now a team of Dchi-chis attempted communication with them. Even more ominous, the N'hlathi were seen to be harvesting poppy seed, storing the great green beads in their burrows. And those burrows themselves were now seen for what they really were; for when the seals on the N'hlathi doors had sprung and the doors had opened, then those massive cylinders – the 'burrows' themselves – had slowly unscrewed from the basalt cliffs. More than mere hibernation cells, those cylinders: thirty feet in diameter and sixty feet long, of a white metal unknown even to Elysia's science, they had commenced to give off certain hyper-radiations – the selfsame energies which powered Elysia's time-clocks! The burrows of the N'hlathi *were* time-clocks – which they now provisioned as for flight!

As for the pattern those doors had duplicated, the great whorl of Andromeda and the emergence of certain stars of ill-omen there:

Now indeed those stars were very nearly right; in fact, only one more was needed to complete the pattern. Its location was well known to Kthanid, its condition, too. For this was a dying star, but a star with a difference. It was the second of twins, the first of which had already self-destructed, and it harboured in its core the seed of universal chaos.

The name of this star?

It was Lith, of course. Lith, where even now Ardatha Ell kept vigil, monitoring the fatal foetal pulse of that which might well signal a new beginning – or a monstrous end . . .

3

The Stars are Right!

When de Marigny slipped the time-clock sideways in space-time and entered their manse in Lith, Exior K'mool and Ardatha Ell were waiting for him. Nor did they fail to note the wisps of greenish mist, materializing into a thin, vapid slime that clung in a sticky layer to the windows of the upper dome, which he brought with him out of the past. The manse was rune-protected, however, and constructed of near-impervious materials, so that they were mainly unconcerned. But Exior sniffed and commented:

'So Loxzor's follow-me spell was effective after all, at least in part. A little of Cthulhu's mind-slime managed to follow the time-clock, and so has found me again. Much weakened now, I note. Why, I could banish it with a simple "get-thee-gone".'

'Let it be,' said Ardatha Ell. 'It changes nothing – indeed, we may even benefit . . .'

De Marigny and Moreen emerged cautiously from the clock, found the wizards waiting. The final stages of their trip had not been uneventful: Tind'losi Hounds had chased them for seven million years, ignoring the time-clock's weapon in a manner de Marigny had never seen before, in a suicidal way that had puzzled and worried and wearied him. They had lost countless thousands tracking him, and had only given up the chase when he reverted to three-dimensioned space over Lith.

But now the time-travellers squared up, nodded their tired acknowledgment to Exior, gazed up in awe at Ardatha Ell.

'Crow's friend,' that towering, slender, powerful person nodded, returning de Marigny's gaze; but though he spoke

214

to them, Moreen and her Earthman noted that his lips moved never a fraction. 'De Marigny The Searcher – and Moreen, whose innocence and beauty shall surely whelm all Elysia. Eventually . . . ' And still his lips hadn't moved.

Moreen blushed and smiled at his compliment, but de Marigny frowned. 'Eventually?' he repeated the wizard's word. 'Soon, we had hoped.'

Ardatha inclined his sharp-featured head. 'Well, it's true that the futures are narrowing down,' he said, 'but until a thing is we can never be entirely certain that it will be. Only the past is fixed, and even that is not entirely immutable.'

'*Ahem!*' said Exior. 'Best remember, Ardatha, that their ways with words are not our ways. Their thoughts run straighter courses than ours.'

He was right in more ways than one; by now de Marigny's thoughts were more than ever one-tracked. 'Ardatha,' he pressed, 'you know why we're here. You yourself hail from Elysia. If anyone can help us get there – '

' – Wait!' said Ardatha, holding up a six-fingered hand. 'Waste no more words, Searcher, the matter is out of my hands – and out of yours – now. Now we can only wait.'

'Wait?' de Marigny cast a puzzled glance at Moreen, who was equally mystified. 'Wait here, on Lith? But wait for what?'

'For whatever will be,' the wizard answered. Bending his ear to his silver-handled sensor, he listened patiently for a moment or two to the strengthening pulse in Lith's core. 'Aye, for what will surely be,' he repeated. 'One thing I *can* tell you, Searcher,' and he straightened up. 'It won't be a long wait. No, not long at all.' And more than that he would not, must not, say . . .

De Marigny slept and dreamed.
In weed-festooned, submarine R'lyeh, Cthulhu's groping

215

*face-tentacles reached for and almost found him before he
fled screaming into time. Bat-winged, like flapping black
rags of evil, the Hounds of Tindalos awaited him there, came
winging out from the corkscrew towers of Tindalos itself at
de Marigny's approach. To escape them he transferred from
time to space, found himself on the shore of a vilely lapping
lake somewhere in the Hyades. Turning his gaze from the
waters of that lake to the sky, he saw the black stars burning
and knew at once where he was. Along the shoreline, coming
his way, a* Thing *in yellow flopped, and in the waters
something monstrous floundered! De Marigny wrenched
himself free of the place, where even now the Lake of Hali's
waters broke in a lashing of loathsome tentacles. Hastur
wallowed in The Searcher's wake . . . And now de Marigny
wandered in unknown space and time, lost and alone in
some weird parallel dimension. But alone for a moment only.
For now, surging out of nameless vacuum, came a frothing,
liquescent, blasphemous shapelessness that masked its* true
horror behind a congeries of iridescent globes and bubbles
– the primal jelly seething forever 'beyond the nethermost
angles' – Yog-Sothoth, the Lurker at the Threshold!*

*De Marigny screamed again as the thing covered him,
folding him into its mass –*

– And found himself like a child in Moreen's arms,
awake, hugged safe to her bosom.

'Henri! Henri!' she rocked him. 'What was it? A dream?'

He shuddered, sat up on his bed in the room Ardatha
and Exior had made for them. 'A . . . a dream? A nightmare!' He hugged her, forced himself to stop trembling.
'Just a nightmare. Yes, that's all it was . . .' But in his mind
he could still hear the thin chittering of the Hounds,
the black gurgling of Hali, and frothing and seething
of Yog-Sothoth, and the – laughter? – of Cthulhu in his
watery sepulchre; all of these sounds, withdrawing now as
he came more fully awake.

'I came to wake you,' Moreen said, 'and found you

shouting and tossing. Henri, Ardatha wants you. He says it's nearly time.'

De Marigny got up at once, followed her a little unsteadily into the communal room. Ardatha Ell was there, his ear pressed to the silver handle of his elongated wand. Exior was also present, but he stood much closer to the time-clock. Both magicians were plainly excited, agitated.

'Ardatha,' de Marigny began, 'Moreen tells me that you –'

'Yes, yes,' said the wizard, cutting him short. And: 'Sit, please sit, both of you. Now, I have a tale to tell – which in itself contains something of an explanation, if you can unriddle it – but just so much time in which to tell it. The stars are coming right, de Marigny – do you know what that means?'

De Marigny drew a sharp breath, let it out more slowly. 'Yes,' he said, 'only too well.'

'They are coming right ... now,' Ardatha nodded, 'at any moment. We shall have – ' he snapped his fingers, ' – *that* much warning!'

De Marigny looked blank, shook his head. 'I – '

'This star, Lith itself, is the final one in the pattern,' Ardatha said. 'And Lith is about to nova, perhaps super-nova!' Even as he spoke the manse rocked, and beyond the tinted windows geysers of molten rock vented fire and steam at a madly boiling sky of smoke and bilious gases. As the floor tilted back to a level keel, de Marigny jumped to his feet, grasped Moreen's hand and headed for the clock.

'Wait!' cried Ardatha Ell, his mouth a thin, hard and immobile slit in his face. 'You may *not* run from this, Searcher – not if you want to enter Elysia!'

De Marigny paused, turned and stared hard at the tall magician. 'I don't run for my own sake, Ardatha Ell. You'd better get that fact fixed firmly in your head. And you'd better talk fast too, while I'm still here to hear you. I don't know about you and Exior, but if this dead sun is about to explode, Moreen and I – '

'It is the *way* to Elysia!' again Ardatha cut him off.

De Marigny opened the clock's door and purple light streamed out.

'Go on then, flee!' Ardatha Ell shouted from a closed mouth. 'Time yet for you to get away, Searcher. Run – and lose everything!'

'Hear him out,' croaked Exior K'mool. 'At least hear him out, son of my sons. You cannot imagine how much depends upon it.'

De Marigny held Moreen close. The interior of the clock was but a step away. 'Go on then,' he said. 'We're listening.'

Ardatha sighed, put his ear back to the sensor for a moment, again straightened up. The manse rocked again, but less violently. Ardatha waited for the disturbance to cease before beginning. Then –

'Once long ago, where now the Milky Way sprawls its myriad stars against the sky, there was nothing. And there, to that vacuous region, came Azathoth.

'Born in billions of tons of cosmic dust, in matter forged by gravity, in the slow seepage of massively heavy metals toward a universal centre, he *was* a Nuclear Chaos. And the report of his coming went out to the farthest stars, so that even now its echoes have not died away! But while Azathoth was of Nature, a true power without sentience, still he spawned others which *had* sentience: he was not only, in a sense, the Father of all "life" as we know it, but also of certain thermal, rather thermo-nuclear beings.' Ardatha paused, shrugged, continued:

'I will not go into nuclear genealogy here; your scientists will one day fathom it in their own way, define it in their own terms – if they tread warily. But just as there may be intelligence in air, and in water, in earth and even in space, so may there be intelligence in fire. Alas, but nuclear fire transmutes all things: metal into liquid or gas or other

218

metals, life into death, time into space and vice versa. Its massive release warps space-time itself. Yes, and it transmuted the thermal beings, too. They themselves were changed by their own chaos of energy. Sanity into madness! They became as mad and ungovernable as the unthinking Father who spawned them. Mercifully their insanity is self-destructive: they are born mad, and on the instant annihilate themselves – and, unfortunately, all who stand near. Which is the reason why even the Beings of the Cthulhu Cycle fear them . . .

'So, what shall we call such creatures, who, when they are "summoned" or born, can turn worlds to cinders and rekindle dying suns to nuclear furnaces? In eons past they were named the Azathi – Children of Azathoth. Now, I have said that they die in the instant of their birth, which is self-evident. But if they can be kept – or keep themselves – in a prolonged or extended foetal condition, then their excess 'madness', their energy, may be drawn off and used. Unwittingly, men have been doing this since the construction of the first atomic pile; though of course theirs is only a synthetic form of the actual Azathoth life-force itself, without the sentience of the Azathi. But not only men have used – are using – this awesome power!

'Long ages past Cthulhu saw a use for such primal forces. He calculated the angles between the Nggr, the Hnng and the Nng, fathomed the warp-energy required to release him and his brethren and their allies from their prisons. Then he searched far and wide in time and space, seeking to learn that precise place and moment when the stars would be *almost* right, when with a little assistance the space-time matrix might be caused to warp sufficiently to break his bonds. And he saw that eventually, in Andromeda, just such an almost-perfect pattern would form itself. A vast equation, complete but for two missing qualities or quantities – forces which Cthulhu himself must insert into the equation. The Azathi, of course!

219

'Cthulhu knew that at least three of Azathoth's primal children had controlled or contained themselves. Oh, they were mad – but not so mad as to will themselves to annihilation. He searched the void for them, at last found two. We shall call them Azatha and Azathe, and they were all the Lord of R'lyeh required to put his eon-formed plan into being, to set ticking his unthinkable cosmic time-bomb! As for Azathu, the third of Azathoth's primal children: he could not be found, perhaps he had after all become unstable, detonated in some remote region.

'But Azatha and Azathe remained, out there in the deepest, darkest reaches, forging ever outward in abysses beyond man's wildest reckoning. And Cthulhu reached out after them – sent his Great Messenger, Nyarlathotep, to parley with them – and made a pact. It was this: that they return, locate themselves in the hearts of certain suns, remain dormant down all the eons and wait on his instructions. Then, at a time of his choosing, he would awaken them, let them be fulfilled, give them glory and life-everlasting, free them of their elemental madness! His reward? – the very multiverse would see how great are the works of Cthulhu, who causes stars to blaze up at his coming!

'Since then . . . the stars have wheeled in their inexorable courses, the pattern has formed, the time is nigh. A little while ago a star exploded, became a super-nova on Andromeda's far flank. That was Azatha. And in the heart of Lith, at this very moment . . .'

De Marigny, despite his urge to get away, had been fascinated by Ardatha Ell's story. Now he completed the wizard's tale: 'Azathe?'

Ardatha nodded. 'And the pattern will be complete. All chains broken, all "spells" unspelled. The Great Old Ones will be free.'

Moreen spoke up: 'But how can that possibly help us? We seek Elysia, from which place Henri hopes to fight the Great Old Ones, assist in their destruction.'

'Wait!' Ardatha commanded. He listened yet again to his wand and his eyes grew huge. 'Soon now!' he hissed. 'Very soon!'

'Exior,' said de Marigny, his voice tense, 'get in the clock. You, too, Moreen.'

Outside, beyond the windows, the lava lake had grown calm. It was an utterly unnatural calm, producing a leaden oppressiveness that came right through the walls of the manse to those within. The lava swirled slowly, sluggishly, red-veined under a crumbling crust of black rock and ash; the smoke- and gas-clouds churned low overhead; in the distance, lightning raced in weird patterns along the under-side of the clouds, springing sporadically to strike the sullenly shuddering surface.

'Well,' said de Marigny, one foot on the clock's threshold. 'Is there an answer to Moreen's question? How *can* the death, or rebirth, of this star help us?'

Ardatha smiled, a strange cold smile. 'You have seen how Cthulhu is a great magician, a fabulous mathematician. Aye, but he is not the only one. The N'hlathi knew Cthulhu's purpose at once, and they fashioned a reminder and a warning in the Vale of Dreams in Elysia. Kthanid is of the very flesh of Cthulhu; when he knew what Cthulhu would do, he set about to maintain a balance. You ask "where is Elysia?" Elysia is where Kthanid and his elder-council desire it to be. When Lith evaporates, space-time will warp and thrust *in the direction* of Elysia, and your time-clock will be propelled through that warp, that frac-ture, *into* Elysia. Don't fight it, de Marigny. Don't try to fly out of it or avoid it. Do nothing! All has been calculated.'

De Marigny knew he must enter the clock, but there was still so much he didn't understand. 'But how do you know all of these things?' he asked. 'How can you be sure?'

Ardatha raised an eyebrow. 'And am I not a magician in my own right? Some of it I have fathomed, unriddled. And some I have had from Cthulhu himself. For have I not eavesdropped on his communications with Azathe? This was Kthanid's reason for sending me here, so that he might know the precise moment when – ' He paused, came instantly alert as never before.

Ardatha's wand began to tremble. The tremors rapidly spread themselves to the entire manse; it shuddered, rocked, was shaken as in the fist of some inconceivable colossus.

'Ardatha!' de Marigny cried out loud over the groaning and grinding of the manse. 'Quick, man – get in the clock!'

'I don't need your time-clock, Searcher,' said the wizard. 'But you do. You need it right now. Good luck, Henri!' He snatched up his wand – which at once retracted to its normal size – saluted the time-clock with a strange gesture, disappeared like a light switched off!

Moreen and Exior dragged de Marigny into the time-clock. And after that –

Lith was no more!

The time-clock was very nearly impervious to all forces and pressures. It had survived, even escaped from, the lure of black holes; it had breached all known temporal and spatial barriers; it had journeyed in weird intermediate, even subconscious dimensions. But even so, it had never before encountered *forces* like those which worked on it now. Ardatha Ell had warned de Marigny not to resist; now, even if he would resist, he could not. Time did not allow. The time-clock itself did not allow. Its controls no longer worked. It was a twig whirled along a gutter in a cloudburst, a canoe caught in the maelstrom.

Light and heat and radiation – even a little matter – exploded outward in such a holocaust of released ENERGY that the clock was simply carried along on its shock wave. For those within – because they were enclosed in an area which was timeless, and yet, paradoxically everywhere and when – it was acceleration without gravity, without the fatal increase in mass which Earthly physics would otherwise demand. But it was more than that. Space-time's fabric was wrenched by Azathe's rebirth and instant death; it was torn, finally ripped asunder. All dimensions of the continuum became one in a crazy mingling, became a new *state*. Barriers Man's science had not even guessed at went crashing, and crashing through the chaos of their collapse came the time-clock.

And it came –

– Into Elysia!

Elysia, yes, but no longer that magical place as described by Titus Crow. De Marigny saw this as soon as the whirling of his psyche settled and his mundane senses regained control. For this was Elysia with all of the magic removed.

Rain lashed the time-clock where it sped of its own accord high above a land grey and sodden. Black clouds scudded in boiling banks, turning the rays of a synthetic sun to the merest glimmer. The sky-islands and palaces floated on air as before, but no transports came and went, no iridescent dragons sped on bone and leather wings through the lowering skies. The aerial roadways of the cities carried no traffic; the streets below shone dully, empty of life; there did not appear to be *any* life in all Elysia.

But then the scanners told de Marigny how he erred, the scanners and Moreen and Exior's combined cry of warning. There *was* life here, behind him, even now bloating monstrous in the wake of the clock!

The blow fell on de Marigny like a crashing, crushing weight. He saw, and was shattered by the sight. For in one soul-destroying moment he saw exactly how, exactly why, the clock's scanners and sensors were now full of the sight and sound and presence of these things: *the massed hordes of the Cthulhu Cycle – including and led by Cthulhu himself!*

It was as simple as this: they had followed him through

the breach! He who had sought only to assist Elysia, had doomed her! Cthulhu was free, he was here, and The Searcher had *led* him here!

It was all so obvious, so very obvious. Everything de Marigny had done since Titus Crow rode his Great Thought to him in Borea might have been designed to draw Cthulhu's attention. Ithaqua the Wind-Walker had doubtless known de Marigny was seeking Elysia; Nyarlathotep, in both his primal and current forms, he too had known; the Hounds of Tindalos had known; and because all of them reported directly to Cthulhu, so too the Lord of R'lyeh. And where better to strike their first blow against universal sanity than Elysia? And how better to get there than by following de Marigny, whose place in Elysia was assured?

'I've betrayed you!' de Marigny cried then in his agony, through clenched teeth. 'All of you ... all Elysia!'

'Oh, Henri, Henri!' Moreen clung to him sobbing.

'*No!*' he put her gently aside. 'I came here to fight, and I can *still* fight!' With his mind he reached out for the time-clock's weapons.

'They won't work for you, Henri,' Exior K'mool shook his head. 'See, the clock has a mind of its own now. It flees before this hideous army. And they follow on, determined to hound us down, and whoever awaits us at the end of our journey.'

Exior was right: the clock's weapons would not fire, the space-time machine refused to respond to de Marigny's touch. And faster than its unimaginable pursuers – answering some unknown, unheard summons – it sped on across Elysia, across the once-Frozen Sea, where now the ice bucked and heaved and waterspouts gouted skyward, toward its goal, the Icelands, where dwelled Kthanid in the heart of Elysia's mightiest glacier. The Hall of Crystal and Pearl: de Marigny saw it again in his mind's eye as once he had seen it in a prophetic dream, that throneroom of

224

Kthanid, spokesman of the Elder Gods themselves. And how would that mighty beneficent Kraken greet him now, he wondered, whose ambition had brought ruin on all Elysia?

The time-clock dipped low and skimmed across ice-cliffs, plunged toward an entrance carved from the permafrost of a vast cavern. But even upon entering the complex of caves and corridors that led to Kthanid's sanctum sanctorum, the clock was slowing down, its scanners dimming, sensors blanking out. The controls were totally dead now, and darkness closing in fast.

'Henri?' In the deepening gloom, still Moreen clung to The Searcher.

'Elysia's finished,' de Marigny felt drained, his voice was cracked. 'Even the time-clocks are running down. This place must be their final refuge – the refuge of Elysia's peoples, I mean, and of their leaders. If Cthulhu can find them here he can find them anywhere, so why run any farther? This is the end of the line ...' Even as he spoke the clock came to a halt; its door swung open and its now feeble purple glow pulsed out; the three gazed upon the interior of the vast Hall of Crystal and Pearl.

Exior K'mool was first to step out. The clock had come to rest deep inside the enormous clamber, close to the curtained alcove where sat Kthanid's throne. The curtains were drawn now and the throne itself invisible, but still Exior felt the awesome atmosphere of the place, knew that he stood at a crossroads of destiny. The shimmering curtains went up, up and up, to the massively carved arch which formed the alcove's façade. And wizard that he was, master of wonders, still Exior went down on his knees before those curtains and bowed his head. 'The place of the Eminence!' he whispered.

De Marigny and Moreen followed him, flanked him, gazed with him as he lifted his head. And as at a signal the curtains swept open!

De Marigny might have expected several things revealed when the curtains swept aside. He might even have guessed correctly, if he'd guessed at all. But in fact it had happened too quickly; his mind had not yet adjusted to his whereabouts: the fact that, however disastrously, he finally stood in Elysia; and so the physical presence of what – of *who* he saw there at the head of the great steps behind the curtains, before the throne and beside the onyx table with its huge crimson cushion and shewstone big as a boulder, was simply staggering.

'*Henri!*' Titus Crow's face had been drawn, haggard – but it lit up like the sun at the sight of The Searcher. 'Henri – you made it – but of course I knew you would. You had to!'

'Titus!' de Marigny tried to say, except nothing came out. On his second attempt he managed a croak, but recognizable anyway. 'Titus . . .'

It shuddered out of him, that word, that name – and in it was contained all the agony of his soul. He swayed, might have fallen. Crow started forward, paused, spoke quickly, forcefully: 'Henri, I know how you feel. Like the greatest traitor who ever lived, like Judas himself. I know, because that's how I've been feeling. Forget it. You're no Judas. You're Elysia's greatest hero!'

'What?' de Marigny's brow furrowed; he knew he was hearing things.

'What?' Moreen was equally confused. 'A hero?'

But Exior K'mool only smiled.

'No time for long explanations, Henri, Moreen,' said Crow. 'You know what's followed you, who's on his way here – to the Hall of Crystal and Pearl – even now. Come up here, quickly! You too, Exior.'

They climbed the steps, de Marigny falteringly, assisted by Moreen and Exior. 'They say a picture's worth a thousand words,' said Crow. 'So look at this – for I've lots to say to you and no time to say it all.'

He touched the great crystal – and milky clouds at once parted.

They gazed upon Elysia. Upon an Elysia falling into ruins!

The drenched, leaden skies had been empty before, but now they were full of death. The Hounds of Tindalos were everywhere, chittering round and about the aerial palaces, the tall buildings, even the lower structures. They were like a cloud of lice around host beasts: the Beings at the head of that monstrous airborne procession. Cthulhu was there, no longer dreaming but awake, crimson-eyed, evil beyond imagination. Flanking him, on his right, Yog-Sothoth seethed behind his shielding globes, unglimpsed except in the iridescent mucous froth which dripped from him like pus; and to Cthulhu's left, there strode the bloated figure of Ithaqua the Wind-Walker, snatched here in an instant from Borea, beast-god of the frozen winds that howl forever between the worlds. And these were but a few ...

They did not fly but seemed half-supported – suspended on the unbreakable strands of Atlach-Nacha's webs, which even now the spider-thing wove fast as the eye could follow across Elysia's drab skies. Yibb-Tstll was there, and Bugg-Shash, both of them close behind their cousin and master Yog-Sothoth; and Tsathoggua the toad crept apace with Cthulhu's shadow. Hastur, eternal rival of the dread Lord of R'lyeh, kept his distance from the main body of the procession, but still he was present, equally keen for revenge. Dagon cruised amid the icebergs of the now melting Frozen Sea, shattering ice floes as he came, and with him Mother Hydra and certain chosen members of the Deep Ones.

Shoggoths surged across the earth like formless towers of filth, while beneath it ran the steaming tunnels of Shudde-M'ell and his burrowers. And all of them converging on the Icelands, closing with the great glacier which housed Kthanid's immemorial palace.

And wherever they moved, each and every one of them brought destruction: sky-islands plummeted and cities went up in gouts of fire; aerial roadways were sliced through, sent crashing, and once golden forests roared into infernos. The waters of a blue, tropical ocean turned black in moments, and mountains long quiescent cracked open and spewed fire, smoke and stinking tephra . . .

'Hero?' said de Marigny dully, flinching from these scenes of destruction. 'I can write my name on . . . on *that*, and you call me a hero?'

Crow grasped his arm, said: 'Let me show you something else, my friend.' Again he touched the shewstone, his hand erasing the scenes of destruction and replacing them.

In the miles-long corridor of clocks, the last of Elysia's exotically diverse peoples and denizens filed into the remaining handful of time-clocks, which then blinked out of existence on this plane. In the Vale of Dreams the last N'hlathi centipede crawled into his life-support cannister, his own time-clock, and was gone from Elysia. With him, as with the rest of his race, he carried life-sustaining – life-assuring seeds of the great poppy, to sow in fresh, far distant fields. High over Elysia, where even now the Tind'losi Hounds streamed ravenously, the silver-sphere manse of Ardatha Ell – in which he had first come to Elysia – slowly faded to insubstantiality, seemed to disappear in drifting wraiths of coloured light. And in the Gardens of Nymarrah, there about the titan wine-glass shape of a Great Tree, a squadron of time-clocks hovered like bees, all perfectly synchronized. In another moment they, too, were gone – and the Great Tree with them. Only the mighty hole which an instant earlier had housed the Tree's taproot remained to show where he had stood.

'He would have been satisfied if we'd taken only his life-leaf,' said Titus Crow. 'Kthanid insisted we take the whole tree.'

'But . . . where to?' de Marigny's mind was still reeling.

'Watch!' said Crow. He put his shoulder to the crystal, and as the three got out of the way toppled it from the table. It jarred, rang hollowly when it hit the floor, but it didn't break. Then it rolled ponderously across the floor of the dais, clanged down the steps and across the massively paved hall toward the several entranceways. There it finally came to rest, spun sluggishly for a moment and was still.

'Come on,' said Crow. He led the way down the steps to the time-clock. 'We're very nearly finished here,' he said, putting his hands on the clock's panelling. Then he smiled wryly, added, 'A million memories here, Henri.'

De Marigny couldn't believe it. He began to doubt Crow's sanity – maybe even his own. For in the midst of all this, Crow seemed completely calm, unpanicked. 'You're thinking of using the time-clock?' The Searcher said. 'But its controls have failed, energy all drained off.'

And Crow's smile was as wide as de Marigny had ever seen it. Incredibly, he suddenly seemed younger than ever! 'What, the old clock finished?' And slowly he shook his head. 'Oh, no, Henri. Even now he leeches warp-energy from Elysia's heart. See?' And sure enough, the familiar purple pulse was building in power, the enigmatic light from within streaming out as of old.

'But where can we go?' De Marigny grasped Crow's shoulders. 'Where? They followed me here – they can follow us anywhere!'

'They?' Crow's eyes narrowed. 'Ah, yes!'

It was then that the centuried odour of deep water hit them. That and the alien stench of things no ordered universe should ever contain. And into the vast hall, squeezing his bulk in under the arch of the main entrance-way, came Cthulhu, the Lord of R'lyeh – now destroyer of Elysia. Behind him and from all quarters crowded the rest.

And there across the floor of the Great Hall of Crystal and Pearl, four human beings gazed into the very eyes of hell itself.

The tableau held, for a moment. Then –

Cthulhu's *mind* reached out, spoke three words, and in so doing paid humankind its greatest ever tribute:

CROW! that awesome, threatening thought rumbled like thunder in their minds. *AND DE MARIGNY!*

The tide of uttermost horror swayed forward – and Titus Crow, a man, held up a hand to stop it. For one and all they remembered, respected him, even though they would now, in the next moment, destroy him.

'Cthulhu!' he called across the sweep of the floor, his voice strong, unwavering. 'You came for Kthanid and the Elder Council and found only me. But Kthanid left you a message. It is written in his great crystal there.' And he pointed.

As the nightmare horde turned to observe the new scene now framed in the shewstone, so Crow whispered to his friends: 'Now, into the clock!'

Moreen and Exior obeyed at once, but de Marigny must see this out. He stood shoulder to shoulder with Titus Crow, and:

MESSAGE? WHAT MESSAGE? Cthulhu gazed rapaciously into the sphere. *I SEE ONLY ... CHAOS!*

'That's right!' Crow yelled, and his laughter rolled out to fill the Hall of Crystal and Pearl. 'It's the legend you brought with you when first you came, Cthulhu – don't you remember? You spoke a word, a Name, and worlds burst into flame. The crazed children of Azathoth destroyed themselves at your command, to light your coming. Isn't that how the story goes? And now you've used two more of these bereft nuclear beings to blast your path into Elysia. Aye, but there's one here who *knows* what you've done. One who doesn't fear you, who fears nothing. One who was satisfied simply to exist and serve, who now

230

is satisfied to sacrifice himself in the name of Sanity! Now *I* speak a word, a Name ... Can you not guess it, Cthulhu?'

The Lord of R'lyeh's octopus eyes bulged hideously, focussed on Kthanid's crystal, where a seething holocaust raged. And so intense his gaze that the shewstone shattered, spilled cold white liquid fire across the paved floor. As if in answer to which –

The floor bucked, heaved – crashed upward and open! Elysia reeled!

NAME? WHAT NAME?

The hell-horde could not be contained; they surged forward.

Crow balanced himself on the tilting, grinding floor, shoved de Marigny toward the clock. And:

'*Azathu!*' he cried. 'Azathu, who has powered Elysia from the beginning – who was sane and sedated, kept that way by Kthanid – and who now takes his revenge, for his poor demented brothers' sake!'

NO! Cthulhu's mental croak of denial followed Crow even inside the time-clock. *NO, NO, NO!*

'Damn you, *yes*!' answered Titus Crow and de Marigny together. And together they piloted the clock a billion miles distant ...

The scanners showed the rest: an area of space-time warped and torn beyond recognition. A supernova to end *all* supernovas, one whose energy could not be contained in this continuum, and so flowed through into another. It brought into being the mightiest black hole ever to exist, which *itself* swallowed up the nuclear holocaust that made it. All that had been Elysia – and all it contained at the end – was sucked into the funnel of that hole and passed into the far, fabulous legend of The Beginning.

And as far as Crow and de Marigny had shifted the clock, still the waves of that massive disruption reached to them. The time-clock tumbled end over end in deepest night, slowly righted itself, warped back into normal space and time. Stars twinkled afar.

'What . . . what the *hell* . . . was that?' de Marigny finally found strength to ask.

Crow's voice was tiny as he answered. 'Creation, Henri. That was Creation . . .'

Epilogue

After some little time, de Marigny said: 'Three questions, Titus – to which you'd better have the answers. Because if someone doesn't tell me the whys and wherefores of it, then I'll surely go out of my mind. I mean, I realize that I was used, that I was made a focus for *Their* attentions, some sort of decoy – and of course I knew that Cthulhu intended to take his revenge on Elysia, and that like me he therefore sought to discover its whereabouts – but *how* did he do it? How did he follow me through, him and all the rest? That's my first question.'

'Cthulhu knew all the angles,' Crow answered at once. 'I mean that literally, not in any sort of slang context. He had had billions of years to calculate the vectors. But it must be done in one fell swoop: all of the greater Beings of the Cthulhu Cycle brought through the gates at the same time.'

'Gates?'

'Yog-Sothoth's department,' said Crow with a nod. 'Yog-Sothoth knew the gates, he *was* the gates. The stars were coming right – made to come right by Cthulhu – when all restrictions would be lifted. Then for a period the Great Old Ones would be able to move at will through the space-time continuum, go wherever they wished to go. It was like that at the beginning – though by the time you have all your answers, "the beginning" as a phrase probably won't make a lot of sense any more. Didn't they come "seeping down from the stars . . . not *in* the spaces we know but *between* them"? And don't we use our time-clocks to achieve the same sort of travel? Anyway, Yog-Sothoth, coexistent with all time and conterminous in all space, would be the guide, would show them the gates.

First they must strike at Elysia, remove all opposition. But in fact Elysia would be the only real opposition. As for the rest . . . a walkover.

'You were a decoy of a sort, yes. They knew you were coming through. It wasn't that you were cleverer than them, simply that in the end you would have Elysia's assistance. In the end you would be *directed*. And so they focussed on you. Oh, if they could they would kill you en route, certainly, for you were a great danger to them. You must be, for why else would Kthanid want you in Elysia? They would kill you in Borea, in the dreamlands, in Theem'hdra, wherever – if they could. In which case Kthanid would have relied on Ardatha Ell. That was Ardatha's other reason for being in Lith: to act as the lure if you . . . if you didn't make it. But the laws of probability said you *would* make it, and of course you did.

'So, when the stars came right – with Lith's termination – when space-time was warped and the gates were opened . . .'

Still de Marigny didn't understand. 'But they all came through together, physically en masse! Teleportation?'

'No,' Crow shook his leonine head, 'though certainly you can be forgiven for that wrong conclusion. It *looks* like teleportation, but it's a world apart. Even Kthanid can't teleport, and neither can Ardatha Ell. Riding their Great Thoughts is about as close as they can come. Likewise Cthulhu, except he uses Nyarlathotep.'

De Marigny nodded. 'I see. They were all in telepathic contact with one another at the moment the barriers went down.'

'Of course. When Lith blew and warped space-time, Cthulhu guided the Great Old Ones along the Vectors and Yog-Sothoth was there – as he is "everywhere" – to bring them through the gates. From there they could go anywhere they wanted to, but this was their main chance. *You* were going to Elysia. So they followed you.'

'That's my second question,' said de Marigny. 'Why Elysia? Couldn't I have been caused to guide them elsewhere? I sought for a dream only to see it shattered, to watch it turn into a nightmare . . .'

For a moment a shadow passed over Crow's face. 'No,' he said then, 'it could only be Elysia. The destruction of Elysia was Cthulhu's greatest ambition. And after Elysia . . . there'd be nothing left to stand in his way. It *had* to be Elysia, surely you can see that? Would you have had him start with the Earth and "clear it off"'? Or with Borea? Or any of the civilized worlds and races you've visited?'

'No,' de Marigny shook his head, 'of course not. But that leads to my third question. I can't believe that we've finally destroyed them. Cthulhu and the Great Old Ones were, they are, and they always shall be. That's the way I'll always think of them. But if not dead, where?'

'Cthulhu, dead?' Crow shook his head. 'Oh, no, not dead, Henri, but only dreaming! Their misguided followers, some of their inexperienced progeny, their lesser minions – these can be destroyed. But not the Great Old Ones themselves. They're beyond death. Truly immortal. Their bodies regenerate, reform, renew themselves. But their minds, their memories, they *can* be damaged, erased! That was why they feared the Azathi: not for their destructiveness but their contamination, their contagion! And they were right to fear them, for now they have scars – mental scars, gaps, erasures – which will be a long time in the healing, Henri. Even billions of years . . .'

Exior K'mool touched de Marigny's elbow. 'Do you recall, son of my most distant sons, what Ardatha Ell said of Kthanid: that he, too, was a miraculous mathematician? Cthulhu wasn't alone in his knowledge of the angles. No, and Yog-Sothoth didn't know *all* the gates. That final "gate" – the great black hole – that was the Completely Unknown . . .'

De Marigny's mind suddenly reeled, somersaulted. He

looked at Exior and Crow and his jaw fell open. 'Dreaming but not dead,' he whispered. 'And that great black hole, a monstrous gateway into the past. *Into their own past!*'

Crow smiled.

'Titus,' said de Marigny, his mouth dry as dust, 'tell me, just exactly *where is* Kthanid? Where is he, and where the others of the Elder Council right now? Where – or when?'

'Ah!' said Crow. 'But that's your fourth question, my friend. And I won't answer it for I know you've already worked it out for yourself.'

De Marigny felt dizzy, feverish with the one gigantic notion spinning like a top in his head. 'Time is relative,' he whispered, more to himself than to the others. 'If anyone knows that, I do. In "the beginning" Cthulhu and the Great Old Ones "rose up against the Elder Gods and committed a crime so heinous ..." '

'Like ... the destruction of Elysia?' said Crow.

'... But the Elder Gods pursued them to punish them. And back there in the dim mists of time ... back there ... memories mostly erased ... they only remember their hatred of the Elder Gods and Elysia ... and ... and ... damn! *The whole thing is a cycle!*'

Crow clasped him by the shoulders. 'But haven't we always known that, Henri? Of course we have – it's the Cthulhu Cycle ...'

A long time later:

De Marigny came out of his mental torpor. He was still a little feverish, but Moreen was there to hold and kiss him. 'Where are we going?' he asked, when he was able.

'There's a world in Arcturus which is a jewel,' said Crow. 'Elysia's peoples are there right now. Tiania, too. They're building new lives for themselves, and for us.'

'But it isn't Elysia,' de Marigny's voice was flat, without flavour.

'It can be, my friend,' said Crow, helping him to his feet,

'it can be. In any case, I'm going there because my woman is there – but we don't have to stay. Elysia? I loved Elysia, Henri – but look out there.'

In the scanners, all the stars of space receded to infinity in all directions. 'Done, Henri,' said Titus Crow, 'a chapter closed. Or perhaps a new one started? And as I believe I've said to you before – '

'Wait,' said de Marigny, no longer The Searcher. His smile was still wan, but at least there was feeling in it now. 'Let me say it this time,' he said. 'Damn it all, it has to be my turn *this* time:

'Worlds without end, Titus – worlds without end!'